A thankless task . . .

By the time he returned to Curzon Street that evening, Pickett was more than ready to surrender his burden. He withdrew the velvet box from his coat pocket and handed it to Julia.

"I wish you would take this," he said without preamble. "I've been as nervous as a cat in a bath, carrying it around all afternoon."

Regarding him with raised eyebrows, she took the box and opened it. A dozen red stones winked up at her in the light. "John, you darling!" she breathed, awestruck. "How did you ever—"

"It isn't yours to keep," he put in hastily, realizing too late how this presentation must appear. "I'm afraid it isn't even yours to wear. It belongs to Lady Washbourn. I need you to put it somewhere for safekeeping."

For the second time that day, he recounted the story of his visit to Grosvenor Square, concluding, "So I have to investigate a murder that hasn't happened, while pretending to investigate a jewel theft that hasn't happened, either."

Mystery Loves Company

Another John Pickett Mystery

Sheri Cobb South

1

A Tale of Two Marriages

A gentleman strode up Curzon Street, a gentleman clearly laboring under some strong emotion, as evidenced by the swift pace of his steps, as well as the muscle twitching in his jaw and the rolled-up paper clenched in his hand, the latter slapping rhythmically against the fine buckskin breeches sheathing his thighs. Upon reaching Number 22, he stepped up onto the front portico and, eschewing the brass knocker, pounded on the door with his fist.

"Rogers," he addressed the butler who answered the summons, giving the man a brusque nod, "a word with Lady Fieldhurst, if you please."

"Very good, your lordship," the butler replied woodenly. "I shall inquire if her ladyship—er, if madame is receiving."

"The devil you will!" Lord Rupert Latham shoved his hat and gloves at Rogers and pushed past him into the marble-tiled hall. "I'll announce myself."

Ignoring the butler's faint noise of protest, he crossed the hall with the directness of one long familiar with the house and its primary resident, and made straight for the drawing room. Just as he expected, a lady sat within, a lovely fair-haired woman who looked up with startled blue eyes at his entrance.

"Why, Rupert! What brings you here?"

"Well you might ask!" he retorted. "Have you seen this?" He opened the broadsheet with a snap of his wrist, and shoved it in her direction.

She laid aside the book she was reading and reached for the bell pull. "Yes, Rogers, it's quite all right," she told the butler when he entered the room in response to the summons. "I thought it would not be long before I had the pleasure of Lord Rupert's company. We'll have the tea tray, if you please."

Not until after the butler had departed on his errand did she take the broadsheet from his lordship's trembling hand. "*Aunt Mildred's Parlour*, " she read aloud. "Why, Rupert, I didn't know you were a follower of Aunt Mildred."

"I'm not," he informed her bluntly. "But it appears I don't have to be. No fewer than three members of my club were kind enough to bring this little tidbit to my attention, after their wives pointed it out to them."

She made no comment, for she was silently perusing the column that made its readers privy to the information that Lady F——, whose husband had been violently done to death only last spring, had apparently not mourned his loss for long before contracting a marriage to the person most instrumental in bringing her first husband's killer to justice; consequently, her ladyship was now to be known by the less exalted title of Mrs. P——. After a brief honeymoon in Drury Lane (of all places!) followed by a trip to the West Country for the purpose of introducing the bridegroom to her family (really, one would have loved to have been a fly on the wall!), the happy couple had taken up residence in the bride's house in C—— Street. Having reached the end of this scrap of gossip, she handed the newspaper back to his lordship.

"Well, Rupert, what of it?"

"What of it?" he echoed incredulously. "Why, it's an insult! I stopped by the publisher's offices in Fleet Street and demanded that they print a retraction, and the editor flatly refused! If I were you——"

He was obliged to break off here, as Rogers returned with the tea tray, followed by Thomas the footman bearing a second tray piled with cakes. Lord Rupert was forced to bide his time in silence, his impatience betrayed by the twitch in his jaw. As soon as the door closed behind them, however, he lost no time in picking up where he had left off.

"If I were you, Julia, I would turn this over to Lord Fieldhurst. Yes, I know there's no love lost between you and your late husband's heir, but do him the justice to admit that he will not swallow this insult to the family name. Depend upon it, he'll have his solicitor slap 'Aunt Mildred,' whoever she is, with a libel suit before she knows what hit her."

"Oh, that we may certainly depend on," she agreed dryly. "Still, I don't believe there is any need for—"

She broke off abruptly, her face lighting up in a radiant smile at some point beyond her visitor's left shoulder. Lord Rupert turned and saw that another man had entered the room—not the butler nor the footman this time, but a tall young man of about five-and-twenty, with curly brown hair tied at the nape of his neck in an old-fashioned queue.

"Well, this is a surprise!" Julia exclaimed, and there was a note in her voice which, combined with the smile, caused Lord Rupert's eyebrows to draw together in a thoughtful frown. "I hadn't expected to see you at this hour."

"I was in Mayfair on a case, and thought I would drop by to see if you could spare a crust of bread for a starving man." The newcomer's gaze fell on the tray of cakes. "Are those the ones with the raspberries?" Without waiting for an answer, he snagged one of them and sank his teeth into it. In the next instant he noticed Lord Rupert glowering at him. "Your lordship," he said around a mouthful of cake, acknowledging him with a nod.

"Mr. Pickett," Lord Rupert said coolly, returning the nod. "You would appear to make yourself very free with her ladyship's hospitality."

Pickett paused in mid-bite. "Is there any reason why I shouldn't?"

By this time Julia had crossed the room to greet him, and now laid a hand on the sleeve of his brown serge coat. "Lord Rupert was kind enough to bring me the latest issue of *Aunt Mildred's Parlour*," she said, offering the broadsheet to Pickett. "It appears we've been given more than a mention. I hope you don't mind it."

"I suppose it was bound to happen," he said with a rueful smile. "Does it bother you?"

She shook her head. "Not so very much. If I am going to be gossiped about in any case, I had much rather it be for marriage than murder."

Lord Rupert had been vaguely disturbed by the smile with which she had greeted the visitor, and the dawning sense that he himself had somehow become invisible had added to his unease. Now he listened to this exchange with growing incredulity. "Good God!" he exclaimed. "Do you mean to tell me it's true?"

Julia blinked at him as if she had only that moment remembered his presence. "But of course it's true! You've known about it—oh, for months now!"

"I knew you had accidentally contracted a marriage by declaration while in Scotland, but it was my understanding that you were in the process of having it annulled."

"Yes, well, we changed our minds." Her eyes met John Pickett's, and if Lord Rupert had any lingering doubts as to their relationship, that look would have settled them.

"But the fellow's impotent!" his lordship exclaimed, with a sweeping gesture in the direction of Pickett's nether parts.

"Oh, he is not," Julia said with unconcealed scorn.

"I tell you, he is," Lord Rupert insisted. "He all but admitted it last November."

"Do we have to talk about this?" put in Pickett, blushing scarlet.

"He was prepared to let my solicitor make such a claim, I'll grant you that," Julia acknowledged. "But the dear man was only trying to free me from a marriage he was persuaded I did not want. There was never any question of his capability, however."

Unconvinced, Lord Rupert pressed on. "It isn't enough for your solicitor to say so, no matter how noble Mr. Pickett's motives. I read for the law some years ago, Julia, and I distinctly remember that, for the purposes of obtaining an annulment, proof of impotence is required, in the form of a physician's verification."

"Is it?" Julia glanced at her crimson-faced husband,

then back at his vanquished rival. "I daresay George bribed a doctor—as you said yourself, he is very careful of the family's honor—but you must allow that in this particular case, I am in a better position to know than any number of physicians."

"Julia—" Pickett protested faintly.

"Inexperience is not at all the same thing as incapacity, you know," she concluded with unassailable logic.

"You aren't helping, Julia," said Pickett.

"You realize, of course, that Lord Fieldhurst will never stand for this," Lord Rupert pointed out. "If he doesn't challenge the marriage in court, I shall own myself much surprised."

Julia nodded. "Yes, we thought so, too, which is why we did the thing properly, by special license, as soon as could be arranged."

"I see." Apparently recognizing a lost cause, Lord Rupert looked from Julia to her husband, and back again. "Well, Julia—"

"Mrs. Pickett, if you please," she corrected him.

"Mrs. Pickett, then, it appears you've made your choice," he said with great dignity. "I wish you joy of it. But when you suddenly find yourself a social pariah—and you will, I make no doubt of it—don't expect me to lift a finger to ease your way."

"I wouldn't dream of it," she assured him sweetly. She

gave the bell pull a tug, and when the butler answered, said, "Rogers, I believe his lordship is leaving us now. Have the goodness to show him out."

Tight-lipped with helpless fury and wounded pride, Lord Rupert turned on his heel and quitted the room without saying goodbye. Pickett, alone with his bride, put his half-eaten cake back on the tray.

"I'm sorry," he began. "I didn't know—I shouldn't have come—it was a bad time—"

"Nonsense!" She sidestepped the tea table that separated them, and wrapped her arms around his waist. "You don't need anyone's permission—least of all Lord Rupert's!—to enter your own home. I am delighted you stopped by, for I didn't expect to see you until dinner."

She lifted her face to be kissed, and he was happy to oblige. At the completion of this pleasant exercise, she withdrew from his arms and sat down on the sofa, patting the place beside her.

"Now then, sit down and let me pour you some tea, and you can tell me what brings you to Mayfair. What is this new case you're on?"

"I don't know yet," he confessed, taking the cup from her hand. "I only know that Lady Washbourn sent a note to the Bow Street office, asking for me by name and requesting that I call 'regarding a matter of the utmost discretion.' "

"That sounds intriguing," Julia remarked, passing him a

small plate containing two more of the raspberry cakes that she had discovered were his favorites.

"Not necessarily. Every case involving the aristocracy is a matter of utmost discretion, at least in their own minds. But maybe you can at least give me some idea of what I'm walking into. Do you know anything about Lady Washbourn?"

"Washbourn, Washbourn," she murmured, her smooth brow creased in concentration. "The name sounds familiar, but I—oh, wait! Now I remember! Lord Washbourn married her two years ago—or was it three? It was quite the *on-dit* of the Season, for she was a mere Miss Eliza Mucklow at the time, and the daughter of a brewer. Her father was enormously wealthy, and everyone knew that the Washbourns had been at *point non plus* for generations. Her dowry was rumored to be in the neighborhood of fifty thousand pounds, all of it in the Funds. Naturally, 'Aunt Mildred' had something highly unflattering to say about the marriage—and whoever she is, she can be quite poisonous when she chooses; in fact, we got off rather lightly, you and I, all things considered. But in Lord and Lady Washbourn's case, Aunt Mildred didn't say anything that the rest of the *ton* wasn't already thinking: that the match had more to do with legal tender than the tender passion."

Pickett withdrew his occurrence book from the inside pocket of his coat, and made a quick notation. "That might be useful to know. Still, I must point out that not every poor man who marries a rich woman is only after her money," he added, with such a speaking look that she had no difficulty understanding to which poor man he was referring.

"Very true—and I only hope Lady Washbourn is even half as happy with her impecunious husband as I am with mine." Setting aside her empty cup, she rose from the sofa and held out her hand to him. "Have you finished? If you will come with me upstairs, I have something for you."

He looked up at her with an arrested expression. "Julia, I—I can't—" he stammered. "I'm on a case—"

"Not that," she assured him hastily, "although I expect it would be interesting to hear you trying to explain to your magistrate your tardiness in returning to Bow Street. In fact, I did not realize you had turned five-and-twenty until you said so during the inquest in Somersetshire. I have a birthday gift for you."

"Oh," said Pickett, not quite certain whether to be sorry or glad. "I'll look forward to it after dinner, then—that, and the other, too," he added with a mischievous grin. He took her proffered hand and allowed her to pull him to his feet, then gave her a lingering kiss before collecting his hat and gloves from Rogers and setting out for the Washbourn residence in Grosvenor Square.

Like so many of the houses in Mayfair, this proved to be a tall, narrow structure connected with its neighbors on both sides. Pickett lifted the knocker and let it fall, and a moment later the door was opened by the butler, a balding individual as short and stout as the house was tall and narrow, who looked askance at Pickett's brown serge coat and inquired as to the nature of his business. Pickett found himself wondering how, given the fact that he himself was the taller of the two by a head, the man still contrived to look down his nose at him.

"John Pickett, of—" He paused, recalling Lady Washbourn's note with its heavily underscored request for the utmost discretion. "John Pickett, to see her ladyship. I believe I am expected," he added, seeing by the butler's expression that he was disinclined to admit the caller.

"I shall inquire," the butler said, making this simple statement sound vaguely like a threat. He returned a moment later with the information that Lady Washbourn would receive him, and Pickett fancied that the butler seemed rather disappointed to admit it. He surrendered his hat and gloves, then followed the man down across a tiled hall to an elegantly appointed drawing room whose windows looked down onto the fashionable square. A lady seated on a crimson brocade sofa sat waiting to receive him, and although she hardly fit the popular conception of a countess, any doubts Pickett might have entertained as to her identity were answered by the large gilt-framed portrait centered over the mantelpiece, for here on canvas was portrayed this same female in all the trappings of aristocracy. Pickett was certainly no expert on art, but eyes far less knowledgeable than his could not have failed to notice the wealth of detail in the painting. The dark blue satin of the subject's Court dress pooled about her feet in folds that looked as if they would have been soft to the viewer's touch, and Pickett suspected that if he took a few steps closer, he could have counted the pearls in her strawberry-leafed coronet.

The lady herself, by contrast, appeared rather ordinary, a young woman whose mouse-brown hair and rather squat figure were redeemed by intelligent grey eyes and a complexion as rosy and clear as a milkmaid's.

"Mr. Pickett," she said, rising to greet him. "Thank you for coming so quickly."

Lady Washbourn dismissed the butler, and invited Pickett to take a seat on the crimson brocade sofa. She sat down on the chair facing him then bent upon him a look no less appraising than the one with which he had considered her. "I must say, you're a bit younger than I had expected," she observed.

"I'm twenty-five," Pickett said, suppressing a sigh at the now-familiar references to his age, or lack thereof. "But I've been with Bow Street since I was nineteen, so I'm not without experience."

"Yes, and you solved the Fieldhurst murder last spring, did you not? And recently married his lordship's widow, if rumor doesn't lie." She glanced toward a broadsheet lying on a side table, and Pickett did not have to guess that Aunt Mildred had another guest in her Parlour.

"I did," he acknowledged with a nod. "But surely you didn't summon me for the purpose of discussing my marriage."

"No, I summoned you for the purpose of discussing mine." She took a deep breath. "Mr. Pickett, I think my husband is trying to kill me."

2

*Which Recounts the Sad History
of My Lord and Lady Washbourn*

*U*tmost discretion,' indeed, thought Pickett, extracting his occurrence book from his coat pocket. "Trying to kill you?" he echoed aloud. "What makes you say such a thing?"

"There have been—accidents," said the lady, choosing her words with care. "And they might well have been no more than accidents, but taken together—well, I can't help wondering."

"I think you had best start from the beginning," Pickett said, settling himself more comfortably on the sofa and readying his pencil to take down her words.

She lifted her eyes, and her gaze drifted past him to the window, although he doubted she was so transfixed by anything she saw in Grosvenor Square. "I suppose it started with our first meeting, in April of '07. We were married two months later, in June."

"A whirlwind courtship," remarked Pickett.

"Hardly that, Mr. Pickett." Her voice held the faintest trace of bitterness. "In fact, Washbourn had been paying court to Lady—to another young lady, one to whom I believe he was sincerely attached. But his estate was heavily encumbered, and Papa was eager to have aristocratic grandchildren, so they arranged the match between them. Still, I couldn't complain, or so I thought. We were happy enough, as these things go, and if Washbourn was unfaithful to me, he was discreet enough that I never knew of it, and was never held up as an object of ridicule—at least, no more so than any other brewer's daughter who aspires to become a countess. And I will do him the justice to own that he seemed genuinely delighted with the birth of our child last year, even though the baby was a girl and not the heir he had hoped for."

It hardly sounded like domestic bliss to Pickett, but he reminded himself that Julia's first marriage had apparently been a good deal worse. "Then—what changed?" he asked.

She sighed. "My father died last year, and since I was Papa's only child, and Mama had died some years previously, the brewery came to me. My dowry was large, but my inheritance far surpassed it."

"But if I understand English law aright, everything a married woman owns becomes the property of her husband," Pickett objected. In fact, it was the only blot on his own happiness, that by marrying the Viscountess Fieldhurst, he had considerably enriched himself at her expense. "What would Lord Washbourn have to gain by, er, disposing of you?"

"Well you might ask! As it happens, Lady—the young lady he had hoped to marry—had wed someone else within a fortnight of our own nuptials, but her husband was thrown from his horse last autumn while hunting with the Quorn, and died of his injuries. So if Washbourn can only find a way to be rid of me, there will be nothing to stand in his way of marrying the lady he'd wanted all along."

Pickett jotted down another note, muttering something under his breath about eating one's cake and having it, too.

"Just so," she agreed bitterly. "And it was shortly after we were out of mourning for Papa that the accidents began. Tell me, Mr. Pickett, do you smell the fresh paint? The ballroom had to be repainted yesterday, for three days ago the chandelier crashed to the floor. The candles set the carpet on fire, and although the blaze was not large, the walls were badly smoked." She inhaled sharply, as if still smelling the acrid scent. "If the chandelier had fallen only seconds earlier, I should have been struck, for I had been standing directly underneath it."

"May I see the room?" Pickett asked.

"Of course."

She rose and shook out her skirts, then led the way

20

upstairs, where the ballroom occupied one entire side of the house. The smell of paint was stronger here, and the damaged carpet had been removed, leaving only bare floorboards beneath a massive gilded chandelier, somewhat the worse for wear. Pickett walked to the center of the room until he stood directly under it, and looked up.

"The chandelier can be lowered in order to change out the candles," said her ladyship, pointing out the cable that led from the chandelier in the center of the room to the wall, where it turned the corner with the aid of a pulley and disappeared discreetly behind the blue velvet curtains framing the window. Pickett crossed the room to the window, drew back the curtain, and found the end of the rope wrapped around a metal cleat set into the wall.

"The rope was changed after the—accident," Lady Washbourn said, stumbling slightly over the word. "The old one had snapped, or else had been cut."

"Was Lord Washbourn home at the time?" he asked.

"No, he was at his club."

"It seems a rather dodgy way of killing someone," Pickett noted. "The murderer would have the advantage of being nowhere near the scene of the crime, but he would have to weigh that against the likelihood of his intended victim being in another room—or out of the house entirely— when the axe fell." He grimaced at his own choice of words. "Forgive me, your ladyship; you know what I meant."

"I do, and I had thought of that. But I have been in and out of this room every day for the past week, as Washbourn must have known I would be. We are hosting a costume ball in three days' time, and I have been kept busy with preparations—meeting with the musicians, consulting with the florist regarding the flowers and then giving instructions to the footmen as to their placement—" She shrugged. "Besides, the blow itself need not have been fatal. Even had I been standing near enough to be struck by shards of broken glass, these could have become imbedded in the skin, and festered."

"Leading to a slow and painful death by infection," concluded Pickett, nodding in understanding. "A charming fellow, your husband!"

Her expression grew wistful. "He can be, on occasion."

"I should like to have a look at the rope, if I may," Pickett said. "Do you still have it?"

She shook her head. "Alas, no. I could think of no excuse for retaining it that would not have aroused suspicion. I did get a good look at it, though, and I must confess that it did not appear to have been cut. It was frayed, you see—not the sort of clean break one might expect to see had it been slashed with a knife."

"And yet one might hack at it in order to make it look frayed, if one wished to make a murder attempt appear an accident," Pickett said, frowning thoughtfully.

22

"My thoughts exactly!" She sounded almost pleased by this observation, and Pickett realized she had probably half expected him to dismiss her concerns as the wild imaginings of a hysterical female.

"I believe you said there have been other such accidents?"

"One other," she said. "I was coming downstairs one morning when I stepped on something on the stairs. It rolled beneath my foot, and had I not been able to grab the banister, I might have suffered a nasty fall. When I regained my balance and looked at the stair, I found three loose pearls on the step."

"Yours?"

"I didn't think so at the time, for I had worn my pearls only the previous Monday, to the Bartleston musicale. I thought they must belong to Lady Washbourn—the dowager, that is, my mother-in-law—but she denied it, and suggested that I take better care of my jewels in the future. And when I looked in my jewel case, my pearl necklace was broken, and three of the pearls were missing. This was the first incident, mind you, so although I thought it was strange, I did not yet suspect any sinister purpose."

"Did you mention the matter to your husband?"

"Yes." Angry spots of color burned in her cheeks. "He promised to take them to Rundell and Bridge for restringing, and read me a lecture—ever so gently, mind you, but a lecture all the same—about the value of money." She gave a snort of derision. "Money! *Me*, mind you, when it is *he* who—but never mind that. Will you help me, Mr. Pickett? I am prepared to offer you the sum of fifty pounds sterling for bringing this matter to a satisfactory conclusion."

Pickett's head spun. Fifty pounds sterling! Almost as much as he could expect to earn in an entire year, although it still fell far short of his wife's jointure from her first husband. He was sorely tempted, but he was loth to take Lady Washbourn's offer under false pretenses. After a few seconds' severe struggle, he answered reluctantly, "I understand your concerns, your ladyship, and don't think I am unsympathetic to your plight, but there is very little I can do with no solid evidence."

"What evidence will it take?" she asked tartly. "My lifeless body discovered at the foot of the stairs? No, Mr. Pickett, I have a better idea. I told you we are to host a masquerade ball; I suspect my husband may think to take advantage of the occasion and make another attempt on my life. You must admit, a houseful of persons wearing masks would offer a rare opportunity."

"Yes, but—"

"I should like you to attend, along with your wife. That is why I requested you in particular. Since Mrs. Pickett is a lady born and bred, no one will wonder at her presence, and you will be on hand to keep my husband under close observation, should he decide to try his hand at murder."

Pickett saw one rather glaring flaw in this plan. "Will Lord Washbourn not be a bit suspicious to discover that you suddenly number a Bow Street Runner and his wife amongst your acquaintances?"

"I've thought of that." She reached into the pocket of her gown and withdrew a long, narrow box covered in black velvet. "Rubies," she explained. "The Washbourn rubies, to be exact, which guarantee that my husband will not think it at all strange that I should summon a Runner when they should suddenly go missing."

"I beg your pardon?" asked Pickett, all at sea.

"Into your possession, to be exact," she said, offering him the box. "I dare not simply hide them, for fear Washbourn or one of the servants should find them, and discover the ruse."

"And how, exactly, will this account for my presence at the masquerade?"

"To ensure that none of our guests suffer a similar loss—at least, so far as my husband is concerned." She smiled mischievously, and her earlier plainness was utterly banished. "After all, when a jewel thief is known to be running amok, one cannot be too careful."

"No, I suppose not." He took the box, not without a pang of misgiving. "With your permission, I will turn this over to Bow Street, to be locked up for safekeeping."

Whatever Lady Washbourn might have said to this suggestion was interrupted by a noise from below. Her earlier animation disappeared, to be replaced by a hunted expression.

"My husband is home," she said, quite unnecessarily. "Come with me, Mr. Pickett, and follow my lead."

Interpreting this command both literally and figuratively, Pickett stuffed the rubies into the inside pocket of his coat, then fell in behind the countess as she exited the ballroom and hurried down the stairs to the ground floor. A stern-looking man in his mid-thirties stood in the hall, divesting himself of hat and gloves, and her ladyship went forward to meet him.

"Washbourn, my love, I did not expect you home so soon."

She presented her cheek for her husband's kiss, and Pickett could not help contrasting the coolness of his lordship's greeting and the rather stilted civility in his wife's voice with the warm welcome he himself had received in Curzon Street only an hour earlier.

As if aware of this assessment, Lord Washbourn's pale blue eyes flicked up from his wife to her visitor. "I wasn't aware that you had guests, my dear," he said. Although he did not go so far as to sneer at the brown serge coat, Pickett had no doubt the earl was fully cognizant of it.

"This is Mr. John Pickett, of the Bow Street Public

Office," Lady Washbourn hurried to explain. "It is the most distressing thing, but I cannot find the Washbourn rubies! I fear they may have been stolen."

The earl's mouth tightened. "Depend upon it, Eliza, you have mislaid them somewhere. We will organize a thorough search of the house, and I have no doubt they will turn up. Really, my dear, you must learn to be more careful. First your pearls, and now this! I'm sure I need not remind you that the Washbourn rubies have been in the family for generations."

"No, indeed! And I hope you may be right, and that they will turn up. Still, just in case they do not, I thought you would have no objection to my summoning Mr. Pickett to try and see if he can discover what happened to them." She took a deep breath. "Mr. Pickett has also agreed to attend our masquerade ball—quite inconspicuously, you know!—to ensure that none of our guests suffer a similar loss. His wife is the former Lady Fieldhurst, so there can be nothing to wonder at in their presence," she added hastily, almost apologetically.

"We will discuss this later, Eliza." Turning to Pickett, he added, "I have every confidence that the rubies will be discovered in my wife's sewing basket, or some such thing, but if I should prove to be mistaken, I'm sure I need not tell you that you will be rewarded handsomely for their recovery."

Pickett nodded in acknowledgement. "I will do my best, your lordship," he promised, knowing quite well that he could not accept any payment for the return of jewels which were at that moment residing in his own coat pocket. He was suddenly eager to be out of the house and out from under Lord Washbourn's too-keen gaze. It occurred to him that if the rubies were to be discovered now, and on his person, his Bow Street career would be over. His life might well be over, too, if Lady Washbourn should choose to sacrifice him in order to save herself: stealing a priceless heirloom from a peer of the realm would almost certainly be a hanging offense.

* * *

"And so with your permission, sir, I should like to lock these away in the safe," concluded Pickett, after recounting to his magistrate Lady Washbourn's plight.

"I see," said Mr. Colquhoun, a bluff white-haired man in his mid-sixties with bushy white brows over blue eyes that could either scowl fiercely or twinkle with good humor, whichever the situation demanded. At the moment, they were frowning down at the long black velvet box containing the Washbourn rubies. "And how long do you expect to keep them here?"

"I don't know," Pickett confessed. "Until I solve the case, I suppose—that's if there *is* a case—or until Lady Washbourn decides her fears were groundless, and asks for them back."

"In other words, it could be a very long time."

Pickett sighed. "I'm afraid so, sir."

"I don't like it." Mr. Colquhoun handed the box back over the wooden rail that separated the magistrate's bench from the rest of the room.

Pickett accepted its return with some reluctance. "Don't like what, sir? The rubies in particular, or the case as a whole?"

"When you put it that way, I can't say I care much for either one. The case—if you want to call it that—is far too ambiguous, to my mind. To be blunt, I can't imagine why you agreed to take on such a thing. There's been no crime committed, at least none that can be proven."

"No, but just last year Mr. Dixon accompanied the Spanish ambassador and his wife to Portsmouth as a bodyguard," Pickett reminded him. "There had been no crime committed then, either, but he took the case never-theless—and picked up a cool thirty pounds for his pains," he added with a trace of envy.

"Let me remind you that the safety of the Spanish ambassador and his wife was a matter of international importance, since Spain had finally had her fill of Napoleon and was prepared to cast her lot with Britain. Naturally, every precaution had to be taken to make sure the new alliance was not threatened by some disgruntled person determined to view the Spanish as our enemies. But I suspect it is not so much international politics that interests you as the prospect of earning thirty pounds."

"Fifty."

The bushy white brows arched toward the magistrate's hairline. "I beg your pardon?"

"Lady Washbourn has offered me the sum of fifty pounds sterling upon the satisfactory conclusion of this case."

"But *think*, John! What, exactly, constitutes a satisfactory conclusion? Granted, if her ladyship is found dead at the end of the evening, I believe we can agree that you forfeit your fifty pounds. But if she isn't? Just how long are you expected to protect her from a crime her husband may have no intention of committing in the first place?"

"I—I don't know," Pickett confessed. "I suppose I shall have to improvise. But—but *fifty pounds*, sir! It's as much as my wife gets in, oh, six weeks," he added with a humorless laugh.

"Mrs. Pickett knew when she married you that you would never be able to match her income," the magistrate pointed out, not unkindly. "One must assume that you held some appeal for her other than the financial."

"Yes, well," said Pickett, willing himself not to blush, "that's not to say I don't intend to do my damnedest— begging your pardon—not to be her petticoat pensioner."

"An admirable sentiment, and one that does you credit—so long as you do not allow it to take control of your marriage."

"And the rubies?" Pickett asked, impatient to abandon a line of inquiry which had become uncomfortably personal. "May I lock them up here?"

"That is another thing I cannot like," the magistrate said, scowling at Pickett in such a way that made him feel very much like the fourteen-year-old pickpocket he had been when first he had made Mr. Colquhoun's acquaintance. "In my experience, deceptions and half-truths only lead to further complications."

"I see your point, sir, but how else was her ladyship to explain my presence? 'This is Mr. Pickett, my dear. I've invited him to see if he can discover whether you are trying to kill me.' " He shook his head. "No, I can't say I like it, either, but I don't see that she had much of a choice."

"Since you are so much in sympathy with the lady, I'm sure you will have no objection to keeping the rubies for her until the business is—what was it?—'satisfactorily concluded.' "

"But sir—"

"But me no buts, Mr. Pickett. Consider, if you will, how many people pass through the Bow Street Public Office every day. Not the criminals, mind you—although God knows there are enough of them!—but the Runners, the foot patrol, the horse patrol—and not a few of them with cause to open the safe from time to time. All it would take for disaster to strike would be for Lord Washbourn to make an unscheduled visit to inquire as to the progress of the investigation, and for someone to recall seeing the rubies and return them to their rightful owner. Lady Washbourn's goose would be cooked, and so would yours. No, having committed yourself to this ruse—and I am willing to concede that, after agreeing to take the case, you could hardly do otherwise—you must see that the fewer people who are privy to the secret, the more likely it is to remain just that—a secret."

"Yes, sir," concurred Pickett with a sigh. "But in the meantime, what am I to do with them?"

"Come, man, your lady wife must have at least a few such baubles of her own; surely she can be entrusted with one more for a few days—weeks—months—however long it takes to reach a 'satisfactory conclusion.' "

Pickett considered the alternative with a thoughtful frown. "And if, in spite of my efforts, there is an *un*satisfactory conclusion? What am I to do with them then?"

"In such an event, the rubies being in your possession might strengthen the Crown's case against Lord Washbourn, as they would serve as evidence of his wife's suspicions—although they would hardly be a testimony to your professional competence," he added darkly.

"Yes, sir," said Pickett, recognizing a lost cause when he saw one.

"Now, if there is nothing else, Mr. Pickett," continued the magistrate, glancing over his shoulder at the clock mounted on the wall above his bench, "I intend to seek my dinner, and I suggest you do the same."

"There is one more thing—" Pickett began.

With an air of resignation, Mr. Colquhoun raked stubby fingers through his thick, snow-white hair. "Why am I not surprised?" he wondered aloud. "Very well, Mr. Pickett, what is it?"

"It's this masquerade, sir. With your permission, I would like to be able to come in late on the morning after. I believe these functions may last into the wee hours."

"And if I know anything at all about women, Mrs. Pickett will not want to leave until the unmasking," predicted the magistrate.

"If I am to protect Lady Washbourn, I must stay until the end of the ball in any case," Pickett pointed out.

"True. Very well, then, you have my permission, provided nothing happens that evening which necessitates your presence here in Bow Street, but I'm sure I need not tell you that. Tell me, what do you intend to do for a costume?"

"Why, nothing, sir," said Pickett, taken aback by the question. "I'll be working, not attending for pleasure."

"Not if Mrs. Pickett has anything to say to the matter,"

Mr. Colquhoun prophesied with grim certainty.

"Forgive me, sir, but why should she?"

"Because even the most rational women lose all sense at the prospect of capering about in fancy dress. Of course, you might attempt a compromise by offering to wear the blue coat and red waistcoat of the foot patrol, but if your wife doesn't have you tricked out as Galahad or Harlequin or some such nonsense, you may call me a Dutchman."

There had been a time when nineteen-year-old Pickett, apprenticed to a coal merchant for five long years, had been awestruck at the magistrate's invitation to trade his coal-blackened work clothes for the uniform of the Bow Street foot patrol. But he had been equally pleased, four years later, to surrender the familiar red waistcoats upon his promotion to principal officer—those elite half-dozen men known colloquially as Runners—even though this advancement meant that a sizeable portion of his twenty-five shillings a week had to go toward supplementing his wardrobe, for the Runners were a plainclothes force. No, to appear once more in uniform as a member of the foot patrol would be, at least in his own eyes, an enormous step backwards. He would make his case for regular evening attire, and trust his Julia to possess a more rational mind than that with which Mr. Colquhoun credited her.

3

*In Which John Pickett
Looks a Gift Horse in the Mouth*

B y the time he returned to Curzon Street that evening, Pickett was more than ready to surrender his burden. He withdrew the velvet box from his coat pocket and handed it to Julia.

"I wish you would take this," he said without preamble. "I've been as nervous as a cat in a bath, carrying it around all afternoon."

Regarding him with raised eyebrows, she took the box and opened it. A dozen red stones winked up at her in the light. "John, you darling!" she breathed, awestruck. "How did you ever—"

"It isn't yours to keep," he put in hastily, realizing too late how this presentation must appear. "I'm afraid it isn't even yours to wear. It belongs to Lady Washbourn. I need you to put it somewhere for safekeeping."

For the second time that day, he recounted the story of

his visit to Grosvenor Square, concluding, "So I have to investigate a murder that hasn't happened, while pretending to investigate a jewel theft that hasn't happened, either."

"You'll do it," she predicted confidently.

He grimaced. "I wish I could be so sure."

"You'll do it because you're brilliant—and everyone seems to know it but you." She punctuated this statement with a quick kiss, and he took her in his arms and finished the job properly.

"Of course, there may be nothing to investigate," he said at last, when they finally drew apart. "It may be nothing more than two unrelated accidents."

She shook her head. "I don't know about the chandelier, darling, but I can assure you the pearls were no accident."

"Weren't they?" he asked, puzzled. "What makes you say so?"

"Because when pearls are strung—good ones, any-way—the thread is knotted between each pearl, so that if the string breaks, the things don't go bouncing and rolling about all over the place. One would certainly come off, and I suppose two might, if the knot came undone at the point of the break, but I can't imagine how three might have done so—not without help, anyway."

He regarded her intently. "And you're sure of this?"

"I'm quite certain." She glanced down at the box in her hand. "I must take these upstairs and put them away. If you'll come with me, I can show you my own pearls, and you can see for yourself."

He followed her up the stairs and waited while she stored the Washbourn rubies safely in her jewel case. When she turned back toward him, she held a strand of creamy white pearls.

"Here they are. If you look closely, you can tell they don't rest against one another."

He took the necklace and carried it to the window, examining it in the afternoon sunlight. Just as she had said, there was a small but unmistakable space between each pearl where the string was knotted.

"Will you need to snap the thread to make sure?" she asked, moving to the window to look over his shoulder. "I don't mind making certain sacrifices in a worthy cause, but since they were a gift from Mama and Papa, I should insist on their being restrung, and at Bow Street's expense."

If they had been a gift from her first husband, Pickett might have been tempted. "That won't be necessary," he assured her, returning the pearls to her. "I think even Mr. Colquhoun would consider destroying my wife's jewelry to be going beyond the call of duty. There is something else I am going to ask of you, though. Would you be willing to accompany me to Lord and Lady Washbourn's masquerade ball?"

"A masquerade?" Her face lit up in joyful anticipation,

and Pickett's hackles rose as he recalled his magistrate's prediction. "I've always wanted to attend a masquerade, but was never able to do so! Before I was married, Mama was persuaded they encouraged licentious behavior, and afterwards Frederick—well, I suppose Frederick merely wished to be disagreeable. Lord Rupert offered to escort me to a masquerade at the Argyle Rooms once, but I *knew* it was licentious behavior he had in mind, and so I was obliged to decline the invitation. But to attend such a function with you sounds delightful!"

"Delightful for you, maybe, but not for me," Pickett said. "I'll be working. Lady Washbourn is afraid her husband might take advantage of the occasion to make another attempt on her life."

Her blue eyes grew wide. "Surely donning a disguise in order to murder one's wife is taking licentiousness to extremes!"

"Yes, well, you can hardly deny that being in fancy dress might afford one opportunities that would be too chancy to attempt otherwise."

"I suppose it depends on what sort of costume the would-be murderer chooses. Anything too remarkable would only attract unwanted attention. But speaking of fancy dress, what should we wear?"

"I'll be working, Julia," he said again. "There's no need for me to don fancy dress at all."

"Nonsense! If you were to attend in plain clothes, you would be far too conspicuous to be any help to Lady Washbourn at all. What do you think of Romeo and Juliet?"

"What am I supposed to think of them?" Pickett asked, blinking at the sudden *non sequitur*.

"As costumes for you and me," she said with exaggerated patience. "I can be Juliet, and you can be Romeo."

"I'm sure you would make a very fetching Juliet, my lady, but much as I love you, I'm *not* capering about in doublet and hose for your sake!"

Her face fell. "I suppose you're right," she acknowledged with a sigh of regret for what might have been. "Since there is no time to have anything made up, we will be obliged to hire costumes, and I daresay your legs are too long for anything that might be available in the shops."

"Thank God for that, anyway," Pickett muttered under his breath.

"Still," continued Julia, not to be deterred, "I am persuaded you would make a very dashing cavalier, and such a costume would have the advantage of allowing you to make do with your own boots, besides merely leaving your hair loose instead of wearing a wig. And," she added, warming to this theme, "you could wear a sword, which might be useful in case you should surprise Lord Washbourn in the act, and be obliged to defend Lady Washbourn—or yourself."

Much as Pickett hated to admit it, she did have a point. Of course, he did own a pistol—had even used it, on occasion—but it would be difficult to invent a compelling reason for carrying a firearm into a ballroom.

"Very well," he conceded with obvious reluctance, "you have my permission to turn me out as a cavalier, and I'll try not to disgrace you."

"As if you could!" she retorted, smiling. "But in the meantime, I promised you a birthday gift. Close your eyes."

He did, and she took his hand and led him across the room, pausing before the place where, he estimated, the tall mahogany clothes-press stood against the wall. This theory was confirmed a moment later, when a faint creak suggested the opening of the wardrobe's doors.

"You can open them now," she announced.

Blinking in the afternoon sunlight after the self-imposed darkness, he found himself staring into the open clothes-press, where her gowns had been moved to one side to accommodate half a dozen new garments, none of which appeared to be meant for the adornment of the female form.

"You went to a tailor's shop?" he asked in some consternation, recalling the decidedly masculine environs of Mr. Meyer's establishment in Conduit Street.

"Of course not! I had only to send round a note, and Mr. Meyer was so obliging as to call upon me here."

"Oh, of course," he agreed in a flat voice.

She pulled one of the garments free and held it to her bosom so that he might admire a double-breasted tailcoat of fine bottle-green wool. "Try it on," she urged. "Or would you prefer the mulberry? Or perhaps the russet?" She reached toward the clothes-press as if to extract another garment.

"How—how many are there?" he asked, eyeing them with misgiving.

"Five coats, and as many waistcoats, three pairs of breeches and one of pantaloons, half a dozen fine cambric shirts, a full dozen cravats, and an equal number of stockings—pairs, that is—and two pairs of Limerick gloves. Oh, and this." She draped the green coat over her arm so that her hands might be free to withdraw from the wardrobe a crimson-and-gold brocade dressing-gown of Oriental design.

"Julia, how much did all this cost?"

"It is very bad form to inquire as to the cost of a gift," she informed him. "Suffice it to say that we can well afford it."

"*You* can well afford it, perhaps, but I doubt you'll find many other Bow Street Runners with so lavish a wardrobe."

"John, you cannot deny that you needed new clothes! Recall, if you please, that I've darned your stockings; I know quite well the sad state of your attire. You possess three coats to your name! Why, Frederick was used to go through as many in a day."

He stiffened. "I wasn't aware that I was to pattern myself after your first husband."

"Oh, John, of course you aren't," she said impatiently. "But still—"

"Julia, no one at Bow Street dresses so fine as this, except perhaps for Mr. Colquhoun, and even he—"

"So fine as what?" she demanded. "It isn't as if they came from the hand of Weston in Old Bond Street, you know."

"No, I *don't* know. In fact, I wouldn't know Weston from a hole in the wall, which is rather the point, isn't it? It's bad enough that some of the men on the foot patrol have taken to calling me 'Lord John,' without me starting to dress as if I thought I were better than the rest of them."

She dumped the garments onto the bed. "Oh, John, I didn't know! Has it been so very dreadful for you? Forgive me—I never meant—"

"There's nothing to forgive," he said with a sigh, drawing her into his arms and pressing his lips to her hair. "As for the foot patrol, well, they don't mean any harm, not really, so let's consign them to the devil, shall we? You only meant to do something nice, and I ripped up at you. I'm an ungrateful brute, Julia. It's you who should forgive me."

"Is it so wrong of me to want to show off my handsome husband? Well, except for the dressing-gown. I shall take it

42

very ill if anyone sees you in that besides me."

"I don't know about that," Pickett said, looking over her head to regard this gorgeous garment with a speculative gleam in his eye. "If I'm to look like the Grand Turk, I might decide I need the harem to go with it."

"That settles it," she declared. "That thing is going back to the tailor's tomorrow!"

"No, no," he protested, laughing. "You bought it, my lady, and you shall have to suffer the consequences. Come, I'll make you a bargain: I'll try it on, if you'll have dinner served up here." His smile faded, and when he spoke again, it was with unwonted seriousness. "What do you say, Julia? It'll be almost like we were back in Drury Lane."

He saw the color that rose to her cheeks, and knew he did not have to elaborate further. She had told Lord Rupert Latham that they had changed their minds about the annulment, but that had not been the whole truth. In fact, he had been seriously injured during the course of an investigation, and it was while she was staying in his shabby little Drury Lane flat and nursing him back to health that they had consummated their marriage. It had been a strange way to begin married life, perhaps, but they had been happy—far happier, in some ways, than he was now, living in luxury in her Curzon Street town house.

"Very well, John," she said breathlessly. "You take off your coat, and I'll ring for Rogers."

It was not until several hours later, lying next to her in the big canopied bed, that he remembered one last bit of unfinished business.

"My lady?" he whispered into the darkness. "Are you awake?"

"I am now," she said sleepily. "What is it?"

"Julia, I—I'm sorry about the rubies."

A rustle of bed linens gave him to understand that she had turned over in the bed.

"I don't mind, John, truly I don't," she assured him. "It will be no trouble to keep them, at least for the nonce. Unless, of course, Lord Washbourn grows suspicious and comes looking for them. That might be a bit difficult to explain."

Pickett, lying on his back and staring upward in the direction of the canopy overhead, paid no attention to this attempt at humor. "No, not that. I made you think—I know you were disappointed—"

"Pray don't dwell on it, darling. It was entirely my own fault, for leaping to conclusions."

"You married a man who will never be able to give you gems."

Another rustle of sheets, and suddenly he was enveloped in soft, warm woman, her fingers pushing back a tangle of brown curls so that she might drop a feather-light kiss on his forehead.

"I married a man who *is* a gem," she said tenderly. "Anything more would be superfluous."

He did not for one minute believe it, but as he rolled over in order to answer this claim as it deserved, he resolved never to give her reason to change her mind.

4

*In Which John Pickett
Dons Fancy Dress in a Worthy Cause*

I look ridiculous," pronounced Pickett, eyeing with disfavor the masked figure who regarded him disapprovingly from the looking-glass. His own brown curls were allowed to fall free to his shoulders, where they spilled over the white lace of his wide collar and onto the back of his red velvet coat. His breeches were cut very full, and were gathered at each knee with a knot of ribbons. Studying his reflection, he could understand why the cavaliers had worn swords; they had probably spent a lot of their time defending themselves against ridicule. "My only consolation is that no one will know who I am."

"I think you look rather delicious."

His eyes met Julia's in the glass, and he turned to admire in person the vision she presented. Like him, she was masked, but where his was made of black satin, hers was white, and covered with silver spangles. Eschewing the high-waisted fashions that had been favored by ladies for the past decade, she wore a blue gown made in the style of a hundred and fifty years earlier, with a bell-shaped skirt falling from the natural waistline, billowing sleeves gathered at the elbows with ribbons, and a wide, round neckline revealing an expanse of creamy bosom. Her blonde hair had been parted in the middle, and over each ear a cluster of curls fell from a tiny bunch of forget-me-nots. If all seventeenth-century ladies had looked like this, Pickett decided, and if they had found his own rather effeminate costume attractive, he could see why the courtiers of Charles's court were happy to oblige them, whatever the cost to their own dignity.

Seeing the appreciative gleam in his eye, Julia spun around in a little pirouette that made her skirts flare out, exposing trim ankles in white silk stockings. "Do you like it?"

"I like it," he said emphatically. "Can't we just stay here tonight, so I can appreciate it in private?"

"Lady Washbourn might have something to say about that," she reminded him. "Don't forget your hat," she added as he turned, bareheaded, away from the mirror.

He gave her a speaking look which left her in no doubt as to his opinion of the wide-brimmed black hat with its jaunty red ostrich plume, then snatched it off the chair and set it on his head. He felt for the hilt of his sword, just to assure himself that it was still there, then offered his arm to his lady and escorted her down the stairs.

Rogers waited at the front door, beaming paternally upon them. "Very nice, sir, madam, if I may say so."

"Thank you, Rogers, you may," Julia said, smiling mischievously at the butler.

He threw open the door with great ceremony, revealing the closed carriage that was already awaiting them. Pickett handed Julia inside and then climbed in after her, albeit not without banging his sword on the doorframe.

"Do you realize," she said, once the carriage started forward, "we haven't made a social appearance in London together since that night at the theatre?"

"Probably not the best comparison, when you consider that the theatre burned to the ground that night," Pickett observed.

She smiled at him. "You acquitted yourself rather well on that occasion, if I recall."

"I didn't have much choice, did I?"

They could laugh about it now, the harrowing escape from the balcony of the burning building, the blow to his head that had left Pickett unconscious for the better part of a week, and Julia's adventures in fending for herself (and him) in a two-room flat without servants or any of the amenities to which she was accustomed. And Pickett could hardly regret the experience, given the fact that during that time Julia had decided, against every stricture of the class to which she belonged, that she wanted to remain his wife, and in more than name. Still, it could not be much of a life for her, cut off from the fashionable world of which she had once been a part. Small wonder that she had seized with such enthusiasm upon the opportunity to attend a ball! For that reason alone, he supposed it was worth making a fool of himself in fancy dress.

"I hope you will enjoy yourself," he told her. "I wish I could spend more time with you, but I'm afraid Lord Washbourn's movements will dictate my own."

"Will you have to follow him the entire evening?" She wrinkled her nose. "How tedious for you!"

" 'Follow' is probably too strong a word," he said, considering the question. "I can't appear to be tailing him too closely, lest he notice and get the wind up, but I will certainly have to keep my eye on him. I'll need to keep a weather eye out for Lady Washbourn, too; both of the earlier attempts—assuming they *were* attempts, and not merely unfortunate accidents—were carefully orchestrated to take place when Lord Washbourn was nowhere near, and could not be connected to them."

"And yet Lady Washbourn managed to connect him. John, you will be careful won't you? I'm glad you'll have a sword, anyway."

It was probably not the best time to mention that he'd had no training at all in fencing. "Swords wouldn't be much use against falling chandeliers or strategically placed pearls on the stairs," he pointed out.

She grimaced. "Is that supposed to make me feel better?"

"No." He caught her arm to steady her as the carriage lurched to a stop before the Washbourns' Park Lane residence. "It's to remind you to keep your wits about you. Falling chandeliers aren't particularly choosy about whom they land on, and I may not be there to protect you."

A liveried footman opened the door at that moment, rendering further private conversation impossible. Still, Julia tucked her hand into the curve of his elbow once they had disembarked, and gave his arm a little squeeze. Pickett interpreted this unspoken message (quite correctly) as a warning to him to heed his own advice.

At the top of the stairs, they were admitted to the house, where Julia divested herself of her evening cloak and Pickett shed his plumed hat before they followed a stout King Henry VIII and one of his queens (Pickett was not quite certain which one she was supposed to be, although the red "bloodstains" on her starched ruff suggested her fate) up yet another flight of stairs to the ballroom above. Here Lord and Lady Washbourn waited to receive their guests, along with a somewhat older lady who bore a marked resemblance to his lordship.

As the event was a masquerade, guests were not

announced, anonymity being (as Julia said) half the fun. Instead, the new arrivals presented their engraved invitations to the butler in order to be granted admittance. Unfortunately, the invitations had gone out weeks before Lady Washbourn had sent to Bow Street, and so she had been obliged to drop a word in her butler's ear to ensure that the Picketts, man and wife, were not turned away at the door in spite of their lack of an invitation. Now, as they reached the top of the stairs, Pickett had only to inform this individual of his identity to be ushered at once to his hostess.

"Mr. and Mrs. John Pickett, my lady," murmured the butler, in accordance with the instructions he had received earlier in the day.

"Mr. Pickett, I'm so glad you could come," Lady Washbourn, charmingly attired in the guise of a rosy-cheeked milkmaid of the previous century, greeted him warmly before turning to Julia. "And Mrs. Pickett, I'm pleased to make your acquaintance. May I offer my felicitations on your recent marriage?"

"Mr. Pickett." Lord Washbourn had eschewed a costume (lucky man, thought Pickett) in favor of a long black domino and black half-mask. The eyes that glittered through the slits seemed to regard Pickett with some misgiving, but the earl shook his hand nevertheless. "Since she lost those blasted rubies, my wife has taken the idea into her head that there's some jewel thief lurking about waiting for the chance to strip our guests bare of their baubles. I appreciate your willingness to humor her in this matter, but I trust your professional services will not be needed."

Pickett stammered something about prevention being better than cure.

"I think it very wise of you, Lady Washbourn," Julia said warmly. "One can never be too careful."

"Quite so, Mrs. Pickett," put in the older woman standing beside her hostess, a tall, slender female who appeared even taller in the flowing gown and great horned and veiled headdress of a medieval lady.

"Mother Washbourn, allow me to present Mr. and Mrs. John Pickett. Mr. Pickett, Mrs. Pickett, my husband's mother, the Dowager Countess of Washbourn."

"La, my dear, that title makes me sound so old!" the dowager protested laughingly as she offered Pickett her hand, upon which a great red stone winked. "Had Edward chosen a less agreeable female to marry, I must have been quite cross with him for taking a bride and relegating me to dowager status."

Pickett had put the woman's age at about forty, but now he realized that, if she were indeed Lord Washbourn's mother, she must be at least fifty, and very likely more. He found himself mentally contrasting her with his own mother-in-law; Julia's mother, Lady Runyon, was a tiny woman whose head didn't even reach his shoulder, and whose figure was so frail she looked as if a strong wind might blow her away. She was also the most terrifying woman he had ever met. Looking into the elder Lady Washbourn's smiling eyes, he hoped the younger knew how fortunate she was.

A fat Friar Tuck, red-faced from his climb up the stairs, "harrumphed" behind them, and so the Picketts were obliged to cut short their conversation and free their host and hostesses to greet the new arrivals. Once inside the ballroom, Pickett blinked at the transformation of the room he had stood in only a few days earlier. The scorched carpet had not been replaced, but then, the carpet laid down to protect the floor at other times would have been rolled up on this occasion to permit dancing. The chandelier overhead, apparently none the worse for its recent adventures, glowed with the light of dozens of wax candles, while at the far end of the room, massive floral arrangements adorned Ionic pillars strategically placed to conceal the small orchestra providing music from a raised dais.

More remarkable than the decorations, however, were the guests that milled about the crowded room. A harlequin in motley performed the complicated movements of the quadrille with a nun whose severe black habit contrasted sharply with the jeweled cross that bounced on her breast with every step, while a Turkish sultan in a feather-topped turban was similarly partnered with a well-endowed angel whose broad, sequined wings caused no small degree of inconvenience to the other couples in the set. Some of the costumed guests declined to dance altogether. A Roman centurion paused in his conversation with Cleopatra long enough to snag a glass of champagne from the tray of a liveried footman, while on the other side of the room, a crusading knight in silver cloth cleverly constructed to resemble armor paid extravagant court to a Greek goddess wearing a clinging linen chiton with very little underneath it. As Pickett watched, an Egyptian Pharaoh separated himself from the crowd and approached the place where they stood.

"Madame, your most obedient," the Pharaoh addressed Julia, making an elaborate leg. "Will you allow me the infinite pleasure of being the first to lead you onto the floor?"

Insufferable ass, thought Pickett, even as he answered Julia's silent query with smiling acquiescence. Too late, he realized that he had let himself in for a long night of observing Lord Washbourn from a discreet distance while watching out of the tail of his eye as men in various disguises attempted to practice the promised "licentious behavior" with his wife.

"I fear I must beg your pardon, Mr. Pickett," Lady Washbourn observed, joining him against the wall. "I had not realized how very dull this must be for you, not being able to join in the dancing."

"It is your safety, not my own amusement, that concerns

me," he assured her. "As for the dancing, I don't know how in any case, so it is a relief to be excused."

She nodded in understanding. "Papa engaged a dancing master for me when I was seventeen, but I have never become entirely comfortable with it. Perhaps if I had begun earlier—" She broke off, shrugging. "I suppose it is just as well that I can claim my duties as hostess as an excuse."

They were joined at that moment by Lord Washbourn, bearing a glass of pale champagne in one hand and another of a somewhat darker beverage in the other. "Accept my compliments, my dear," he said, offering the amber-colored liquid to his wife. "You have surpassed yourself. It is a splendid party."

She accepted the glass with thanks. "Do you really think so?" she asked, her fine grey eyes filled with mingled hope and fear.

"I'm sure of it. I overheard no fewer than five ladies speculating as to the name of the florist who created the magnificent arrangements adorning those pillars, and I have no doubt that come tomorrow morning, they will be lined up at our door to inquire. Will you tell them the truth, my dear, or will it amuse you to keep the information to yourself, and send them chasing after mares' nests by naming some fellow who doesn't exist?"

"As if I could be so cruel! If they ask, I will furnish them with his name and direction, and take their interest as a compliment."

The earl unbent sufficiently to smile down at her. "Somehow I expected nothing less of you. All the ladies of the *ton* could take a lesson from your kind heart."

Blushing rosily, Lady Washbourn covered her confusion by seeking recourse to the glass in her hand. Her lips had scarcely touched the rim when an interruption occurred in the form of a serving girl in a starched and ruffled cap.

"Begging your pardon, ma'am," she said, twisting in her hands the white apron covering her dark dress, "but Lady Carrington has fainted."

"Oh, dear!" Lady Washbourn set her glass down on a nearby table. "Where is she?"

"One of the footmen fetched her into the ladies' retiring room and laid her on the sofa. It seemed better than just leaving her there on the floor," she added apologetically.

"Yes, he did exactly right. I shall go there at once. In the meantime, Annie, go upstairs and have my abigail bring my smelling salts."

Annie bobbed a curtsy and took herself off. A short time later, Pickett saw Lady Washbourn return to the ballroom with one arm tucked solicitously beneath the elbow of a pale female who appeared not only unharmed by her ordeal, but actively relishing the attention it had won her, as those guests who were aware of the crisis flocked around to inquire as to her health. Shaking his head at the vagaries of

56

gently bred females, Pickett turned his attention back to the task at hand, and found Lord Washbourn leading the scantily-clad goddess into the set just forming.

As the night wore on and the champagne flowed more freely, the behavior of the guests grew more abandoned: the voices more boisterous, the dancing more reckless, the flirtations more brazen. Pickett, allowing himself nothing stronger to drink than the very mild peach ratafia flavored with almonds, watched as Lord Washbourn led one lady after another into the increasingly rowdy sets (including, on two occasions, Julia, her face becomingly flushed with champagne or exertion, Pickett was not quite sure which), but saw no actions on his host's part that might be considered suspicious, either of murderous intent toward his lordship's own wife, or amorous interest in Pickett's.

And then, just as he had decided the entire evening was a waste of time, and wondered how long it might be before he could collect Julia and return with her to Curzon Street, he realized the set was over and the dancers were dispersing—and Lord Washbourn, whom he had last seen partnering the angel with the large, er, wings, was nowhere in sight.

Grumbling under his breath, he pushed his way through the crowd in search of his host, to the considerable displeasure of those persons whom he accidentally whacked in the shins with his sword. He recalled the numerous small alcoves that lined the perimeter of the ballroom and, seeing no sign of Lord Washbourn anywhere else, charted a rather circuitous course for the nearest of these when his sword once again made violent contact with one of his fellow guests.

"Pardon me," a feminine voice said coldly, turning to glare at him. Upon getting a good look at her attacker, however, she took a step toward him, and her eyes took on a rapacious gleam. "Pardon me!" she said again, in a rather warmer tone.

"I—I beg your—I'm sorry," Pickett stammered, falling back a step, as he recognized the insufficiently garmented Greek goddess. "I didn't mean to—it's this sword—I'm not used to it—"

"What a waste," she purred, giving Pickett to understand that she was less concerned with the sword in his belt than she was the one in his breeches.

She closed the distance between them with another step in his direction, and once again Pickett fell back—and found his shoulders brushing the blue velvet curtain that closed off the small anteroom from the ballroom proper.

"Who are you?" she asked, reaching up as if she would untie his mask then and there. "I've never met you before, have I? I'm sure I would remember."

"That—that would be telling," Pickett said, casting a desperate glance over her shoulder, for Lord Washbourn, or

Julia, or anyone else who might rescue him from the predatory Persephone who was now pressing her insufficiently contained breasts against his chest.

"Is that your real hair?" she cooed appreciatively, running her fingers through his unbound curls. "Have you the least notion how many hours I spend with my hair tied in rags to make it curl like that?"

"No, I—I can't say that I do." Having caught sight of Julia across the room, Pickett strove without success to catch her eye.

"So much time that could be better spent," she continued, gently but inexorably backing Pickett through the curtain and into the alcove.

"You—you don't understand," he protested, trying (and failing) to keep the determined Diana at arm's length. "I'm married."

"Lud, so am I! What difference does that make? Come along now, sweeting, and you can show me your sword!"

One more step, and the light suddenly grew dim. Pickett realized with something akin to horror that they were now completely enclosed within the antechamber, and the heavy curtain had fallen into place behind them, blocking out the light from the ballroom. He wondered fleetingly, as the amorous Aphrodite set upon him in earnest, if it would also stifle the sound of his screams.

No sooner had the idea formed in his brain than a high-pitched shriek rose over the muffled sounds of music and conversation beyond the curtain, and for one dreadful moment, Pickett feared the thought had given birth to the deed. An instant's reflection was enough to reassure him on this head and, finding the interruption had momentarily distracted the goddess from her single-minded pursuit of his person, he seized the opportunity to free himself. Tossing a hasty "excuse me" over his shoulder, he ducked through the curtain, and found most of the Washbourns' guests huddled in one corner of the room. He hurried to join the crowd, making a beeline for a familiar figure in a blue satin gown.

"*There* you are!" exclaimed Julia in some relief, finding him at her elbow. "Where have you been?"

"Hell," was his emphatic reply. "What happened? Who screamed?"

"I don't know. That is, I don't know who screamed, but as to what happened, it's one of Lady Washbourn's maids. John, she's dead!"

5

*In Which a Masquerade Ball
Comes to an Abrupt End*

S tay here, my lady."
Pickett set his wife gently aside, then pushed his way
to the front of the crowd, whacking several people in the legs
with his sword (quite deliberately this time) in order to clear
a path. A petite young woman—or what was left of her—lay
facedown on the floor near the wall. Beneath her, and
apparently brought down by her fall, a small table had
tumbled onto its side, littering the floor with broken glass,
spilled liquid, and stained table linens.

Hearing a faint sound resembling something between a
gasp and a whimper, Pickett glanced around and saw Julia
standing right behind him, in spite of his instructions. He
handed her the cumbersome sword, then dropped to one
knee and carefully turned the girl over onto her back, but
when he brushed back the ash-blonde hair that had escaped
from her starched and ruffled cap and fallen across her face,

he suffered a check. This was the same serving girl who had interrupted his conversation with Lady Washbourn to inform her of Lady Carrington's fainting fit. More surprising than the girl's identity, however, was her condition. In almost six years with the Bow Street force, he had seen his share of dead bodies, but most of them had been gray of countenance. This girl's face was flushed with an unnaturally rosy hue that put Lady Washbourn's apple-cheeked milkmaid to shame. She might have been supposed to be in the bloom of health, had it not been for the unseeing eyes staring up at the ceiling, eyes which had rolled back in her head so that only the lower edge of the pale blue iris was visible. Bending nearer, Pickett caught a whiff of almonds; clearly, the girl had been availing herself of her employers' ratafia.

Pickett felt a bit ill as he realized he'd put away one or two glasses of the same beverage, and that his wife was even now holding just such a drink. It was this last that spurred him to action. He stood up and snatched the glass from Julia's hand, then tipped its contents into the base of a nearby potted plant that had somehow escaped the debacle.

Julia observed this wasteful operation in bewilderment. "John? What—?"

If he heard her at all, he gave no sign. "What happened?" he asked the gaping crowd. "Did anyone see?"

There was no response. Of course no one saw, he thought bitterly. She was a servant, and the Washbourns' guest list comprised the flower of British aristocracy. Unless they wanted something from her—another glass of champagne, perhaps, or a quick tumble in the cloakroom—they would have paid no attention to her at all.

"I—I saw."

Pickett looked up to identify the timid speaker, and found another maid standing at the dead girl's feet. To his chagrin, he realized that he had not noticed her; amongst Lord and Lady Washbourn's gorgeously costumed guests, her plain black dress and white chintz apron rendered her all but invisible.

"And what is your name?" It didn't really matter at this point, but Pickett was painfully aware of having committed the same error for which he had just been mentally castigating his betters.

"Mary."

"Very well, Mary, can you tell me what happened?"

"I'll try, sir. Mrs. Milliken—the housekeeper, you know —she sent me and Annie upstairs to collect all the dirty dishes. She was afraid we might run out of glasses before the ball was over, see, and so she wanted Bess—she's the scullery maid, Bess is—to wash the ones that the guests was done with. And so me and Annie come upstairs and was gathering up the dirties when Annie starts shaking fit to be tied, sort of jerking back and forth like, and the stuff what's left in the glass she's holding spills all over the place. And just when I'm thinking as how I'll be the one to have to clean up the mess after she's put to bed ill, she falls down just like you see her there, and it don't take no doctor to see that she's dead!" With this pronouncement, she buried her face in her apron and burst into loud, gusty sobs.

"There, there, Mary." Lady Washbourn, followed by her husband, moved through the crush of people to join them. "I'm sure no one blames you. Perhaps you had best go to bed yourself. Go downstairs and ask Mrs. Milliken to give you a dose of sleeping draught."

"But, ma'am, the mess—" protested Mary, gesturing toward the broken glass and spilled liquid on the floor.

Lady Washbourn shook her head dismissively. "We will deal with it later."

"I'm sorry, your ladyship," Pickett put in, "but I'm afraid Miss, er, Mary will have to postpone her sleep until after the coroner has spoken to her."

"The coroner?" echoed the maid and both her employers, like a Greek chorus.

"You need have nothing to fear from him," Pickett assured the trembling Mary. "All you have to do is answer whatever questions he may ask."

"Surely the coroner's presence won't be necessary." Lord Washbourn protested. What could be seen of his face beneath his half-mask was frowning in disapproval.

"I'm afraid it will, your lordship. The coroner must be

called in the event of any sudden death." Seeing the earl inclined to argue the point, Pickett added, "If it turns out that the girl died of natural causes, you need have nothing to worry about."

"What do you mean, 'if'?" demanded Lord Washbourn. "Of course she died of natural causes!"

"Nevertheless, when an apparently healthy young woman drops dead without warning, every possibility must be considered."

"*Apparently* healthy," echoed the earl, latching onto this qualifier. "I daresay the poor girl suffered from some illness, and never told us for fear of losing her position. What else could it be? Who would have any reason to do her harm?"

"I'm sure the coroner's inquest will answer any such questions," Pickett said, giving his best imitation of Mr. Colquhoun in a mood to brook no argument. "The sooner you send a message to the coroner, the sooner we can put the matter to rest."

Grumbling under his breath, the earl turned away to summon a footman.

"Mr. Pickett," said Lady Washbourn, lowering her voice. "Could it be possible that—do you think perhaps—?"

"I think the possibility must be considered, your ladyship," Pickett responded in like manner, "but I must ask you not to make any mention of the matter—not here, nor at the coroner's inquest."

"Will I be asked to give evidence, then?"

Pickett shook his head. "I don't know. That will be up to the coroner."

The coroner, when he arrived twenty minutes later, proved to be one Mr. Bartholomew Bagley, a cadaverous man of middle age, who seemed mildly offended that a Bow Street Runner should be on the scene before him, as if Pickett were somehow poaching on his own preserves.

"And what, pray, might you be doing here?" he asked, regarding Pickett with undisguised hostility.

After advising Mary to answer the coroner's questions as truthfully as she could, he could hardly balk at doing the same himself. "My wife and I are the guests of Lord and Lady Washbourn," he said. "More than that, her ladyship charged me with seeing to her guests' safety."

"I see." Mr. Bagley's beady eyes shifted from Pickett to the body on the floor, and back again. "A pity your protection didn't extend to the household staff."

Pickett opened his mouth to protest this unjust insinuation, but the coroner had by this time turned his attention to Lord Washbourn.

"There will have to be an inquest into the young woman's death, your lordship. I will require the services of half a dozen men to serve on the jury."

Lord Washbourn nodded in resignation, and Pickett noticed that somewhere along the way the earl had shed his costume. Uncomfortably aware of his own flamboyant silks and velvets, and their stark contrast to the dead woman at his feet, Pickett wished he might have done the same. At the very least, he wished he might tie back his hair; unbound curls seemed somehow frivolous and unprofessional at such a time.

"I understand the necessity, Mr. Bagley," the earl said, nodding, "and I stand ready to serve."

The coroner shook his head. "I appreciate your willingness, your lordship, but seeing as how the deceased was in your service, and the death took place in your house, I'm afraid you're a bit too closely involved—a conflict of interest, you might say." He looked beyond Lord and Lady Washbourn to their guests. Some of these still hung about the scene of the tragedy, while others had lost interest in the proceedings and wandered off in search of more diverting entertainment. "Is there anyone else who might agree to serve?"

"I'll do it," announced the red-faced Friar Tuck eagerly. "Most exciting diversion I've had all Season." He made a wobbly bow in Lady Washbourn's direction. "Congratulations, ma'am. Everyone will be talking of your ball for weeks to come."

One by one, other men consented to serve on the coroner's jury, their demeanors ranging from enthusiasm to curiosity to a bored obligation to duty. Having got the half-dozen he'd asked for, plus another beside, the coroner invited these men to step forward and examine the body more closely.

"No blood, you'll notice, nor any other sign of a wound," he pointed out, after cautioning the men to step carefully around the broken glass. "But note, if you will, the flushed face of the deceased."

"There's also a strong odor of bitter almonds," put in Pickett.

The coroner glared at him. "Yes, thank you, Mr. Pickett, when I need your assistance in conducting an examination, I'll ask for it. I daresay you will find that particular odor on the breath of half the people here." He turned to Lady Washbourn for confirmation. "You did offer your guests a beverage flavored with almonds, did you not, your ladyship?"

"I did, Mr. Bagley, but at no time in the evening did I invite the servants to share it," the countess said with some asperity.

"Still, I daresay it's not unheard of for a servant to indulge without an invitation." He scanned the assemblage for the little maid Pickett had questioned earlier. "You, there, do you know if the deceased drank any of this beverage before her unfortunate collapse?"

"Yes, sir, she did," confessed Mary, with an apologetic glance at her mistress. "She was clearing the dirties away when she noticed one that looked like it hadn't even been touched. She said as how it were a right shame to let it go to waste, and then she turned her back so no one could see, and drank it right down." Another guilty glance in Lady Washbourn's direction gave Pickett to understand that Annie was probably not the only one to help herself to the leavings of her betters.

"And that explains your almond odor, Mr. Pickett," concluded the coroner. "No reason to make a mystery where none exists."

Pickett was by no means convinced, but since he could hardly argue the point without voicing his own suspicions regarding Lord and Lady Washbourn, he was obliged to bite his tongue and trust to the coroner's jury to be more open-minded than the man himself.

"Are there any more questions? No? Very well, then," pronounced the coroner at last. "The inquest will be held tomorrow morning at nine of the clock, in the public room of the Bull's Head in Covent Garden. I shall look forward to seeing all of you there. The jurors, that is," he amended hastily, frowning at Pickett. "Mr. Pickett, I am sure you have other responsibilities, so we will not trouble you to attend."

The devil you won't, thought Pickett, resolving that wild horses would not keep him away from the Bull's Head at nine o'clock the following morning.

69

6

In Which Is Seen the Calm before the Storm

T he next morning, Pickett awoke to find himself alone
in the bed.

"Julia?" he called, turning toward the adjoining dressing
room.

There was no answer. He stretched and rubbed the sleep
from his eyes, then rose and donned (albeit not without a
certain self-consciousness) the gorgeous new dressing gown
and tying its belt about his waist. He slid his feet into
slippers of buttery soft Moroccan leather (yet another token
of his wife's affection), then headed downstairs in search of
her.

He found her in the breakfast room, clad in a pink satin
wrapper and dispensing hot, fragrant coffee into a delicate
Sevrès cup. "Good morning, John," she said, reaching for a
second cup and beginning to pour. "I hope I didn't disturb
you when I got up."

"Not at all," he assured her, stealing an arm around her waist and dropping a kiss onto her bright hair. "You're not troubled by all this, are you?"

She didn't have to ask what "all this" was. "No, darling, not really. That is, one never likes to see someone die, especially when the someone was as young as Annie. Still, dead bodies do seem to have a habit of following you, so I suppose I might as well accustom myself to it. In fact, I awoke early, and couldn't get back to sleep." She sighed. "But it doesn't seem to make any difference, for by noon I can hardly hold my eyes open, no matter how late I might have slept. Do you want one sugar, or two?"

"Two," he said, and pulled her into his arms and kissed her twice.

"Mmm," she purred, leaning into his embrace. "I wish I could go with you to the inquest, but I promised to call on Emily Dunnington this morning."

"I thought Lord and Lady Dunnington had gone back to Sussex." He released her so that he might load up a plate of bacon, toast, and buttered eggs from the silver chafing dishes lined up on the buffet.

"They had, but they've returned to London so that Emily may consult with her dressmaker," she told him as they seated themselves at the breakfast table. "Poor Emily! London during the Season can be a dull place when one cannot go out. She is almost five months gone, you know, and her delicate condition is getting more and more difficult to hide. When she begged me to come and alleviate her boredom, well, I could hardly refuse." She grimaced. "Of course, when I agreed, I had no way of knowing we would stumble across a murder the night before."

"We don't know that it was murder," Pickett reminded her.

"No, but you think it was, don't you? That's why you took my drink away."

"Yes, I think it was. There's a particular poison that leaves an odor of bitter almonds. I've never come in contact with it before, but some of the older Runners have. I'm thinking if one wanted to kill someone with such a poison, what better way to administer it than through a drink flavored with the very same almonds whose scent would otherwise point to its use?"

Julia pressed a hand to her abdomen. "That's enough to put me off my breakfast."

"I'm sorry, love," Pickett said, conscience-stricken. "I shouldn't be talking about such things at the table."

"Nonsense! I'm the one who brought up the subject. And it's not as if I've had much appetite lately, in any case. But what will you do now?"

"There's very little I *can* do, especially since the coroner refuses to consider any scenario beyond natural causes, and even if I'm allowed to testify at all—which I doubt—I can't suggest the possibility of willful murder—not without betraying Lady Washbourn's confidence and perhaps even compromising her safety."

"Difficult for you," she said sympathetically, passing him the marmalade. "We must hope that the truth will come out at the inquest."

"Yes, but what it's going to come down to is this: why would anyone wish to murder a maid? And I can't offer an answer to that question without suggesting that perhaps the maid was not the intended victim. Which will raise the further question of who, then, might have been? And I can't answer that without dragging Lady Washbourn's suspicions into it."

"Oh! That reminds me—" Julia quickly choked down a mouthful of buttered toast before continuing. "In all the hubbub last night, I almost forgot to mention it. Just a little while before Annie collapsed, I was searching for you and happened to look inside one of those little alcoves lining the ballroom. You'll never guess what I saw."

Pickett's fork grated against his plate with a loud *screech*, and it was perhaps a good thing that Julia was so eager to impart her discovery that she failed to notice the guilt writ large on his expressive countenance.

"Lord Washbourn himself," she announced, "closeted there with the least angelic angel I have ever seen."

Pickett snapped his fingers in sudden recollection. "The

lady with the, er, wings!"

"The very same."

"Who was she, anyway?"

"Lady Barbara Brennan," she said. "The widow of Sir Roger Brennan, late of His Majesty's diplomatic corps. And I do mean 'late,' for Sir Roger died less than six months ago."

Pickett's eyebrows rose. "She didn't waste much time in mourning, did she?"

"No, but I can hardly criticize her for that, not when one considers the fact that I am already remarried, and Frederick has not yet been gone a year. Still, her behavior was hardly that of a decent woman, much less a grieving widow. When I stumbled across them in the alcove, she had her arms coiled about Lord Washbourn's neck and was cooing something into his ear, but then he became aware of my presence and shoved her away. I begged their pardon—quite collectedly, I thought, under the circumstances—and made my escape just in time to hear a scream, and see everyone rushing over to where Annie had fallen."

"I wonder if this Lady Barbara is the woman Lady Washbourn mentioned, but declined to name," Pickett said. "She told me her husband had once had hopes of marrying another, but was obliged to hold out for an heiress."

"I am not well acquainted with either lady, but from what I saw last night of both Lady Barbara and Lady

74

Washbourn, I should say he got the better bargain—unless, of course, he is one of those gentlemen who values females only for their, er, wings."

Pickett pushed back his plate and rose from the table. "Thank you for telling me. I will certainly bear it in mind, but now I had better get ready for the inquest."

Citing the need to change her own wrapper for a morning gown, she followed him up the stairs. He opened the clothes press and would have extracted from its depths the black tailcoat he favored for appearances at the Old Bailey, when she protested.

"Oh, John! Will you not wear one of the new ones?"

He hesitated. He was not at all comfortable with the idea of puffing himself off as a gentleman when he knew full well that he was no such thing. And yet, given the fact that most of the jurors had handles attached to their names, and the knowledge that the coroner was already inclined to disregard his suspicions, and the pleading look in his wife's blue eyes as she gazed up at him . . .

"Very well." Conceding defeat with a sigh, he stepped away from the clothes press. "You may choose. Which is it to be?"

"Hmm." She rifled through the garments, considering each one in turn. "Nothing so bright as the mulberry I should think, given the solemnity of the occasion. What do you think of the bottle green?" She pulled it out of the clothes press and held it up for inspection.

"If that is what you like, my lady, then who am I to dispute it?"

He dressed hastily in the shirt, breeches, and waistcoat she chose for him, but when it came time to pull on the green tailcoat, she was obliged to lend a hand to coax the close-fitting garment up his arms and over his shoulders.

"You will want to engage a valet, of course," she said, smoothing his collar.

"I will?" he asked, rather taken aback by this revelation.

"Of course," she said again. Seeing he was not convinced, she explained, "John, you'll find that fashionable garments fit much more closely than those you are accustomed to wearing. I confess, I've sometimes wondered how you contrived to dress yourself for our wedding."

"It wasn't easy," he admitted, recalling his struggle with the blue tailcoat he'd worn on that occasion. "Still, you helped me put on that same coat for dinner at your parents' house—more than once, in fact."

"Yes, but you cannot deny that the circumstances were unusual," she pointed out. "We'd only just married, and hadn't yet had time to engage additional staff. For that matter, we'd have had nowhere to put servants in any case, since we were living in your Drury Lane flat. But you cannot expect me to valet for you forever."

"Why not?" he asked plaintively.

She continued as if he had not spoken. "Thomas might oblige, if you don't wish to entrust the care of your person to the ministrations of a stranger. In fact, he would consider it quite a step up in the world. We could then engage another footman to take his place."

"I'm not at all comfortable with the idea of ordering Thomas about," Pickett objected. "After all, I've worn the man's livery."

"Yes, in Yorkshire," she recalled, nodding in remembrance. "And as I recollect, the sleeves were a bit short on you, were they not? Still, Thomas knows you, and likes you, and so is unlikely to look down his nose at you, as a truly fashionable valet might do."

"But the expense—"

"Thomas will need to be given a rise in his wages, of course, but we can well afford it. Besides, his services will cost less than those of a fashionable gentleman's gentleman. Come, I will make you a bargain," she said with a provocative gleam in her eye. "If you will engage a valet to help you into your coat in the morning, I will endeavor to help you out of it at night."

This offer seemed to clench the matter, just as she had intended. Pickett bade her a lingering farewell, and then set out for the Bull's Head, albeit not before she had extracted a promise from him that he would tell her anything interesting that happened at the inquest.

Alone in the bedchamber, Julia watched out the window until she saw him emerge from the house into the street below. Her loving gaze followed his departure until he disappeared from view, then she gave a little sigh and turned her attention to her own toilette.

A quarter hour's walk brought her to Audley Street and the Town residence of Emily, the Countess of Dunnington. The butler opened at once to her knock, and all but fell on her neck in gratitude.

"Lady Dunnington will be pleased to see you, your ladyship—er, madam," he said in a voice that conveyed a wealth of understatement.

He led the way to the drawing room where Julia had partaken of many a cup of tea in company with the countess.

"Julia! Thank God!" declared Lady Dunnington, heaving herself to her feet to welcome her guest. "I thought I should die of boredom. Do come in and sit down."

Julia embraced her friend warmly, and then took a seat on one end of the sofa, from which vantage point she surveyed the elegantly appointed room as if seeing it for the first time.

"What is it, Julia?" Lady Dunnington asked, regarding her visitor curiously.

"Nothing, really, only—I can remember a time when I sat in this room with John, and I had no idea that, through some quirk of Scottish law, we were legally wed." She shook her head as if to clear it. "Was it really only this past November? So much has changed since then!"

Emily studied her keenly. "Are you happy, Julia? Do you regret it?"

"Oh, Emily, how could I? It is true that I sometimes get lonely or bored—I confess, I am too much of a coward to face the prospect of walking in St. James's Park, where I should no doubt be ogled and pointed out, or else given the cut direct." Her gaze grew soft. "And yet when I compare what I have lost with what I have gained—no, Emily, I cannot regret it."

"And *that* is what they cannot pardon, you know. If only you had had the decency to suffer for your sins, it would have been very different. Much can be forgiven a woman who breaks the rules only to die a lingering death of some wasting disease, having been abandoned by her lover and left to languish in solitary misery. But *you*, my dear, had the gall not only to break the rules, but to rejoice in your shame. Why, it threatens the very fabric of Society. Oh! Speaking of fabric—" Emily leaped to her feet as quickly as her increasing girth would allow. "—Mother Dunnington sent the most beautiful little dress for the baby's christening! I suspect she is angling to have a daughter named after her if it should be a girl, and I suppose we ought to do so, since she is the child's grandmother, but I *cannot* bring myself to saddle my daughter with a name like Iphigenia! But let me show you the dress, and you may tell me what you think of it. I'll just dash upstairs and fetch it."

Julia felt compelled to protest. "Had you not better send a servant for it?"

"Pish tosh!" Emily declared inelegantly. "You are as bad as Dunnington! If it were left up to him, I would sit on the sofa for the next four months with my feet on a cushion. One would think it was my first child, instead of my third."

Julia abandoned an argument that she recognized to be futile, and sat back to await her friend's return. The room seemed unnaturally silent after Lady Dunnington's departure, the only sound being the ticking of the ormolu clock on the mantel. Julia suddenly realized how very tired she was. The events of the previous night and her early morning awakening all seemed to catch up to her at once, and she raised her gloved hand to cover a yawn. Perhaps if she were to close her eyes for just a moment . . .

By the time Lady Dunnington reentered the room a few minutes later with a lavishly embroidered gown of whitework on fine batiste draped over her arm, Julia was sound asleep.

"I'm sorry it took me so long. I thought Cummings had packed it in the—" Emily broke off abruptly at the sight of her slumbering guest.

Whether it was Emily's voice that awoke her, or its sudden cessation, Julia returned to wakefulness with a start.

"Late night, Julia?" Emily asked, arching one provocative eyebrow. "Am I to assume, then, that the education of your *enfant prodige* is proceeding apace?"

It would be useless, Julia supposed, to protest that the warmth that flooded her face was simply due to its being flushed with sleep. She had never told Emily in so many words that John Pickett had been a virgin when she'd married him, but she supposed that, given the requirements of the annulment process, it had not been difficult to deduce. "I'll have you know, Emily, that we were in bed before midnight!"

Emily nodded sagely. "Of *that*, my dear, I have no doubt."

"I mean we were *asleep* by midnight," Julia insisted. "We had gone to the Washbourn masquerade—John was on a case, so you need not look like that—and one of the maids collapsed and died, right there in the ballroom. Needless to say, it brought the revelries to an abrupt end."

"Yes, I know about that. I read about it in *Aunt Mildred's Parlour* just this morning."

"What, already?"

Emily returned to her vacated place on the sofa, and removed a single printed page from the piecrust table at her elbow. "Here, you may read it for yourself."

Julia took the broadsheet and scanned it quickly. Sure enough, a third of the way down the page, " 'Lady W— is proving herself to be a Society hostess whom all others will strive in vain to emulate,' " she read aloud. " 'Not content with introducing a Bow Street Runner into her social circle, the former Miss M—'s primary entertainment for the evening proved to be the sudden death of one of her house-maids. While Lady W—'s masquerade will certainly be the talk of the Season, one can only hope that competing hostesses will not feel compelled to slay their servants in imitation.' Oh, poor John!"

" 'Poor *John*'?" Lady Dunnington echoed incredu-lously. "I should say rather, 'poor Lady Washbourn.' Does it not seem to you that there is a particular malice at work whenever Aunt Mildred mentions Lady Washbourn?"

Julia considered the matter, and was forced to agree. "Now that you mention it, I suppose there is. One might argue that certain of her targets almost *ask* to be skewered by Aunt Mildred's pen—individuals who gamble away obscene sums of money at cards, or couples who are indiscreet in their pursuit of *affaires*—but Lady Washbourn is guilty of no greater sin than marrying above her station. She is far from the first person to have done so, and yet whatever the poor woman does, even giving birth to a girl instead of the hoped-for heir, is fair game for Aunt Mildred."

"Yes, I had thought that last was particularly cruel. As if a woman has any choice in the gender of her child! And by all accounts, Lord Washbourn positively dotes on his little daughter, so if *he* is not bothered by it, what cause has Aunt Mildred for complaint?"

"One thing is certain," Julia said. "Whoever Aunt Mildred is, and however much she may despise Lady Washbourn, she had no qualms about accepting the lady's hospitality."

"Julia! You think she was at the masquerade last night?"

"I think she must have been. How else would she have known about the incident in time to write about it and submit it to her printer, who then published and distributed it, all in less than twelve hours?"

"Yes, I suppose you must be right. That narrows the lady's identity down to, what, fifty women, give or take a few."

"You might as well make it an even hundred, for 'Aunt Mildred' might well be a man using a female *nom de plume*," Julia pointed out.

"Very true! I hadn't thought of that. But enough about Aunt Mildred! Tell me what you think of this."

Lady Dunnington spread the christening gown over her knees, and the conversation turned to the countess's approaching confinement. At length, however, Emily noticed her guest's frequent glances at the clock, and was smitten with remorse.

"Oh, my dear Julia, pray forgive me!" she exclaimed,

conscience-stricken. "I had not thought how difficult this must be for you, unable as you are to have children of your own."

Julia placed her hand over Emily's and gave it a squeeze. "Not at all, Emily. I am genuinely happy for you, truly I am—all the more so because it was John who brought it about." Seeing Emily's wide eyes and gaping jaw, she amended hastily, "Not that he is responsible for your condition, of course, but he certainly brought about the reconciliation between you and Lord Dunnington that made it possible."

"I should say so! As for my condition, that must certainly be laid at Dunnington's door." Her satisfied smile put Julia forcibly in mind of the cat that ate the canary. "One thing must be said for gentlemen of a certain age: they know much better than their younger counterparts how best to please a lady."

Julia could not allow this slur against her own very young husband to go unchallenged. "Nevertheless, Emily, there is much to be said for the—the stamina—of five-and-twenty," she insisted, coloring slightly as she glanced up at the clock over the mantel.

"There you go again," Emily accused.

"Oh, Emily, I do beg your pardon," Julia said, much chastened. "It is the inquest, you see. It began an hour ago, and I cannot help wondering—" She could not say more without betraying her husband's confidence. Thankfully, Emily seemed to grasp the situation at once.

"And you cannot help wondering how things are going for your Mr. Pickett," she deduced. "Very well, then, go home and wait for him. And if he should return from the inquest cross and out of temper, then take him upstairs and swive him properly, and all will be well."

"What an excellent notion!" Julia rose to her feet and looked down at her hostess with a mischievous smile. "You do realize, do you not, that he would be utterly mortified if he knew we were talking about him in such a way."

"I do indeed—in fact, that is what makes it so enjoyable. My one regret is that he is not here, so I am denied the pleasure of watching him squirm." Lady Dunnington regarded her friend with a long, appraising look. "In all seriousness, Julia, however much I might have deplored your decision to marry him, I do believe he has been good for you."

"Yes." Julia's smile grew soft. "Yes, he has," she said, and set out for Curzon Street to await his return.

7

In Which an Inquest Is Held

T he subject of this discussion, meanwhile, arrived at the Bull's Head shortly before nine o'clock. He passed through the public room to the more private one in the back, and found that the tables had been shoved against the wall and the chairs arranged in rows. One row of seven chairs stood apart from the rest, and Pickett recognized these as having been set aside for the jury. Adjacent to these chairs, and positioned facing them, was a single chair where those being questioned would sit in turn. As for the other seats, the first few rows were reserved for witnesses, with Lord Washbourn, his wife, and his mother taking up most of the front row. The earl sat tight-lipped, while Lady Washbourn's face was white and strained. A flash of red caught Pickett's eye as the dowager countess toyed with the handkerchief on her lap, and Pickett recognized the same large red stone she'd worn the previous evening. He had supposed the ring was part of her costume, but apparently this assumption was incorrect. Now he found himself wondering if it, too, comprised part of the Washbourn rubies and, if so, how she had contrived to retain it when the rest of the set passed to her daughter-in-law. Pickett found little to interest him in the other seats, most of which appeared to be filled with a motley collection of masquerade attendees who were not on the jury, and regular patrons of the establishment. The former had no doubt been lured there by morbid curiosity; the latter, by the desire for liquid refreshment even at so early an hour. Pickett chose a chair at one end of the second row and sat down to await events.

"Room for one more?"

At the sound of a familiar voice, one whose native Scots accent was still intact despite years spent living in London and, long before that, America, Pickett looked up into the face of his magistrate.

"Mr. Colquhoun!" Pickett quickly slid over to the next chair, leaving the one on the end for his mentor. "What brings you here?"

"Need you ask? Let us say that when my breakfast is interrupted by a communication from the esteemed Mr. Bagley requesting that I instruct my Runners to cease meddling in matters that are none of their concern, I judge it wise to take an interest. No, my lad, let me have the inside chair. I daresay you'll need to be on the end, so you can get out more easily when you're called on to testify."

"*If* I'm called on to testify," Pickett put in bitterly.

"You will be," the magistrate predicted confidently.

Pickett shook his head. "I'm not so sure. Mr. Bagley was not at all pleased to see me at the Washbourn masquerade—never mind the fact that I was the one who instructed them to send for him in the first place," he added with perhaps justifiable resentment.

"Bartholomew Bagley is a fool," declared Mr. Colquhoun, never one to mince words. "His appointment as coroner is strictly on an interim basis, his predecessor having recently retired, and until he is confirmed in the position permanently—a day I hope I may never live to see—he perceives a threat to his authority behind every bush. He doesn't want the sort of messy murder case that might jeopardize his permanent appointment."

"I should have thought a sensational murder would help rather than hinder his cause," Pickett observed.

"A sensational murder, perhaps. But there's nothing particularly sensational about the death of a housemaid. Then, too, if he can prevent any hint of scandal from wrecking Lord Washbourn's chances for his own government appointment, Mr. Bagley might acquire a powerful patron."

"In other words, I haven't a chance," Pickett said bleakly.

"Make no mistake, Mr. Pickett, you will have your say—I intend to make sure of it—but I doubt you will much enjoy it. I shouldn't wonder if Mr. Bagley seizes upon any chance to discredit you."

Pickett gave a humorless laugh. "He won't have far to look, will he?" It was a statement, not a question, but one with which the magistrate begged leave to differ.

"Nonsense! Whatever you might have done before you came to Bow Street, your record since then has been exemplary. You have nothing to fear from the likes of Bartholomew Bagley."

"Thank you, sir," Pickett said with an uncertain yet grateful smile. Mr. Colquhoun, he knew, did not suffer fools gladly (as evidenced by his bluntly stated opinion of the coroner) which made the magistrate's intervention in the life of a juvenile pickpocket all the more incredible—almost as incredible as the idea that, ten years later, a viscountess (and one, furthermore, who might have had any gentleman she wished) could fall in love with and marry that same pickpocket.

"Sir," Pickett began, but whatever he might have said was interrupted when a door on the opposite side of the room opened and seven gentlemen filed in, followed by the coroner himself. The seven took the seats reserved for the jurors with much scraping of chair legs against the wooden floor boards, and it occurred to Pickett that surely never before had the death of a housemaid attracted so exalted a collection of spectators. Once the jurors settled themselves comfortably, the coroner rose. Mr. Bagley looked over the room, which by this time had grown quite crowded, and glared when his gaze fell on Pickett and Mr. Colquhoun. Looking quickly away, he cleared his throat and addressed the gathering.

"Gentlemen—and ladies," he added as an afterthought, seeing Lady Washbourn and the dowager countess seated next to Lord Washbourn on the front row, "the purpose of this assembly is to conduct an inquiry into the death of Ann Barton, kitchen maid, on the twenty-first of April, 1809, at number twelve Grosvenor Square, the Town residence of Lord Washbourn. We will begin with his lordship's testimony. Your lordship, if you would be so good—" Mr. Bagley gestured toward the single chair, and Lord Washbourn left his seat at his wife's side and came forward with measured steps.

"Thank you, my lord. The deceased, Ann Barton, was in your employ, was she not?"

The earl tilted his handsome head as he considered the question. "As the hiring of female servants falls within my wife's purview, it might be more accurate to say that she was in Lady Washbourn's employ."

"Nevertheless, Miss Barton was on your payroll, and lived beneath your roof, is that correct?"

"It is."

"Did she have any enemies that you were aware of?"

Lord Washbourn's eyebrows rose. "My good fellow, I doubt the girl was more than fifteen years old! What could she possibly have done to have made enemies at such a young age?"

"I must remind your lordship that I am asking the questions," Mr. Bagley said pointedly. "Again, did the girl have any enemies that you are aware of?"

"No, not that I am aware of," the earl said with the sigh of a man whose patience is being sorely tried.

"Did she suffer from any illnesses?"

"My good man, if she had shown any indication of poor health, I doubt very much that my wife would have engaged her! If you want more detail than that, I fear you must ask a physician."

"All in good time, your lordship, all in good time," the coroner assured him. "Now, tell the gentlemen of the jury, as clearly as you can recall, what happened last night to Miss Barton."

"I'm afraid I can't tell you much, because the girl was already dead when I arrived on the scene. I was dancing with one of our guests—Lady Barbara Brennan, if memory serves —when I heard a shriek and a sound of breaking glass. Needless to say, I considered it my duty as host to discover the cause of the disruption. A crowd had gathered at one corner of the ballroom, and when I pushed my way to the front of it, I found Annie—Miss Barton, that is—lying on the floor, with Mary Soames, another housemaid, standing over her sobbing, and Mr. John Pickett examining the body. It was Mr. Pickett who suggested—although 'ordered' would not be too strong a word—that you be sent for."

"Hmph," was Mr. Bagley's only response. He dismissed the earl and summoned the countess to take his place. He asked her the very same questions he had put to her husband, and received the same answers.

"This Mr. John Pickett is a principal officer at Bow Street, is he not? A Runner, in other words?"

Lady Washbourn confirmed that this was so.

"You might say it was a very good thing Mr. Pickett was present," Mr. Bagley observed smoothly.

"Yes, it was," she agreed.

"Tell me, your ladyship, are you in the habit of entertaining Bow Street Runners, or was Mr. Pickett there in some official capacity?"

Lady Washbourn's eyes met Pickett's for the briefest of moments before returning to the coroner. "In fact, Mr. Bagley, I have recently—lost—a valuable ruby necklace. If there should happen to be a thief in the house, my guests would very likely have offered the fellow more temptation, perhaps, than he could resist. Mr. Pickett was invited as a deterrent against theft."

"And not, you are quite certain, as a deterrent against any attempt on the life of one of your servants?"

"Indeed not!" exclaimed her ladyship, bristling with indignation. Pickett could not help admiring her cool-headedness, for she had spoken no less than the truth: it was her own life, not that of one of her servants, that he had been engaged to protect.

"Thank you, Lady Washbourn, you may return to your seat. We will hear next from Miss Mary Soames."

A brief silence reigned while the little maid shuffled forward, her face white and her whole demeanor fearful. Pickett could not help wondering if her fear was nothing more than a timid girl's discomfort at finding herself the center of so much attention, or a very real dread that Annie's death had indeed been murder and that, by testifying, she was somehow placing herself in danger.

"Miss Soames," the coroner spoke to the girl, "how long had you been acquainted with the deceased?"

"Beg pardon, sir?"

"The dead girl," the coroner explained with poorly concealed impatience. "How long had you known her?"

"I'd known Annie for almost three years, ever since she first come to work for Lord and Lady Washbourn. Her parents had just died, see, and so she had to find some way to support herself."

"And the two of you were working last night at the

93

masquerade ball?"

"Oh, aye, sir. That is, we was mostly working in the kitchen, but Mrs. Mitchum—she's the housekeeper—she said as how we was going to run out of glasses soon, and so she sent us—Annie and me, that is—upstairs to collect the dirties and bring them downstairs for washing."

"And this was a regular part of your duties, yours and Miss Barton's?"

"I wouldn't say as how it was *regular*, sir. In the usual way of things, it would be the footmen bringing the dirties downstairs. But they was all upstairs, passing around drinks on silver trays, so Mrs. Mitchum sent Annie and me instead."

"Thank you, Miss Soames. You will please tell these good men, to the best of your recollection, what happened when Miss Barton collapsed. No conjectures, if you please."

"No sir, of course not, only—what's conjectures?"

"Guesses," he explained impatiently. "Don't try to guess at anything, or make assumptions as to what Miss Barton might have done, or thought. Only tell what you saw."

"Yes, sir," she said again. "As I said, we was gathering up the dirties to take downstairs, and Annie noticed as how some of the glasses was still almost full. She picked up one glass of rataffy that looked like it hadn't even been touched, and said it was a right shame to let it go to waste." She cast an apologetic glance at Lady Washbourn, sitting in the front row as if turned to stone. "Before I knowed what she was about, she turned up that glass and drunk it right down. Mind you, she never would have done such a thing if it wasn't going to be poured out in any case," she added hastily.

"No conjectures, Miss Soames," the coroner reminded her. "And what happened after she drank the ratafia?"

"Well, she had just offered me a glass that had a bit left in the bottom, thinking as how I might want to do the same, when suddenly she started twitching like she was having some kind of a fit. She dropped the glass, and the tray of dirties in her hand, and a regular mess it made, what with the glasses breaking and what was left of the drinks spilling everywhere." She sniffed loudly and wiped her nose on her sleeve. "And then she just fell down on the floor and laid there still, and I knowed then that she was dead."

"You did?" The coroner regarded her keenly. "Have you ever seen a dead body before, Miss Soames?"

"No, sir, and I hope to God I never see another!"

"How, then, did you know she was dead?"

"She was so still, sir, and her face so red, and her eyes all rolled back in her head, like."

"I see. Miss Soames, were you aware of any health conditions from which Miss Barton might have suffered? Any illnesses, perhaps?"

Mary Soames's gaze dropped to her hands twisting

together in her lap. "I don't like to speak ill of the dead, sir."

"Of course not," Mr. Bagley said soothingly. "We are not here to judge Miss Barton, who surely must have done nothing to deserve so gruesome a fate. But anything you can tell us may help us to determine the cause of her death."

"Well, sir, when you put it that way—Annie, well, you might say as how she had one in the oven."

The coroner scowled at her. "A rather cryptic utterance, Miss Soames. I assume you do not mean to tell us that Miss Barton had been assisting Cook with the baking."

A bark of bawdy laughter from one of the jurors broke the silence, and was quickly stifled.

"No, sir. I mean Annie was going to have a baby."

Pickett had taken no notes thus far, as the inquest had told him nothing that he had not already determined for himself, but at this revelation, he fumbled in the inside breast pocket of his coat for his occurrence book and pencil and began to scribble furiously. Of course, it proved nothing, and might have been no more than a tragic coincidence. Still, there was just a chance that Annie's lover (one of the male servants? Lord Washbourn himself?) had been less than pleased to learn of his impending fatherhood, and had killed his mistress before her condition could become an embarrassment. In any case, it would certainly have to be looked into.

"Thank you, Miss Soames, you may—"

"One moment, Mr. Bagley, if you please."

All eyes turned toward Mr. Colquhoun as the magistrate heaved himself out of his chair.

"What is the meaning of this?" demanded the coroner.

"I'm sure you don't dispute that witnesses may be questioned by persons other than the coroner, so long as they have a legitimate interest in the case. The manual describing the protocol to be observed even goes so far as to list several examples of such individuals: family of the deceased, companies underwriting insurance policies, beneficiaries of any such policies—"

Mr. Bagley shook his head dismissively. "No, Mr. Colquhoun, of course I don't dispute it. But it can hardly matter, given that Miss Barton had no family, and no such insurance policy—"

"Oh, but that list of 'properly interested persons' leaves room for a certain amount of discretion on the part of the coroner. At the bottom of the list, you will find 'any other person who, in the opinion of the coroner, is a properly interested person.' Surely you will agree that if one of my men did indeed examine the body—and, in fact, examined it long before you or any of these men on the jury had the opportunity to do so—then it follows that I must be 'properly interested' in the case."

The coroner screwed up his face in what was no doubt intended to be a fierce scowl, but gave him instead the appearance of a sullen toddler. "Well, yes, I suppose so, but—"

"Excellent!" Mr. Colquhoun squeezed past Pickett's knees and joined Mr. Bagley at the front of the room. "I have a question I should like to put to Miss Soames."

"Very well, then," conceded Mr. Bagley, glancing a bit desperately about the room as if seeking some way to be rid of his fellow magistrate. "Ask it."

"Thank you, Mr. Bagley. Miss Soames, did you watch as Mr. Pickett examined Miss Barton's body?"

Mary's head bobbed up and down. "Aye, sir."

"Would you say he made a thorough job of it?"

She hesitated, glancing uncertainly at the coroner. "Mr. Bagley said I wasn't to go putting in my own opinion."

"Very true, Miss Soames, and right you are to remind me of it." He turned to the coroner for confirmation, and received a rather cautious nod. "Let me rephrase the question. Tell me, as nearly as you can recollect, what were Mr. Pickett's observations regarding the deceased?"

"Mr. Colquhoun!" expostulated the coroner. "You must know as well as I do that secondhand testimony is not admissible!"

The wily Scot heaved a sigh of regret and spread his hands in a gesture of helplessness. "In that case, Mr. Bagley, I suppose there's nothing for it but to have Mr. Pickett up here and have his account from his own lips."

"As you wish, Mr. Colquhoun," said the coroner, giving

him a very ugly look. "But I'll do the questioning. If there is anything I forget to ask, why, you may have your chance when I've done with him."

With this vaguely threatening promise, Mr. Bagley summoned Pickett to the witness's chair. Pickett rose, gave a tug to the bottom of his new waistcoat, and took the chair Mary Soames had just vacated.

"You will state your name and place of residence for the jury, if you please," commanded Mr. Bagley.

"John Pickett, of Drury—that is, of Curzon Street. Number twenty-two."

"And you have been with Bow Street for how long?"

"Six years—almost four on the foot patrol, and the last two as a principal officer."

"A Runner, in other words?"

"Yes, sir."

The coroner gave him a long, appraising look that took in the bottle green tailcoat, the buff-colored breeches, and everything in between. Pickett had the feeling he was being weighed in the balance and found wanting.

But no; in fact, the opposite appeared to be true. "You look very fine today, Mr. Pickett," the coroner said.

"Thank you, sir," Pickett said warily, suspecting there was more behind the compliment than admiration of his appearance.

And so it proved. "A bit *too* fine, if I may say so. What

are they paying Bow Street Runners these days?"

Pickett, assuming the question to be purely rhetorical, made no response.

"Well, Mr. Pickett?" prompted the coroner.

"Am I to understand, sir, that my answer to that question is required as part of my testimony?"

"I would not have asked it otherwise."

Pickett glanced at his mentor. Smoke was all but coming out of the magistrate's ears, but he gave an infinitesimal nod.

"The current base salary for a principal officer is twenty-five shillings a week," Pickett said tonelessly, fully conscious of how meager this amount must seem to the seven men sitting on the jury. "A Runner may also accept private commissions for a guinea a day plus expenses. Some further reward is usually paid upon the satisfactory conclusion of the case, with the amount being left to the discretion of the person or persons doing the commissioning."

"Hmm," was the coroner's noncommittal reply. "A guinea a day, eh? One wonders how many days it took you to purchase those togs on your back."

"I fail to see what bearing my clothes may have on this case," Pickett said, bristling.

"On the contrary, Mr. Pickett, I believe your finery may have a great deal of bearing. We have established, have we not, that you attended the Washbourn masquerade on just such a private commission from her ladyship?"

"Yes, sir, what of it?" Pickett asked testily, heedless of the warning frown from his magistrate.

"I suggest, Mr. Pickett, that your purpose in attending the masquerade has been misrepresented."

As this was quite true, Pickett could not deny it. Instead, he listened in mute horror, fully expecting the coroner to blast his cover—and, quite possibly, Lady Washbourn's safety—to perdition. To his surprise, Mr. Bagley's thinly veiled accusations took an entirely different turn.

"We have heard that Lord Washbourn is being considered for an important government post. I submit that there are any number of persons—political adversaries, for instance, or rival candidates for this position—who would pay well for the opportunity to create the sort of scandal that might cost his lordship this appointment."

"Surely you do not mean to imply that Miss Barton's death was politically motivated!"

"Mr. Pickett, it is not my place, nor yours, to imply that Miss Barton's death was anything but a natural, albeit unfortunate, occurrence. But a clever man, particularly one with much to gain financially, might seize upon the incident to create a tempest in a teacup. Masquerades have long had a reputation for the sort of immoral conduct that might wreck the political ambitions of an indiscreet man; I submit, Mr.

Pickett, that a third party, upon learning that you were to be present on a private commission for Lady Washbourn, paid you handsomely"—again the coroner's glance darted to Pickett's well-tailored coat—"to keep an eye out for any such behavior, or to invent it, if necessary, and to make sure that it became public knowledge. Miss Barton's death, and the opportunity to create a murder case from whole cloth, must have appeared a godsend—if one can imagine the Almighty involved in such nefarious dealings."

"Begging your pardon, sir," Pickett said with some asperity, "but the only one who appears to be creating anything from whole cloth would seem to be you." He had not wanted to drag Julia's name into a coroner's inquest, but neither could he sit silently by while his integrity was ripped to shreds. He told himself that she would not expect him to do so. "In fact, the clothing you seem to find so objection-able did not come to me through the machinations of any third party, but through the generosity of my wife. I have recently wed, and my wife gave them to me as a birthday gift."

Mr. Bagley lifted one skeptical eyebrow. "Expensive birthday gift, wouldn't you say?"

He could hardly deny it, having thought the same thing himself. "Yes, sir," he conceded with a sigh. "But Mrs. Pickett is a lady, and no doubt wants me to appear worthy of her." Recalling certain words of Julia's, he added, "It is not as if they came from the hand of Weston in Old Bond Street, you know."

Mr. Bagley conceded the point with a nod. "The court offers its felicitations on your marriage, Mr. Pickett, and congratulates you on attaining your majority."

A smattering of laughter greeted this announcement, and Pickett fumed. *'The court offers,'* he thought bitterly, *just as if Mr. Bagley, a lousy interim coroner, were presiding over a trial at the Old Bailey!* As for his majority, he had reached it four years earlier, for the birthday he had celebrated was not his twenty-first, but his twenty-fifth.

But it appeared Mr. Bagley had made his point, for he apparently lost interest in Pickett's age, clothing, and marital status. Pickett could only hope the jury realized that Mr. Bagley did not believe the wild theories he had proposed, that they were, in fact, nothing more than an attempt to discredit his own testimony, just as Mr. Colquhoun had predicted.

"You examined the dead girl, as Miss Soames claims?"

Pickett nodded. "I did."

"Tell us, if you will, the result of your examination."

"Her face was flushed, as Miss Soames said, and there was no sign of a wound—no blood, nor any visible bruises."

"It appears you can tell us very little that the jurors could not see for themselves," observed the coroner.

"Perhaps not, but there was one curious circumstance

that has not been mentioned," Pickett said. "When I bent over Miss Barton's body, I detected an odor of bitter almonds."

"Interesting, Mr. Pickett, but hardly surprising under the circumstances. We know from Miss Soames that the girl had been drinking the same peach and almond ratafia that Lady Washbourn had offered her guests."

"Yes, sir, but I had taken a couple of glasses of that same ratafia myself."

"Drinking on duty, Mr. Pickett? Fie on you!"

"As you have said yourself, I was present in both a professional and a social capacity," Pickett pointed out, "and it would have been very unusual for a guest not to avail himself of the refreshments his hostess offered. Since I must drink something, I judged the ratafia a safer choice than the champagne."

Mr. Bagley nodded in agreement, muttering something about casting pearls before swine. "And your point, Mr. Pickett?"

"If I'd had the same almond odor on my own breath, how could I have smelled it on Miss Barton's?"

"Exactly what are you suggesting, Mr. Pickett? That Miss Barton was killed by eating bad almonds?"

There was another smattering of laughter from the assembly, which Pickett ignored.

"No, sir. But there is a particular poison—prussic acid,

to be exact—that leaves behind it an odor of bitter almonds."

"I see," Mr. Bagley said with a sneer. "And supposing that one were inclined to go about poisoning housemaids, how do you suggest someone at the masquerade contrived to obtain this prussic acid?"

Pickett regarded him with limpid brown eyes. "I shouldn't like to offer personal opinion as testimony, sir."

Muttering under his breath something that sounded suspiciously like curses, the coroner instructed him to step down. Pickett's victory, however, was short-lived as Mr. Bagley called for his next witness.

"Will Dr. Edmund Humphrey please take the stand."

8

In Which a Verdict Is Rendered

It was a name Pickett had hoped never to hear again. *Humphrey is a common name*, he thought desperately. *Surely it can't be—*

It was. The middle-aged man who rose to his feet, adjusting his wire-rimmed spectacles as he made his way to the front of the room, was no stranger. Pickett had met Dr. Humphrey only once before, but that one time had been more than enough. The feeble hope that the physician might not remember him died when they passed one another in the makeshift aisle. Their eyes met, and the doctor smiled toothily at him.

"Friend of yours?" Mr. Colquhoun asked, when Pickett collapsed onto his chair.

"We've met," Pickett muttered.

It had been the worst time of his life, that period when Julia had sought an annulment of their accidental marriage.

The only grounds available to them had been impotence—
his, to be exact, since she had been married for six years,
while his capabilities in that regard had been at that time still
unproven. He'd been obliged to submit to a particularly
humiliating physical examination, quite literally at the hands
of two prostitutes enlisted for the purpose. That the
examination had in fact proved quite the opposite had been
small comfort, since Dr. Humphrey had been bribed by the
Fieldhursts to falsify the results.

Now, as the physician took his place in the witness's
chair, Pickett wondered if Dr. Humphrey had made a
lucrative career of telling the aristocracy what they wanted to
hear. As the direction of the coroner's questioning became
clear, Pickett became certain of it.

"Your name and residence, please?"

"Edmund Humphrey, physician, of Harley Street."

"You have examined the body of Ann Barton?"

"I have, although not until some time after these gentlemen did," Dr. Humphrey said, indicating the men of the jury.

"Tell us, if you will, your conclusions regarding that
examination."

Dr. Humphrey removed his spectacles and peered
through them at the light streaming through the windows,
then polished them on the tail of his coat, peered through
them again, and replaced them on the bridge of his nose.
"Most of what I could detect has already been described by

other witnesses: the patient's, er, the deceased's unnaturally flushed face, the lack of any blood or bruises which might indicate a wound—"

"And this almond scent that Mr. Pickett mentioned?"

The physician shook his head. "I noticed no such scent, but as some time had elapsed by the time I was summoned, it is possible that any odor might have dissipated."

"I see." The drooping of his mouth indicated that Mr. Bagley was not best pleased with this disclosure. "Tell me, Doctor, are you familiar with the acid described by Mr. Pickett?"

"I have read about it in medical texts, but I have never come in contact with it, sir."

The coroner pondered this admission for a long moment before asking an apparently unrelated question. "Dr. Humphrey, how long have you practiced medicine?"

"More than thirty years." He flashed the toothy smile Pickett remembered so well. "With so much practicing, perhaps one day soon I'll perfect it."

The coroner was in no mood to be amused. "And in more than thirty years, you have never come in contact with this prussic acid Mr. Pickett describes. One must suppose, then, that such poisonings must be quite rare."

Some spark of professional integrity must have remained, for Dr. Humphrey apparently felt compelled to add a qualifier to this assumption. "They are certainly not common, but one must bear in mind that death comes so swiftly that there is no time to send for a physician—except, of course, for a *post mortem* examination."

"In your professional opinion, then, could Miss Barton have died of such a poison?"

Dr. Humphrey pondered the question with a thoughtful frown. "I suppose she might have done, although such a conclusion must raise more questions than it answers: who would have wished to kill a humble kitchen maid and why, as well as how they might have obtained the poison—"

"Yes, Doctor, may I remind you that I am the one conducting this inquest," Mr. Bagley said impatiently. "You said *most* of your observations had already been made by others. What additional facts can you relate that the other witnesses might have missed?"

The physician gave a self-satisfied smile. "I meant no disparagement of young Mr. Pickett's powers of observation, you understand. It is only that I have the advantage of him in one regard—that is, a professional acquaintance with the risks associated with early pregnancy."

"You believe, then, that Miss Barton's death is related to her, er, unfortunate condition?"

Dr. Humphrey inclined his head in agreement. "I think it very likely. The first *trimestre* is of particular danger to both mother and child, particularly since the mother may yet be unaware of her condition, and may fail to care for herself and her unborn child as she should. Indeed, in such cases as Miss Barton's, where there is no father, one wonders if such a tragic conclusion may be a judgment of God."

The coroner nodded soberly. "Indeed, one does. Thank you, Doctor, you may step down. Gentlemen of the jury, let me remind you that it is your duty to render one, and only one, of the following verdicts as to the cause of death." One by one, he ticked them off on his fingers. "Natural causes; accident or misadventure; suicide; or unlawful killing. Are there any questions? No? Good."

Having been dismissed, the jury rose as a body and shuffled out the same door through which they had entered at the beginning of the proceedings. With their departure, most of those remaining (including the coroner himself) adjourned to the public room to fortify themselves for the verdict. Left in relative privacy with his mentor, Pickett found himself the recipient of a look of silent sympathy.

"Sir?" he asked, having a very fair idea of what was coming.

"I did warn you," Mr. Colquhoun pointed out.

Pickett nodded glumly. "You did, sir, but—well, I couldn't live with myself if I hadn't told what I know." He sighed. "Whether the jury chooses to believe it or not is another matter. What verdict do you think they'll bring in?"

"You already know, don't you?"

"I'm afraid so."

After a brief silence, Mr. Colquhoun spoke again. "The physician, Dr. Humphrey—I gather he's the same doctor who, er—"

"Yes," Pickett said, flushing. "And while he didn't go quite so far as to say, 'Pay no attention to that fellow from Bow Street; he's impotent, you know,' he might as well have done. I expect the result will be the same."

The magistrate stared fixedly straight ahead. "And does Mrs. Pickett have any complaints in that area?"

Pickett gave him a rather smug smile. "She does not."

Chuckling under his breath, Mr. Colquhoun patted him on the knee. "Good lad!"

The jury had been gone for hardly a quarter-hour before the door opened and they filed back in. Pickett could tell nothing from their bland expressions, and reminded himself that these men regularly played cards for exorbitant stakes in the gentlemen's clubs of St. James's and, sometimes, the gaming hells of Jermyn Street; they would have long since learned to school their features so as not to give anything away.

"Gentlemen of the jury," Mr. Bagley paused to set down the tankard from which he'd fortified himself during the jury's deliberations, and wiped the foam from his upper lip with his sleeve. "Have you reached a verdict?"

"We have," declared the fat Friar Tuck of the previous evening, who had obviously been delegated as spokesman for the group. "We find that the deceased, Ann Barton, died of natural causes."

* * *

Julia was in consultation with the cook regarding meals for the coming week when she heard the front door open and then close with unusual force.

"That will be all for now," she told the woman. "We'll finish up later."

She dismissed the cook hastily and hurried to the hall, reaching it just in time to see her husband casting off his hat and gloves as if their very existence offended him.

"Welcome home, darling. How did the inquest go?" Even as she asked, she knew the answer would not be good.

"Natural causes," he announced, with contempt in every syllable.

"John, no!"

"Surely you don't mean to doubt the judgment of seven good men and true," he said bitterly, bending rather mechanically to receive her kiss.

"But there must have been some mistake!"

She followed him into the drawing room, where he collapsed onto the sofa.

"If there was a mistake, then I'm the one who made it. After all, who cares whether a mere housemaid gets justice, so long as there's no scandal to spoil Lord Washbourn's government appointment?"

"*You* care," she said softly. "It's one of the things I love about you."

He took her hand and drew her closer, then pulled her down onto his lap and buried his face in the curve of her neck. "Sometimes I wonder why I bother," he said, his voice muffled by her shoulder.

She stroked his hair, recalling Lady Dunnington's advice. She'd thought her friend was merely being outrageous, but now she realized she'd been given a very sound piece of wisdom. In her six years of marriage with the late Lord Fieldhurst, the sole purpose of intercourse (indeed, its *only* purpose) had been the conception of an heir—the long-awaited event that had never taken place. By contrast, the consummation of her second marriage had been the joyful and passionate expression of a deep and unexpected love. It had never occurred to her that a woman might comfort her husband through the conjugal act, and she found the realization curiously empowering.

She cupped his face in her hands and set herself to the sweet task of comforting.

* * *

"So, what happens now?" she asked some time later, lying within the circle of his arm in drowsy contentment.

He idly twisted one long golden curl around his finger. "I suppose we'd better get dressed and go back downstairs before we shock the servants."

"Not that, silly!" She gave his bare chest a playful swat. "I meant the case. What will you do now?"

His smile faded. He disentangled himself from her with a sigh, then sat up and reached for his breeches. "There isn't a case, Julia. 'Natural causes,' remember? A jury has said so."

"But Lady Washbourn—?"

"I'll have to see her sometime—preferably when her husband isn't at home—and arrange to return the rubies to her. And pray to God that if Lord Washbourn was behind that maid's death, then his accidentally killing the wrong person will make him afraid to try again."

It was, he feared, a very slender thread to which to tie a woman's life.

* * *

Pickett awoke the following morning filled with a vague sense of dread. As the sleep cleared from his brain, the events of the previous two days came back to him: the maid's death, the jury's verdict, and, still ahead of him, the meeting with Lady Washbourn, at which time he would have to tell her ladyship that there was nothing more he could do for her. Conceding reluctantly that there was no point in delaying the inevitable, he pushed back the counterpane and sat up. A slender white hand emerged from the covers and trailed its fingers down the length of his spine. He captured the hand and raised it to his lips.

114

"You make it very hard to leave," he said.

"You don't have to, you know," Julia's voice came from somewhere beneath the counterpane.

"Mr. Colquhoun might have something to say about that."

She pushed the covers off, revealing a head of tousled blonde curls. "Really, John, you don't have to," she insisted.

He realized with some consternation that she was quite serious. "Give up my position at Bow Street? What would I find to do all day?" In answer, she arched one provocative eyebrow at him, and her lips curved in a seductive smile. "Yes, but not all day, every day," he said hastily.

"If you are unhappy in your work there—and after yesterday, you cannot deny it—you can walk away any time you wish. We could live quite well on my jointure, you know."

It would have been a delicate subject to broach under any circumstances; coming on the heels of the coroner's inquest, it was a disastrous one. Pickett stared at her with something akin to revulsion. "Is that what you think of me? That I could be content to live as my wife's pensioner?"

"But you already are, in a way," she pointed out with unassailable logic. "After all, your wages wouldn't begin to cover the cost of this house, much less the servants, or—"

"I thank you, my lady, for the reminder," he said, tight-lipped. "Now, if you'll excuse me, I'll away to Bow Street without further ado. I wouldn't want to trespass in your house any longer than I must."

"I didn't mean it that way, John," she insisted, watching helplessly as he dressed hastily in his old brown serge coat and its usual accoutrements. "You know I didn't."

"I know," he conceded with a sigh. "I can hardly fault you for speaking the truth."

Still, the kiss he gave her was rather perfunctory, and he left the house without eating breakfast.

Alas, no relief was to be found in Bow Street. As he entered the Bow Street Public Office, he was hailed by a couple of Runners, along with several members of the night patrol just going off duty. All were several years his senior, and between them were exchanged several bawdy references to "Lord John, the blushing bridegroom."

"Pay them no heed," recommended Mr. Colquhoun, when Pickett joined him at the magistrate's bench. "They don't mean any harm, you know. It's only that most of them have known you since you were nineteen years old. They're not accustomed to thinking of you as a married man, let alone the husband of a viscountess."

"And they would be right," Pickett grumbled, leaning against the wooden railing as was his usual habit. "I may be married, but I'm no husband. I'm a petticoat pensioner, a kept man, a—"

Mr. Colquhoun's eyebrows rose. "Nice work, that, if

one can get it."

"You might think so, but I can assure you it's nothing of the sort."

"John"—the magistrate's use of his Christian name, particularly at the Bow Street office, was enough to capture Pickett's attention—"may I suggest that your wife is the proper person to whom you should voice these complaints?"

"I have tried," Pickett confessed, recalling several aborted conversations that had taken place—or rather, that had *not* taken place—over the past six weeks. "But whenever I broach the subject, she—she—"

"She what?"

Pickett flushed scarlet. "She seduces me."

"The harpy!" exclaimed Mr. Colquhoun, the revulsion in his blue eyes utterly belied by the fact that he was struggling, not entirely successfully, to keep a straight face.

Pickett grinned sheepishly in answer. "Yes, well, laugh if you must, but it's—it's emasculating, living off my wife's income—particularly when that income is derived from her first husband."

"Has she given any indication that she resents the fact that you cannot support her in the style to which she is accustomed?"

"No," he admitted.

"Then perhaps you are creating a problem where none exists."

"Oh, it exists," Pickett said. "Whether or not she chooses to recognize it, it exists."

Mr. Colquhoun turned to look up at the big clock mounted on the wall behind him. "Be that as it may, it's much too early in the morning for a philosophical debate on real versus perceived truth." He turned back to Pickett. "On a related subject, however, what do you intend to tell Lady Washbourn?"

In fact, Pickett had pondered this question all the way to Bow Street in an unsuccessful attempt to forget the discord between himself and his wife. Along the way, he had determined to prove that he was not so incompetent a creature as the coroner's inquest had made him out to be—although whether this proof was for the benefit of Lady Washbourn, the coroner, Julia, or himself, he could not have said.

"That girl was murdered, sir. With your permission, I should like to do what I can to prove it."

"According to the jury, she died of natural causes," the magistrate reminded him, his voice carefully neutral. " 'A judgment of God,' if our friend the doctor is to be believed."

"Juries can be wrong, sir, and this one was. You know it as well as I do."

The bushy white brows lowered ominously. "You do realize that if Lord Washbourn gets wind of it and lodges a complaint against you, I will have to disavow all knowledge of any investigation—reprimand you—send you back to the foot patrol—possibly even release you, all for the sake of appearances."

Pickett nodded resolutely. "I do, sir, and if it should come to that, I will accept any such punishment with a good grace."

"Good God, but you're a stubborn lad!" Mr. Colquhoun grumbled.

"Begging your pardon, sir," Pickett said with a hint of a smile, "but I learned from a master."

A bark of laughter managed to escape before the magistrate contrived to disguise it as a cough. "Impertinent whelp!" He reached over the wooden railing, adding in a more serious vein, "For God's sake, John, try to be discreet."

"I'll do my best," Pickett promised, and took his hand.

9

*In Which John Pickett and Mr. Colquhoun
Pursue Separate Lines of Inquiry*

M r. Colquhoun watched through the tall windows
until Pickett was out of sight. Once he'd judged his
protégé to be well en route to the Washbourn residence in
Grosvenor Square, he left Mr. Dixon in charge of the Bow
Street Public Office and set out on his own for Curzon
Street. He stopped before Number 22 and sent up his card to
the lady of the house, and a moment later was shown into the
drawing room.

"Why, Mr. Colquhoun, what an unexpected pleasure!"
Julia exclaimed, glancing over his shoulder and beyond him
as if expecting to see an additional caller there. "John does
not accompany you? Is he—?"

"No accident has befallen him, if that is your concern,"
he assured her hastily. "In fact, he is away on an investigation."

"Of course—the Washbourn affair," she said, nodding

in understanding. "It sounds like a thoroughly bad business. But will you not sit down? It is a bit early for tea, but perhaps coffee?" She reached for the bell pull.

"No, no, nothing for me, thank you," he said, seating himself on the sofa nevertheless. He regarded her in silence for a moment, then asked bluntly, "Mrs. Pickett, how much did your husband tell you about yesterday's inquest?"

"He told me the jury had returned a verdict of death by natural causes, which did not best please him. In fact, he was quite indignant about it, as I am sure you are aware."

"And that was all? He said nothing, for instance, about his own testimony?"

"No." She considered this omission with growing unease. "Is there some reason why he should have?"

The magistrate shook his head. "It's not my place to bear tales. I'm sure he would have told you anything he wished for you to know."

"Mr. Colquhoun, you have known him much longer than I have. If something happened yesterday that I need to know about, for heaven's sake, tell me!" she pleaded.

He sighed. "How much easier marriage would be if we could crawl inside the minds of our spouses! Very well, Mrs. Pickett, I'll tell you—but remember, you never heard it from me."

She agreed to this caveat, and so he proceeded to recount to her all those details of the inquest which her husband had chosen to withhold: most particularly, how the coroner had seized upon Pickett's new finery as a way of casting doubt upon first his integrity, and then his competence.

"He wasn't going to wear it," she confessed, conscience-stricken. He would have worn the black coat he reserves for court appearances, but I—well, I'm afraid I made it impossible for him to do so without hurting my feelings."

"And so you hurt his instead," the magistrate pointed out with brutal candor.

She bristled at the charge. "I should rather say the coroner did! Surely you don't mean to accuse me of a lack of feeling where he is concerned—why, I gave up everything to be with him!"

"Of course you did," he said soothingly. "Everything but your house, and your servants, and your—"

"That is not fair, Mr. Colquhoun!"

"No, no, Mrs. Pickett, hear me out. I do not doubt the depth of your affection for your husband—no one who had witnessed your tender care of him following the Drury Lane Theatre fire could do so—but I fear you don't understand how galling it is for him to be beholden to you for financial support."

Given that morning's disagreement, she could hardly deny the charge. But she was not afforded the opportunity to do so in any case, for Mr. Colquhoun was not finished yet.

"In fact," he continued, "from something he said to me at your wedding, I had the impression that he had every expectation of supporting you, rather than the other way 'round. Surely you could not have been so foolish as to withhold the information from him!"

She cast her mind back to the days in Pickett's flat following the Drury Lane Theatre fire: the long, tense hours of nursing him back to health, followed by the blissful week between the consummation of their accidental marriage and the formal exchange of vows held at the home of the magistrate. No, she had not withheld anything, at least not on purpose, but she could not honestly say that the matter of money had been addressed. Between the constraints of the sickbed and the pleasures of the marriage bed, there had been little time for (or interest in) serious discussion; in fact, what conversation *had* taken place had been of the "when did you first know . . . ?" variety so beloved of lovers. Given the severity of his injury, the future had been too uncertain, and the present too precious, to waste a moment of it worrying over such mundane matters as household income.

"I didn't 'withhold' it," she insisted. "It's just that—the subject somehow never came up."

"I see," the magistrate said drily, and Julia colored, fearing he saw a great more than she had said.

Still, she was quite certain that Mr. Colquhoun was

overstating the case. "But it's so—so *absurd!* I could show you any number of impoverished gentlemen who married ladies with fortunes far greater than mine, and it bothered them not at all."

"Impoverished *gentlemen*, yes. But I would wager that in most, and very likely all, of those cases, the gentleman in question had something else of value to offer in exchange: a title, for instance, or a large estate, or an ancient lineage. Your husband has none of those things."

"And no woman could possibly find anything of value in a clever brain and a sweet temperament, especially not when those attributes are contained within the person of a handsome young man," she retorted. "Really, Mr. Colquhoun, you presume too much."

Mr. Colquhoun lifted a hand in acknowledgement. "Perhaps I do. I suppose it is not surprising that you should view him in such a light; in fact, it is only right that you should do so. But I"—he heaved a reminiscent sigh—"I sometimes catch glimpses of a fourteen-year-old pickpocket with a black eye and a broken nose."

She laid her hand over his, and patted it in understanding. "I know you mean well, Mr. Colquhoun, and I honor you for it, but I think you are worrying over nothing. It is not as if my jointure is all that large, you know. I can think of many people who have far more, and I daresay you can, too. I should call mine a competence, rather than a fortune."

He leaned back against the sofa cushions and regarded her with an appraising expression in his keen blue eyes that made her feel uncomfortably like a miscreant brought before the bench. "Your husband—your first husband, that is—left you an income of four hundred pounds a year, did he not?"

"Yes, along with a house in Kensington, which I sold in order to purchase this one. If I had been obliged to pay for lodgings out of my jointure, I should have been hard pressed."

The magistrate, however, appeared unmoved by this argument. "And if you consider four hundred pounds per annum a mere competence, what would you call twenty-five shillings per week?"

Rather nonplussed by this question, Julia sought refuge in counterattack. "But Mr. Colquhoun, it's so—so *unimportant!*"

"I understand your first marriage gave you a very poor example of what that institution ought to be, so I will give you one piece of advice: if it is important to one of you—and I can assure you that this is extremely important to him—then it had better be important to the other." He rose to his feet and held out his hand to her. "Be kind to him, Mrs. Pickett. That is all I ask."

* * *

Pickett, in the meantime, reached Grosvenor Square and

sent up his card to Lady Washbourn, who received him in the fashionable drawing room with the formal portrait over the mantel.

"Your ladyship," he said, bowing over her hand. "I trust Lord Washbourn is well?"

She inclined her head. "He is indeed, Mr. Pickett. He has gone out driving with the Four Horse Club today, so I do not expect him back until late this evening. He will be sorry to have missed you."

Pickett rather doubted this, but silently blessed the lady's perspicacity in recognizing his unspoken query.

"My mother-in-law, too, has taken to her bed, so you find me quite alone today," she continued blandly.

Pickett made some patently insincere remark expressing regret at the dowager's absence, then added, "I trust she is not ill."

"No, it is only that she has been greatly upset by Annie's death." She grimaced. "Or else by the realization that her son might be a murderer."

"You believe she suspects him?"

The countess shook her head. "If she does, she has said nothing of it to me. But then, I would not expect her to. After all, it would be a rare woman who would take her daughter-in-law's part over her son's."

"Everyone else seems to be satisfied, then, with the verdict regarding Miss Barton?"

"Yes." She frowned thoughtfully. "I only wish I could be so accepting. I keep remembering Washbourn bringing me a glass of ratafia, which I was obliged to set down to deal with a minor crisis in the ladies' retiring room."

"Lady Carrington's fainting fit," Pickett said, nodding in understanding. "I remember."

She shuddered. "I can't help wondering if it was the same glass Annie drank from. I suppose I shall never know."

Here was the opening Pickett had hoped for. "Lady Washbourn, I await your instructions. If you want me to return the rubies, I will, and you can fob your husband off with some tale of their having been found, but unless you have some objection, I would prefer to do what I can to discover what happened to that poor girl."

"Thank you, Mr. Pickett. I would prefer it as well. If you would be willing to keep the rubies a bit longer, their supposed theft would give you a pretext for calling from time to time to keep me informed as to your progress."

"I'm afraid I'll have to call for more reason than that, your ladyship. If I'm to investigate Annie's death, I must learn more about her life. For that, I will need to question your servants."

"But I thought we were agreed that I was the intended victim, and that Annie's death was no more than a tragic accident!"

"I think it likely, but by no means certain. Given

Annie's preg—er, delicate condition, there is always the possibility that she was killed by the father of her child." There was a moment's awkward pause as he considered how to phrase his next question. "I don't suppose she was—that is, do you have any idea who the father might have been?"

"I daresay it was Ben Bradley—one of the stable hands. Annie had been walking out with him for some time, but they could not yet afford to marry. Mrs. Mitchum, the house-keeper, told me she was obliged to speak quite sharply to Annie about slipping out to the mews at night to meet him. I think she expected me to dismiss the girl—in fact, I'm afraid I rather lost face with her when I didn't—but I couldn't help feeling a bit sorry for Annie and her beau. It must be very hard on young people of the serving class, having all the natural urges of persons that age, and yet being financially unable to wed."

"Did Ben know about the baby?"

Lady Washbourn shook her head. "I'm afraid you are asking the wrong person, Mr. Pickett. I was not in his confidence."

"May I speak to him? I have a few questions I should like to ask."

"Of course. You will find him in the mews behind the house." She reached for the bell pull. "I shall have the butler direct you there, and give instructions that all the servants are to answer any questions you may wish to ask them."

"Thank you, your ladyship."

The butler arrived in answer to Lady Washbourn's summons and, upon receiving his orders from his mistress, led Pickett down the stairs and through the servants' hall (where he was the object of many a curious stare), and finally out the rear door of the house into a small garden. A gate in the back of the garden wall led to the mews, where Pickett was turned over to Jenkins, the head groom, who led the way past rows of stalls. At last he stopped before a stall wherein a strapping blond lad drew a currycomb in long strokes down the side of a fine bay. A black armband was tied about the young man's sleeve halfway between elbow and shoulder.

"Ben," the head groom addressed this individual, "this here's Mr. Pickett, from Bow Street. He wants to ask you a few questions."

The stable hand looked up from his task, and Pickett saw that Lady Washbourn had not exaggerated when she referred to the couple's youth. In spite of his large size, the boy appeared to be still in his teens. His light blue eyes were red-rimmed from crying, and Pickett thought he'd never seen anyone less likely to have killed his sweetheart and her unborn child. Even if he were not the father, and had been driven to murder his faithless lover in a jealous rage, one look at Ben's beefy hands was enough to inform Pickett that he could have done the job much more efficiently by choking the life out of her, rather than going to the trouble of not only obtaining prussic acid, but then finding some way to administer it.

"Thank you, Jenkins," Pickett told the head groom, nodding in dismissal. Alone with Ben, he added, "You need not stop what you're doing on my account." He suspected Ben was not accustomed to idleness, and thought the boy might be more forthcoming if he had something to do with his hands.

"I've never had no dealings with Bow Street before," Ben said, with another sweep of the currycomb. "What do you want to know?"

"I believe Miss Barton was a special friend of yours," Pickett began. "Let me say how sorry I am for your loss."

"Annie was more than a friend," Ben said, swiping the long sleeve of his smock across his eyes. "We was going to be married just as soon as we had enough money saved up."

"It's expensive, setting up household, especially in London," Pickett remarked sympathetically.

"Aye, it is at that."

Remembering that he was supposed to be investigating the theft of a supposedly stolen ruby necklace, Pickett remarked, "It's a shame Miss Barton couldn't have found Lady Washbourn's missing jewels."

Ben scowled fiercely. "Are you suggesting Annie might have stolen them?"

"Not at all," Pickett assured him with perfect truth. "I only meant that, if Miss Barton had discovered them and been rewarded by her mistress, it might have helped your cause." After a delicate pause, he added, "I understand there was a particular reason why the two of you needed to marry as quickly as possible."

"Aye," Ben agreed, nodding. "The babe."

"Then you were the father?"

It was a tactical error. Ben took a menacing step forward, and it was only through sheer force of will that Pickett held his ground.

"Just what are you getting at?" demanded the outraged lover. "She was a good girl while she was alive, my Annie, and I'll not let anyone say otherwise now she's dead, do you hear?"

"Of course," Pickett said hastily. "I meant no disrespect. It's only that, well, one hears stories about housemaids being put in uncomfortable positions by men who have no scruples about preying on pretty girls—other servants, houseguests, even their employers."

"That's true enough," Ben conceded, relaxing somewhat. "But Annie was safe enough below stairs, for there aren't too many fellows on the staff who'd be willing to cross me. As for upstairs, well, Annie counted herself right fortunate in that respect. Lord Washbourn might be a bit of a cold fish, but he's a good man at heart, and Lady Washbourn is as kind as she can be, for all she ain't Quality-born."

"She certainly is. But you say Lord Washbourn is a good man. What makes you say so?" Realizing how this question must sound, Pickett added quickly, "I mean no disparagement of your employer, of course. I suppose Miss Barton will have given you the benefit of her own opinions regarding her mistress, but I should not have thought your position in the stables would give you much opportunity to form an estimation of his lordship's character."

Ben waved one arm in the direction of the rows of stalls, each with its sleek and well-groomed four-legged occupant. "It's his horses, isn't it? No man who treats his animals so well can be what you'd call wicked."

It was an interesting standard for judging human nature, but Pickett discovered he could not dispute it. He once again offered his condolences to Ben, then left the stables and returned to the house via the servants' hall. He had almost reached the stairs going up to the family's rooms above when he was hailed by a voice that sounded vaguely familiar.

"Why, if it isn't Mr. Pickett, from Bow Street!"

He turned and saw a rather scrawny young woman with wisps of mouse-brown hair escaping from beneath her starched white cap. The left sleeve of her dark stuff gown bore a black armband much like the one Ben had worn.

"Miss—Soames, is it?" he asked.

"Lord love you, sir, I'm just 'Mary' when I'm working," she said, twisting her hands in her apron. "But what brings you here?"

"I just wanted to offer my condolences to Ben, the stable hand," Pickett said with perhaps less than perfect truth.

Mary shook her head. "Poor Ben, he's that cut up over Annie's death. If you're thinking he might have had something to do with it, Mr. Pickett, you just put that thought right out of your head. Well nigh worshipped that girl, he did, and wouldn't have harmed a hair on her head."

"Yes, that was my impression as well." In fact, he was hardly listening to Mary at all. His attention had been distracted by the butler, who had unlocked a door just off the hall, pushed it open, and disappeared inside. Through the gap, Pickett caught a glimpse of a small room lined from floor to ceiling with shelves containing gleaming black or green bottles. This, then, was where the champagne and ratafia would have been stored prior to being served at the masquerade ball.

"Miss Soames," said Pickett, interrupting a lengthy account of Annie and Ben's clandestine courtship, "where do Lord and Lady Washbourn buy their wine?"

She blinked at him in surprise. "Why, from Berry Brothers, in St. James's Street." She didn't add, "Doesn't everyone?" but her tone certainly implied it.

"And the butler takes charge of the deliveries?" This much he knew from his own brief stint working incognito as a footman the previous summer.

"Aye. Mr. Forrest checks the shipment against the invoice, and then makes sure the bottles are properly stored." Mary's brief glance toward the room whence the butler emerged at that moment with a dusty black bottle confirmed Pickett's theory.

"I suppose the wine cellar stays locked most of the time?" he asked.

"Aye, and Mr. Forrest keeps the key."

Difficult, then, for anyone to slip into the wine cellar and add prussic acid to one of the bottles, Pickett noted, even assuming one might have been able to obtain the poison itself. As master of the house, Lord Washbourn could certainly have got his hands on a key, but his responsibilities as host would have kept him above stairs during the masquerade. Even if his lordship had contrived to duck down the stairs and add poison to one of the bottles before the festivities began, his presence in the servants' domain would certainly have been unusual enough to attract attention. Then, too, there was the likelihood that the contaminated beverage would find its way to the wrong throat, which Pickett was convinced had been precisely what had happened. It didn't seem right. It was sloppy, messy, careless —none of which adjectives seemed to apply to Lady

Washbourn's husband, based on Pickett's admittedly limited interactions with that gentleman. Still, it was worth making inquiries.

"Tell me, Miss Soames, did anyone—any of the family, I mean—come downstairs, let us say, within an hour or two of the time the masquerade was to begin? To ensure that everything was in order, perhaps, or to make some last-minute changes to the arrangements?"

"Only her ladyship. She came down about half an hour before the guests was to begin arriving, with orders that her own peach ratafia that she makes special was to be served along with the from Berry Brothers."

It was a curious circumstance, Pickett thought, making a note of it in his occurrence book, but he was at a loss as to what significance it might hold. Of course, if it had been Lord Washbourn, instead of his wife, who had issued such instructions, it would have been a very different matter.

"Did it strike you as, I don't know, unusual, this substitution?"

"Oh, no, sir, not at all." Mary's curious expression was enough to warn Pickett that he was in danger of tipping his hand. "She's that proud of her ratafia, you know, for she makes it from a receipt that belonged to her own mama."

He thanked Mary Soames for the information, then went upstairs to take his leave of Lady Washbourn.

"You are welcome to call and make inquiries anytime

you need," she assured him, giving him her hand in farewell, "only—Mr. Pickett, I must beg you not to let my husband discover what you are about. I think—I hope poor Annie's death will offer me some protection, at least for a while." She gave him a strained smile. "After all, two sudden deaths in the same household within a matter of days would be rather difficult to dismiss, even for Mr. Bagley."

Pickett pondered the possibility of this tragic outcome for a long moment. "Your ladyship, do you think perhaps it might be wisest for you to go away for a bit? I know you can't return to your father's house, since he is deceased, but could you contract some unspecified illness that requires sea air, or else discover some need to take the waters at Bath?"

"I understand what you are saying, Mr. Pickett, but what if my husband were to decide to accompany me? Such a journey might even offer more opportunities than he might find here in Town. Then, too, the dowager's presence in this house offers a certain degree of protection; after all, no man wants his mother to see him as a monster."

"And yet your mother-in-law's presence has failed to protect you thus far," he pointed out. He proposed several other scenarios, each more unlikely than the last, by which she might escape her husband, even temporarily, but she remained adamant.

"No, Mr. Pickett, I must stay where I am," she insisted, gently but firmly. "Only promise me that if I should die suddenly, whatever the circumstances, you will not allow a coroner's jury to dismiss it as merely natural causes, or else a tragic accident."

Pickett agreed reluctantly, confounded by her determination to remain with a man who was in all likelihood trying to kill her. He wondered if Lord Washbourn's finances were arranged in such a way that his wife was rendered incapable of supporting herself independently. He supposed he might inquire as to the name of the solicitor who had been charged with writing up the marriage contract, but rejected this notion at once; even if Lady Washbourn knew the solicitor's name, any attempt by Pickett to question this individual would certainly be reported back to the earl, and would put paid to his investigation—and, quite possibly, to his career as well.

There was, however, one other person of his acquaintance who was not without experience in these matters. And so, after taking his leave of Lady Washbourn, Pickett turned his feet toward a destination he had not visited in many years: Cecil Street, and the residence of his former master, Mr. Elias Granger.

10

In Which an Old Acquaintance Is Renewed

I t was a strange feeling, in a way, lifting the iron knocker on the front door of the house where, only six years earlier, he would have descended the steep and narrow service stair to the tiny basement room where he'd slept. The butler answered his knock, and if the manservant recognized Mr. Granger's erstwhile apprentice, he gave no outward sign. Pickett handed over his card.

"John Pickett, to see Mr. Granger," he said, and had the satisfaction of seeing the butler's eyes widen in surprise.

"One moment, John—er, Mr. Pickett," said the butler, clearly uncertain as to what attitude he should take toward this unexpected guest, given Pickett's former position in the house. He disappeared into the interior, and returned a moment later. "If you will follow me, er, sir?"

Elias Granger had grown somewhat stouter and his hair was rather grayer than Pickett remembered, but in all other aspects, he was unchanged. As Pickett entered the drawing room, the older man cast aside his newspaper and heaved himself to his feet.

"Well, stap me if it isn't young John Pickett!" he exclaimed, shaking his former apprentice warmly by the hand. "I'd have known you anywhere, for you haven't changed at all—oh, you're a bit cleaner, I'll grant you that, but otherwise the very same. Come and sit down, and tell me what you've been doing with yourself. Are you still with Patrick Colquhoun at Bow Street?"

"I am," Pickett said, seating himself in the chair Mr. Granger indicated. "In fact, that's what brings me here—not that I wasn't pleased to have an excuse to call on you."

"Anytime you choose to call, you can be sure of a welcome," the coal merchant assured him, then turned to address the butler, who was still hovering in the doorway. "Smithers, fetch a bottle of port, there's a good man, and young John and I will drink it in friendship."

"I thank you, sir, but I'm working," Pickett demurred.

"Very well, then. Make it tea, Smithers."

As Mr. Granger gave instructions to the butler, Pickett glanced around the room. The walls were still covered from wainscot to ceiling with well-known works by Old Masters, and the bookcases were filled with the calf-bound volumes he remembered so well, volumes that still looked new even after six years; he wondered if anyone had read them since he had left Mr. Granger's employ. Everything was almost exactly as he remembered it, with one significant difference. When he'd first been brought to this room as a fourteen-year-old pickpocket, he'd thought Mr. Granger's house a veritable palace, and was quite certain there could be no finer residence in all of London. Having made the acquaintance of the Viscountess Fieldhurst, however, and become at least somewhat familiar with the world she inhabited, he now recognized the paintings as copies of indifferent quality, and the books as more for show than for education or entertainment. In fact, every detail of the house's interior existed for no other purpose than to lend an illusion of gentility to a family whose fortune was founded in Trade, and a gritty and grimy Trade at that.

Not that he saw the Granger family's pretensions as deserving of condemnation; on the contrary, he found much to admire in a man who had enriched himself by his own efforts. In fact, Mr. Granger's rise in the world was much more admirable than his own. After all, Mr. Granger had worked and invested to build a coal empire through which thousands of homes and businesses were warmed. He, John Pickett, had done nothing more than make love to a lady whom he had adored since first setting eyes on her. As a result, an accidental marriage by declaration had been rendered invulnerable to annulment, and his own fortunes were forever changed.

He suddenly became aware of an unnatural silence, and realized Mr. Granger had asked him some question for which he was now awaiting an answer.

"I beg your pardon," he said hastily. "Being in this room again brings back so many memories that I'm afraid I was wool-gathering. You were saying—?"

"I was merely wondering what brings you here. I believe you said it was connected to your work at Bow Street?"

"Yes, sir. I wondered if you might be able to give me some insight into a situation that has come up in a case I'm investigating."

"I'll do my best, but I can't say I know much about crime. I hope you'll remember me as an honest man." The merchant's ample belly shook as he laughed at his own witticism.

"I do, sir, else I would not be asking your advice. As I recall, at the time I left your employ, your daughter was about to go to her aunt in Tunbridge Wells in the hopes of making an advantageous marriage."

There was more than that, of course—much more. Sophy Granger had set her sights far higher than an advantageous marriage; she wanted a brilliant one. Nothing less than a lord would do, and she had not hesitated to say so to the nineteen-year-old apprentice who had begged her to marry him instead. He had not thought of Sophy for years—

certainly not since he'd laid eyes on the widowed Lady
Fieldhurst—but he was surprised at how clearly all the pain
of Sophy's rejection came back to him, even after six long
years.

"Aye and she did exactly that," Sophy's proud papa
said, oblivious to Pickett's long-buried hurt. "Married Lord
Gerald Broadbridge, she did, him as is the fourth son of the
Duke of Aldrington. Mind you, she was a bit disappointed to
learn that she would be 'Lady Gerald' instead of 'Lady
Broadbridge,' and that any son of hers would be a mere
'mister.' Still, the boy's paternal grandfather is a duke, and
that's no small thing."

"And the boy's maternal grandfather is a good man, sir,
and that's no small thing, either."

"Bless you, my boy." He regarded his former apprentice
with a look of regret. "Sometimes I can't help wishing—but
that's neither here nor there. What did you want to know?"

"I assume marriage negotiations between Sophy—er,
Miss Granger—and Lord Gerald must have been fairly
complicated—"

"Aye, that they were, I'll not deny it."

"So I thought you might be able to tell me, in such a
case, when a young woman of property marries a gentleman,
what terms the woman's father might include for his
daughter's protection. In plain words, sir, what is to prevent
the gentleman from pocketing the bride's dowry and then

getting rid of her?"

Mr. Granger's piercing black eyes, so like those of his daughter, narrowed thoughtfully. "Divorce, you mean?"

"Actually, I was thinking of something rather more permanent."

"Bless my soul!" exclaimed Mr. Granger. "Has some blackguard killed his wife?"

"No—at least, not yet—but the lady fears that may be his intention."

"Who—?"

Pickett shook his head. "You must know that I can't tell you that."

"No, no, of course not," conceded the coal merchant with a sigh of regret. "As to whether any precautions were taken that might ensure the lady's safety, that would depend on what terms were made part of the marriage contract. The solicitor who drew up the agreement would know."

"Yes, but even if I knew the solicitor's name—which I don't—I can't be sure any inquiries on my part wouldn't get back to the lady's husband. In fact, I think it very likely that they should. I know you can only answer me in the most general of terms, but even that might be helpful."

Both men lapsed into silence as the butler returned bearing the tea tray.

"I'm afraid I'll have to pour," Mr. Granger said apologetically, picking up the teapot. "My wife succumbed to a putrid fever last winter."

"I'm sorry to hear it, sir," Pickett said with perhaps less than perfect sincerity. Mrs. Granger had never liked him—in fact, Pickett had always had the impression that she fully expected him to steal the silver at the first opportunity—and her presence at this interview would have done nothing to aid Pickett's cause.

Once tea and sandwiches had been distributed and Smithers had departed, Mr. Granger leaned back in his seat and clasped his hands over his belly. "Where were we, now? Oh, yes, marriage contracts. I should say that in most cases, it would be to the gentleman's advantage to keep his wife alive. My Sophy came to Lord Gerald with forty thousand pounds, but I didn't just hand it over in cash, you know; it's in the four per cents, and if his lordship is wise, he'll leave it there and make do with just the interest. In addition, he's guaranteed five thousand pounds per year for my lifetime, or, if Sophy should predecease me, for hers. Such arrangements are fairly common, so I can only assume your mystery lady's father would have offered something similar."

"And if the lady's father died at some point after the marriage had taken place, and she inherited his business enterprise?"

Mr. Granger rubbed his nose. "Well now, that's a different matter. A married woman can't own property independently of her husband, you know, so even if the business had been left to her, it would belong to her husband in the eyes of the law." This much was no surprise to Pickett, who had acquired legal ownership of his wife's house in just such a way. "Still, I suppose a cautious man could prevent his son-in-law from getting his hands on it by leaving it in trust for her—that way her husband couldn't touch the principal—or better yet, leave it in trust for her children and skip over their father altogether, but I'll admit such a set-up is unlikely."

"How so?"

"Because to put it bluntly, no gentleman needing a wealthy bride would ever agree to take the girl under those conditions. They have mighty high opinions of themselves, these 'lordships' do, and if one merchant isn't willing to cough up the ready in order to see his daughter get a handle to her name, there's a dozen others that are. Then there's the girls to consider, too." He grimaced. "I would have taken a firmer line in negotiations myself, for Lord Gerald struck me as a gamester and a spendthrift—still does, for that matter—but Sophy had the bit between her teeth, and nothing would do but we must give Lord Gerald whatever he asked for, in exchange for the privilege of hearing her called 'my lady.' "

That sounded very much like Sophy Granger as Pickett had last seen her, and it occurred to him that in being rejected by her, he had actually had a very lucky escape.

"And if the marriage should fail?" he asked. "Might

there be any provision for the lady to establish a separate household?"

Mr. Granger fairly goggled at the very suggestion. "I doubt there is a man alive of *any* class who would agree to such a thing! Why would a man make it possible for his wife to abandon him?"

Pickett merely nodded, for he had expected as much. It appeared his suspicions were correct: Lady Washbourn was trapped in a potentially dangerous situation because she hadn't the wherewithal to escape.

"So there is nothing the lady can do except wait, and trust either that she is mistaken, or that I can find sufficient evidence to arrest her husband before his next attempt proves more successful than his previous ones."

Mr. Granger regarded him with narrowed eyes. "I said you hadn't changed, but I was wrong. There is something different about you. Your speech is part of it—my Sophy, bless her, has never quite got the hang of talking like the nobs, although it appears you've taken to it readily enough— but there's something else, too. Or maybe it's just that you left here as a boy, and now you've come back a man." He wagged his head regretfully. "I should have made Colquhoun pay me fifty pounds for your release, like I asked, or else refused him outright and kept you for my Sophy."

Pickett had known that Mr. Colquhoun had paid generously in order to persuade Mr. Granger to release him from his apprenticeship, but he felt compelled to protest this casual assumption that his master could have ordered his future so easily. "I'm not a lapdog!"

Mr. Granger chuckled, and his belly shook. "No, but I'll wager there was a time you'd have come to heel readily enough at Sophy's bidding."

Pickett couldn't deny it, but neither did he like being reminded of the fact. "Yes, well, as you said, that was a long time ago. But why would you wish Sophy had married me, when you've got, what did you say, the fourth son of a duke for a son-in-law? Is she not happy with him?"

"Oh, she's as merry as a grig, but—"

His account of Sophy's marriage was interrupted when the door opened, and the lady herself flounced into the room. "Papa, Smithers says—" She broke off abruptly at the sight of her father's visitor. "*John!*"

Pickett had stood at her entrance, just has he would have for any lady, and now executed a little bow. "It's been a long time, Sophy."

She gave him a coy smile as she offered her hand. "Actually, I'm called Sophia now." She pronounced it with a long "i," so that it rhymed with "pariah," which was what Julia had become when she'd married him.

His first impression was that Sophy had not changed much, but a closer inspection proved that this assumption, like her father's impressions regarding himself, was

147

erroneous. Her glossy black hair, once worn simply and fetchingly in loose curls, was now crimped into ringlets according to the latest fashion, and her demure schoolgirl dresses had yielded to stylish gowns lavishly bedecked with ribbons and lace. Nineteen-year-old John Pickett might have been dazzled by this display of wealth, but then, nineteen-year-old John Pickett had not yet met Julia, Lady Fieldhurst, who had worn the severest black mourning with more grace and elegance than Sophia, Lady Gerald Broadbridge, in all her modish attire.

More telling than Sophy's clothes, however, was her face. Sophy—or rather, Lady Gerald—was still a very attractive woman, but the black eyes that had once sparkled with mischief had grown hard and calculating, and lines of discontent now bracketed her mouth.

"You are called Sophia?" Pickett echoed in surprise. "Your father had given me to understand that you were called Lady Gerald Broadbridge."

"Oh, *that!*" she flapped one hand as if to rap him on the arm with an imaginary fan. "I'm sure we need not stand on ceremony, John, such old friends as we are. After all, if it hadn't been for my dear Gerry, I might have been called Mrs. Pickett."

"Speaking of which," her father put in, "is there another female of that name?"

"There is," Pickett said with some satisfaction, and

148

found himself wishing he'd dressed for the day in some of the new clothes his wife had given him.

"You're *married?*" Sophy's mouth tightened in displeasure, deepening the creases in her cheeks.

"Congratulations, my boy!" exclaimed Mr. Granger, seizing his hand and shaking it with enthusiasm. "How long has it been?"

Pickett was not quite certain how to answer. Should the length of the marriage be calculated from October, when he and Julia had claimed to be husband and wife as a matter of expedience, not realizing that in Scotland such a claim might constitute a marriage by declaration? Or should he date it from the end of February, when they had thrown away all the arrangements that had been made for obtaining an annulment, and consummated the union?

"Not quite two months," he said, opting for the latter.

"Still newlyweds, in fact," Mr. Granger observed. "Well, I hope you and Mrs. Pickett will be very happy."

"Thank you, sir, we are."

"But who is your wife?" Sophy demanded in dulcet tones belied by her brittle smile. "Someone I know? One of the downstairs maids, perhaps? I always suspected Betty, the second chambermaid, of casting lures in your direction."

"If she did, I never knew of it. No, my wife is the former Lady Fieldhurst, widow of the sixth viscount of that name," Pickett said, trying unsuccessfully to keep the

149

smugness in his voice to a minimum.

"A *lady?* Do you mean to say you've married a *lady?*" Sophy had never been one to conceal her feelings, and her consternation was all too clear for a moment, until she recollected herself and gave a little titter of laughter. "How strange to think that, if we were all invited to the same dinner party, I should take precedence over your viscountess."

He knew exactly what she was about, but found he had no interest in playing the sort of games in which she apparently still delighted. "I'm afraid you're fair and far off there, Sophy."

"I can assure you, I'm right," she insisted, thrusting out her full lower lip in a pout. "Younger sons of dukes take precedence over viscounts, and so their wives take precedence over viscountesses. I've made quite a study of these things, you know."

Of that, Pickett had no doubt; in fact, he wouldn't have been in the least surprised to learn that she had picked out her husband from the pages of *Debrett's Peerage.* "But my wife is no longer a viscountess," he pointed out. "She is now Mrs. John Pickett, and seems happy with her new title, humble though it is."

"Oh, I see!" Sophy exclaimed, brightening. "But it is quite cruel of you to tease me so. What a pity that women become ladies when they marry lords, but men do not become lords when they marry ladies! Then you could be 'Lord John.' Wouldn't that be droll?"

"Hilarious," muttered Pickett, and rose to take his leave, citing his need to return to Bow Street.

"I say, John," put in her father, "I wonder if you would be willing to take Patrick Colquhoun a copy of the *Observer* I promised him. I know he takes an avid interest in manufacturing, and there's an article on cotton production I think he'll find interesting."

Pickett nodded. "I would be glad to, sir."

"One moment, then, while I fetch it from my study."

"That's what you have servants for, Papa," Sophy scolded him.

"Nonsense! I can get it myself in less time than it would take to summon a footman and tell him where to look."

Suiting the word to the deed, he took himself off, leaving Pickett alone with his first love for the first time in six years.

"Allow me to offer my belated felicitations on your marriage," he said, breaking the strained silence. "You said you would marry a lord, and you did."

"Yes, but—oh John, I've been so unhappy!" she cried, casting herself onto his chest.

"Unhappy?" Under the pretext of looking her in the eye, he seized her by her upper arms and pried her loose from his chest—no easy task, since she clutched the lapels of his coat with both hands. "Whatever happened to 'dear Gerry'?"

"I had to say so for Papa's sake," she insisted. "He paid out so much to allow me to marry a lord, you know. But Gerry is simply *ancient*—forty-five if he's a day—and I need so desperately to be loved by a man my own age. Oh John, you know I have never truly loved anyone but you!"

Pickett suspected Sophy had never truly loved anyone but Sophy, but as he had no desire to provoke further histrionics, he refrained from saying so. Besides, he could hardly fault her for hypocrisy when he had been no better; from a distance of six years, he could look back and realize that it was not Sophy he had loved, but what she had represented: prosperity and respectability wrapped in a lovely and vivacious package. It had been a rude awakening, but he'd eventually discovered that her vivacity hid a streak of cruelty, and her respectability was only the thinnest of veneers overlaying the soul of a courtesan.

"Anything between us was over long ago," he said gently but firmly, resisting the urge to point out that it had been her own ambition that ended it. "We're not the same people we were then. You're married now, and so am I."

"Yes!" She seized with desperation upon this change in their circumstances. "Gerry is a fourth son, so I am under no obligation to provide heirs of his blood. We've made our brilliant matches, you and I, and now we can please ourselves!"

"I think you mistake the matter, Sophy. I might have made a brilliant match, but I married Julia because I love her. I would have married her even if she'd had nothing."

"Hmph!" Sophy snatched her arm free of his grasp, then withdrew an embroidered handkerchief from her sleeve and dabbed at suspiciously dry eyes. "That I can readily believe, for you always were a romantic fool."

"If marrying for love and being faithful to one's spouse is being a romantic fool, then I suppose I must plead guilty."

Before Sophy could make some fresh attack, the door opened and her father entered the room bearing a folded broadsheet. Pickett didn't see how his former master could fail to notice Sophy's flushed cheeks or the angry glint in her eyes, but then, for all his business acumen, Mr. Granger had always been astoundingly obtuse where his daughter was concerned.

"Here we are," the merchant declared cheerfully, handing over the paper. "Give this to him with my compliments, and tell him to take all the time he needs with it."

"I will, sir," Pickett promised. He took his leave of Mr. Granger, who wrung his hand in farewell, and Sophy, who shot daggers at him with her hard black eyes, and felt a stab of pity for both of them: for Mr. Granger, whose daughter would never live up to her father's rosy imaginings, and for Sophy, who, though she might marry a dozen lords, would never, ever, be a lady.

11

In Which John Pickett Must Pay the Piper

A fter leaving the Granger residence, Pickett returned
to Bow Street. He had much to think about on the
walk, and very little of it concerned the Washbourn case.
Upon entering the Bow Street Public Office, he waited until
Mr. Colquhoun was free, then approached the magistrate's
bench and handed the journal over the rail.

"Mr. Granger sends his compliments, sir, along with
this. It contains an article on cotton production he said he'd
promised you."

"Oh, yes, I remember. So you've been to see Elias
Granger, have you? Since you're on duty, I'm assuming it
wasn't merely a social call."

"No, sir, I was learning what I could about the
intricacies of marrying a daughter of industry into the
aristocracy."

"And?" prompted the magistrate.

Pickett shook his head. "Little of use, I'm afraid. I wondered why Lady Washbourn refuses to leave her husband, even though she may be putting her life in danger by staying with him. I can't help feeling there's something she's not telling me. After talking to Mr. Granger, I suspect Lord Washbourn holds the purse-strings so tightly that she can't escape, even on peril of her life."

"I daresay she isn't the only woman in that unhappy position. Not that there are that many homicidal husbands— at least one must hope not—but there are certainly more than a few women who are forced to endure cruel treatment from the men they married, and with little legal recourse available to them."

Pickett, leaning against the wooden rail, offered no response beyond a distracted nod. Mr. Colquhoun peered closely at him.

"Is something troubling you, John?"

"Not 'troubling,' exactly. It's only that, well, Sophy Granger was there visiting her father, and—" He broke off abruptly, and looked beseechingly up at his mentor. "Sir, tell me I didn't make a fool of myself over that girl!"

A hint of a twinkle lurked in the too-perceptive blue eyes. "You want me to lie to you?"

Pickett groaned. "I did, didn't I?" It was an acknow-ledgement, not a question.

"We all do at one time or another. Why should you be

any different from every other man?"

Pickett regarded the magistrate with mingled admiration and resentment. "I can't imagine *you* being so taken in."

"Only because my temporary insanity took place long ago, and an ocean away in Virginia, so the few remaining witnesses can't bear tales." His expression grew distant, and his eyes took on a reminiscent gleam. "Good Lord, she must be sixty years old by now."

"Sophy Granger is very much present in London," Pickett said. "Only she's called 'Sophia' now—that is, when she isn't being called 'Lady Gerald Broadbridge.' "

"Bah!" Mr. Colquhoun gave a snort of derision. "His grace of Aldrington has five sons, and every one of them is a bigger fool than the one before. If that was what Miss Granger wanted, I'd say she got no more than she deserved."

"I should say rather that Lord Gerald has earned every farthing he got from the marriage settlement," said Pickett, with feeling.

"As for your falling under Miss Granger's spell, John, don't take it so much to heart," Mr. Colquhoun advised. "It was five years ago—"

"Six," put in Pickett, determined to distance himself from his youthful folly as much as possible.

"Six, then. And under the circumstances, I should say it was almost inevitable. Miss Granger could be quite fetching when she made up her mind to it—how else did she manage to keep her father wrapped around her finger all those years?—while you were of an age ripe for falling in love, and no more likely candidate in sight. At least you stopped short of actually marrying her."

"Not for lack of trying." He shuddered at the thought.

"Ah, well, she wouldn't have you then, and she can't have you now, so there's no harm done. What do you intend to do next?"

"Kiss the hem of my wife's garment," replied Pickett without hesitation.

Mr. Colquhoun gave a bark of laughter, which made two Runners on the other side of the room look up from their own conversation. "I meant what do you intend to do on the case, young Lochinvar! Mind you, whatever you may choose to kiss on your own time is your own affair."

"Oh," Pickett said, blushing.

"You *are* on a case, you know," the magistrate reminded him with mock severity.

"Yes, sir." Pickett looked up at him suddenly, and grinned. "Maybe I should introduce Lord Washbourn to Lady Gerald Broadbridge. He'll learn to appreciate his countess, once he sees what he might have got instead."

* * *

While he stopped short of actually kissing the hem of her garment, Pickett did greet Julia that evening with even more warmth than usual, continuing to hold her close long after he would normally have released her in order to dress for dinner.

"What's all this?" she asked, making no very visible effort to free herself from his embrace.

"Nothing, only—I love you, Julia. You know that, don't you?"

"I'd had my suspicions," she said, lowering her voice to a conspiratorial whisper. Her smile invited him to share in the joke, but he spoke again in the same serious tone.

"I would have married you even if you were as poor as I am," he insisted.

"I have never doubted your love for me, John, not even for a moment," she assured him with mingled affection and exasperation. "You proved it a hundred times over, before you ever spoke the words. Darling, what is the matter?"

He shook his head in an attempt to banish Sophy from his thoughts. "Don't mind me. I'm not making much progress on this case, that's all."

"I'm glad of that," she said flippantly.

"You're glad?"

"For a moment there, I thought you'd found another woman." Seeing guilt writ large upon his expressive countenance, she exclaimed, "John! Who is she? Not Lady Washbourn, I presume?"

"No, she isn't Lady Washbourn—that is, I haven't found another woman—at least, not exactly." Realizing he was digging himself deeper with every word, he broke off and started over. "I wanted to pursue a line of inquiry that took me to the home of an old acquaintance. Before Mr. Colquhoun brought me to Bow Street, he arranged for me to be apprenticed to a coal merchant—"

"Yes, I know all about that," she said, nodding.

"You do?"

"Mr. Colquhoun told me while we were in Scotland."

Pickett frowned. "It wasn't his story to tell."

"On the contrary, he had your best interests at heart. He thought I was trifling with your affections, and warned me to keep my distance."

"Oh," Pickett said, rather taken aback by this revelation. "I'm glad you didn't listen, anyway."

"But what were you saying? About the coal merchant, I mean."

"What? Oh yes—Sophy. As I was saying, I was apprenticed to a coal merchant. He had a daughter my age—still has, for that matter—and when I was young"—she smiled at the implication that his youth lay in the dim and distant past—"well, I guess you could say I lost my head over her."

"Did you?" she asked, wide-eyed at this unknown and entirely unexpected chapter of his history. "What happened?"

"She told me in no uncertain terms that she had set her sights on bigger things."

"Oh, poor John!"

"Believe me, it was the best thing she could have done," he added hastily, "but it didn't feel that way when I was nineteen."

"Of course it didn't!" Her voice was warmly sympathetic as she took his arm and led him toward the stairs. "But will you think me very selfish if I say I'm grateful to her for leaving you for me? I feel I should send her flowers, or something. Will you have to call on her again?"

"I didn't call on her; I called on her father, and it was just my bad luck that she happened to stop by for a visit while I was there. And no, I didn't find out much of value today, so I shouldn't think a second visit would be any more productive than the first was."

They had reached the bedchamber by this time, and after following Julia into the room and closing the door behind them, Pickett stripped from the waist up, then poured water from the pitcher into the bowl and sponged himself off before putting on a clean shirt and breeches before attempting to do something with his hair. It was yet another indication of his sudden rise in the world, this nightly ritual of dressing for dinner.

"I hate that spot," he grumbled, stooping so that he might glare at his reflection in the mirror atop his wife's delicate rosewood dressing table.

"What spot?" asked Julia, who had watched his

ablutions with an appreciative gleam in her eye, and had seen nothing in his person to provoke such an outburst.

"*That* spot." He poked disapprovingly at the crown of his head, where a tuft of hair much too short to be tied back into his queue stuck up through the longer strands, a lingering reminder of the injury he had suffered following the Drury Lane Theatre fire.

"I'm sorry for it, John, but the doctor had to shave that spot in order to clean and treat your wound."

"I know," he conceded with a sigh. "I know he did what he had to do, and I don't blame you for giving him permission. But now it's grown out just enough to make itself a nuisance."

She gestured toward the chair before the mirror. "If you would care to sit down, I'll see what I can do with it."

"I wish you joy of it," he said, taking the seat she indicated and surrendering his head to her ministrations.

She untied the ribbon holding back his queue, then picked up her silver-backed hairbrush and began running it through his long brown curls. "Of course, the one short spot might be less noticeable if the rest of your hair were not so long," she pointed out. "I confess, I have sometimes wondered why you still wear a queue, when most men your age cut their hair years ago."

His eyes met hers rather sheepishly in the mirror. "I'll tell you, if you really want to know, but you'll laugh," he warned her.

"No, I won't."

"It has to do with my days delivering coal."

"For the beauteous Sophy's father," she said, nodding sagely. "Yes, I remember."

"My hair was already rather long—Moll, my father's woman, couldn't often be persuaded to put down the bottle long enough to cut it—but once I started working for Mr. Granger, I let it grow and began tying it back. It made sort of a shield, you see, for keeping the coal dust from getting down the back of my neck."

She set the brush down and picked up a fresh ribbon of black velvet. "And after you left Mr. Granger for Bow Street?"

"Habit, I suppose," he said with a shrug. "My landlady, Mrs. Catchpole, would give me a trim when I needed it. But if ever I had it cut short, I'd have to *keep* it cut. Besides the time and expense involved, I wouldn't even know where to go," he confessed.

"John, you don't have to 'go' anywhere," she pointed out, regarding his reflection with some exasperation. "Every gentleman I know arranges for his barber to come to *him*."

She tied the ribbon, gave one last tweak to the loops of black velvet, and stepped back to survey her handiwork. "There," she pronounced. "It isn't perfect, but it's better than it was, and you are tall enough that unless you are seated, few people can see the top of your head in any case. Shall I send a message to Monsieur Albert, requesting him to wait upon you? He was always used to cut Frederick's hair you know. I'm afraid I don't know any other barbers, but I can always inquire of Emily who cuts Lord Dunnington's hair, if you prefer."

"That—that won't be necessary," Pickett said, and was both surprised and relieved when Julia accepted this answer without protest.

Having completed his toilette, Pickett rose from the dressing table and rang for Thomas to help him into a coat and waistcoat more suitable for dinner than his brown serge had been. Julia pronounced him presentable, and both Picketts, man and wife, quitted the bedchamber and descended the stairs to the dining room.

From the day she had installed her low-born husband in her Curzon Street residence, Julia had been careful to see that he was afforded every courtesy which the master of the house might expect as his due (and indeed, more than one servant had been quietly dismissed for failing to obey this stricture), including surrendering to him the seat at the head of the table which had been her own place since she had first taken up solitary residence there some months after her first husband's death. Pickett seated himself there now, and she eschewed the corresponding place at the opposite end of the table in favor of the chair at his right hand, as was her usual habit. Conversation was temporarily suspended while Rogers served the evening meal, assisted by Andrew, the footman who had been hired to replace Thomas upon that young man's promotion to valet. Once the servants were dismissed and they were once again alone, however, Julia resumed the thread of their earlier discussion.

"What did you hope to discover? From Sophy's father, I mean."

He sighed. "I can't understand why Lady Washbourn is so determined to stay with her husband, even though she thinks he may be trying to kill her."

"And you thought Sophy's father would know?" she asked, bewildered by this leap in logic. "Are they acquainted, then? I didn't know coal merchants moved in such exalted circles."

"No, but I hoped he might be able to offer some insight into what financial arrangements might have been made, having negotiated a similar marriage for his own daughter."

"Wouldn't it be simpler just to ask Lady Washbourn?"

"Of course it would—if I could be sure that she knew, or would tell me the truth if she did. But when I suggested she might remove herself to Brighton or Bath for a few weeks, she refused even to consider it. I thought perhaps she couldn't afford to set up an independent household. After talking to Mr. Granger—Sophy's father, that is—I still think that is the most likely explanation."

"But not the only possibility," Julia remarked.

"No, but I've been at a loss to think of anything else that might keep her in Town against her own best interests."

"Perhaps she doesn't want to leave her husband because she loves him."

He paused with a forkful of roast beef halfway to his mouth. "Julia, she thinks the man is trying to kill her!"

"And of course no one *ever* loved someone who was no good for them! John, our own histories must tell you such things do happen, and more often than one might think."

He had to acknowledge this home truth, but was still not entirely convinced of its application to the Washbourn case. "To Sophy's credit, she never tried to kill me, at least not to my knowledge. I think that would have ended my calf-love in very short order."

"And you say she married into the aristocracy?" Julia asked thoughtfully.

Pickett nodded. "She is now Lady Gerald Broadbridge."

"*Sophia* Broadbridge? Oh John, you didn't!"

He grimaced. "I did. Julia, I'm afraid your husband is a fool."

Julia did not know Lady Gerald well—in fact, they had never been formally introduced—but she did remember her own first Season in London as the bride of Lord Fieldhurst, and she well recalled witnessing the spectacle of the former Miss Sophia Granger pursuing the middle-aged Lord Gerald

Broadbridge from Tunbridge Wells to London, until at last he caught her. Given her own husband's background, Julia suspected he would have stood little chance against Miss Granger if that rather ruthless young woman had set her sights on him.

In fact, knowing of his past history with the merchant's daughter gave Julia some unexpected insight into his character: she remembered his conviction (still not entirely banished, she feared) that he was unworthy to aspire to marriage with her, and wondered to what extent the faithless Miss Granger was responsible for his feelings of inadequacy. In the light of this revelation, Julia revised her earlier thinking: instead of presenting Lady Gerald Broadbridge with flowers, she contemplated with pleasure the thought of putting her hands around the woman's throat and choking the life out of her.

Although she said none of this to her husband, something of her thoughts must have shown in her face, for Pickett set aside his fork and laid his hand over hers. "My lady, don't think you need have anything to fear from Sophy, for nothing could be further from the truth! What I felt for her—it seemed real to me at the time, but only because I had no idea then—" His voice was filled with wonder. "I didn't know how it could be, between a man and a woman."

She turned her hand over so that she might give his a little squeeze. "No more did I, and I had been married for six

166

years! You need not regret Sophy, for she and Frederick were necessary, in their way, so that we would recognize what we'd found in each other." Turning back to the business at hand, she asked brightly, "What will you do now? About the investigation, I mean."

"I'd like to learn a bit more about poisoning with prussic acid, if I can," he said. "What was the name of the doctor who treated me while I was injured—Portman, was that it?"

"Good heavens, no! Dr. Portman was that horrid man who wanted to drill a hole in your skull. Dr. Gilroy is the one you want—Thomas Gilroy. I believe he has offices in Harley Street."

Pickett made a note of the name, and the conversation turned to other things. It was not until much later that Julia's thoughts turned again to her husband's first love. She had got up in the middle of the night to use the chamber pot—an increasingly frequent occurrence of late; really, it was no wonder she was tired so much of the time—and had just come back to bed. The evening was mild for late April, and so the bed curtains had been left open. Curzon Street had not yet been fitted with the gas street lamps that lit Pall Mall near St. James's, but the moon was almost at the full, and its silvery light spilled through the window and illuminated the face of her sleeping husband. The sheer beauty of the man took her breath away, and she stood there for a full minute, just watching him as he slept.

Be kind to him, the magistrate had said, and she realized that he, too, knew about Sophy, who had not been kind at all. Small wonder Mr. Colquhoun had disapproved so strongly of her own friendship with his protégé! She hardly knew whether to curse the girl for hurting him, or to bless her for the ambition that had blinded her to the treasure that might have been hers. But as for her own treatment of him, she might have assured Mr. Colquhoun that they were two very different things. Sophy had only been out for what she could get; she, Julia, wanted only to lavish on him all the things that life had heretofore denied him. Unfortunately, it appeared that her stubborn, foolish love had no desire to be lavished upon. She stifled a sigh and climbed back into bed.

"Julia?" Pickett mumbled. "Is anything wrong?"

"It's nothing, darling, only answering nature's call." She kissed him on the forehead. "Go back to sleep."

He muttered something unintelligible and rolled over, apparently taking this advice to heart. But she lay awake for some time afterward, thinking of a pair of mocking black eyes and a nineteen-year-old boy with a broken heart.

12

Which Finds Mr. and Mrs. Pickett at Cross-Purposes

T he following morning, Pickett stopped in Bow Street
     only long enough to acquaint Mr. Colquhoun with his
plans before setting out for the Harley Street office of Mr.
Thomas Gilroy, Physician. His recollections of the doctor
were of necessity vague, given the fact that he had been
unconscious during much of his time under Dr. Gilroy's
care, but at the sight of the doctor's tall, lean figure and
wire-rimmed spectacles, what few memories Pickett retained
emerged from the fog. By contrast, the physician seemed to
remember him quite well, as was evidenced by the warmth
with which he was greeted.

"Why, Mr. Pickett, it's a pleasure to see you again," he
exclaimed, offering Pickett a firm handshake. "But you need
not have come in person. A message would have brought me
to you. Tell me, are you still troubled by headaches? They
will pass with time, I assure you."

"Only very rarely," Pickett answered him. "I can't even remember the last time I had one. But I'm in no need of medical care today. In fact, I wanted to consult with you on a—a matter of some delicacy."

Dr. Gilroy's eyebrows rose. "Mrs. Pickett, then? Is she—?"

"No, no," Pickett put in hastily, eager to put an end to any expectations the doctor might have of ushering a bouncing baby Pickett into the world. "Nothing like that."

"Ah well, it's early days yet. I daresay it will happen in its own good time."

Privately, Pickett rather doubted it. After all, six years had not been enough time for Julia and her first husband to conceive a child. But he had not come to Harley Street to discuss his wife's fertility or lack thereof.

"Actually, I wonder if you can advise me regarding a case I'm investigating," he said.

"I can certainly try," the doctor promised, waving him to a chair. "Pray sit down, and tell me what it is you would like to know."

Pickett sat. "I should like you to tell me the symptoms of poisoning by prussic acid."

The physician gave a short laugh. "The most striking symptom is death." Seeing Pickett rather taken aback by this speech, Dr. Gilroy hurried to explain himself. "That is, death usually occurs before any symptoms can manifest themselves. Consequently, its influence is easier to identify *after* death than before."

"I see," Pickett said, rather daunted by this information. "And what identifiers might one expect to see then?"

The physician regarded him keenly. "If you examined the victim shortly after death occurred, you probably know them as well as I do: the unnaturally flushed face, the almond odor—" Pickett's eyes lit up in recognition, and Dr. Gilroy added, "Perhaps it is I who should be asking you. I must confess that although I recall studying that particular substance in medical school, I have never actually seen a case."

"Then Dr. Humphrey—Edmund Humphrey, that is—he was correct when he said such occurrences are rare?"

The doctor hesitated a moment before replying. "Professional ethics make it impossible for me to tell you what I think of Edmund Humphrey, but in this instance, at least, he was telling the truth."

Pickett was as gratified by the knowledge that someone shared his low opinion of Dr. Humphrey as he was by the information itself. "And where might one obtain such a poison? From an apothecary?"

"I suppose one might ask," Dr. Gilroy said, with such a lack of conviction that Pickett put no very great faith in this source. "Better yet an artist, or a seller of art supplies."

"An artist?" Pickett echoed incredulously. "Why would

an artist be in possession of a deadly poison?"

"Because the substance is derived from the pigment Prussian blue, which may be found in any artist's paint box."

"An artist," Pickett repeated thoughtfully, recalling the large portrait holding pride of place over the mantel of the Washbourn drawing room, the portrait in which Lady Washbourn was depicted wearing a dark blue gown. It would be interesting to know who had painted it and when, and how active Lord Washbourn had been throughout the process: if he had observed the painter at work; if he had asked any questions or otherwise taken an unusual interest in the proceedings; or, perhaps most intriguing of all, if the artist had noticed his blue paint missing at the conclusion of this commission.

* * *

Pickett returned to Curzon Street that evening eager to share his findings with his wife over dinner; however, it soon transpired that Julia had made other plans. She usually greeted him at the door, having kept an ear cocked for his return, but on this occasion he was met by Rogers, who relieved him of his hat and gloves and informed him that the mistress awaited him upstairs with what she termed a "little surprise."

"A surprise?" echoed Pickett, regarding the butler with an arrested expression. "Upstairs, you say?"

Rogers inclined his head. "Yes, sir."

As most of the rooms on the upper floors were still unfurnished, "upstairs" could only mean the bedchamber. Pickett promptly lost all interest in dinner. He stammered his thanks to the butler and climbed the stairs, resisting the urge to take them two at a time. He reached the door to the bedchamber and froze on the threshold. The room was empty.

"John, is that you?" Julia called from a room further down the corridor. "I'm in here."

Pickett followed the sound of her voice, and found her in one of the unfurnished spare rooms. A large white sheet had been spread on the floor, and the chair that usually stood before her dressing table had been brought from the bedchamber and placed squarely in the middle of the sheet. Julia stood at one corner, smiling proudly up at him—and she was not alone. She was accompanied by a dapper little man wielding a hairbrush in one hand and a scissors in the other.

"John, this is Monsieur Albert. Monsieur, my husband, Mr. Pickett." As if further explanation for the Frenchman's presence was required, she explained, "Monsieur Albert is going to do something about that spot you dislike so."

"*Bonjour*, Monsieur Pickett." He pronounced the name "pee-*kay*," as if Pickett were as French as himself. "If it will please monsieur to take off his coat and sit down?"

He gestured toward the solitary chair. Feeling rather

foolish (to say nothing of sexually frustrated), Pickett shrugged out of his brown serge coat and sank numbly onto the chair.

"As for you, Madame Pickett," he continued in a heavily accented mixture of English and his native tongue, "if you will please to leave us?"

"Of course." Julia took Pickett's coat, then gave him a wink and a smile and removed herself from the room.

"And now, monsieur, *voila!* We begin." Suiting the word to the deed, he began to ply his brush.

"There's a short spot at the crown," Pickett said, finding his tongue at last. "It had to be shaved—"

"*Oui, oui, madame* has told me all," Monsieur Albert assured him. "It is not difficult. *Madame's* first husband, *le vicomte*, had a thin spot, oh, of the smallest, which I had the honor of helping him to conceal. But this—" He ran one hand through Pickett's thick curls. "This will be *un plaisir*. Monsieur has hair for which many a lady would commit murder."

"So I've been told," Pickett muttered, remembered the lascivious lady at the Washbourn masquerade. Being favorably compared to Julia's first husband, however, had gone some way toward reconciling him to the process, and he relaxed somewhat in his chair—until he heard the metallic whisper of blade sliding against blade, and realized to his dismay that his head felt curiously light.

He whirled about in the chair, and stared with horrified disbelief at the sheet covering the floor. On its pristine folds lay a hank of long brown curls, tied at one end with a black ribbon.

"You cut off my hair!" He clapped one hand to the back of his head, and narrowly missed being stabbed with the Frenchman's scissors.

"Have a care!" Monsieur Albert exclaimed. "You will do yourself an injury, *non?* But *oui*, I give *monsieur* a coiffure of the most fashionable, as *madame* has desired. I will now trim the ends, if you will permit."

"My permission doesn't seem to be necessary," Pickett grumbled under his breath. Still, the damage had been done, and so he had no choice but to let the man finish what he'd begun.

At last Monsieur Albert pronounced himself "*fini*." He gave Pickett a hand mirror and stepped back, confidently awaiting the expressions of praise and gratitude that must surely follow when his client gazed upon his reflection. His client, however, was speechless, and not necessarily with admiration. Pickett, looking into the mirror with some trepidation, was relieved to discover that from the front, at least, he did not look so very different. It was only when he turned his head to the side, and saw the ends of his hair just curling over the collar of his shirt, that he could tell the extent of the violation that had been perpetrated on his unsuspecting head. He reached back gingerly and fingered the shorn ends at the nape of his neck.

"If *monsieur* will notice," the hairdresser put in, "the spot he so deplored is quite hidden."

That much, at least, was true. Now that the curls at his crown were no longer confined to their ribbon, the tuft of short hair was easily lost among them. He supposed he should be grateful, but it was the principle of the thing that offended him. He had never agreed to have his hair cut, had never even said he *wanted* to have his hair cut, and yet Julia had taken it upon herself to—

"Oh, my," breathed a soft feminine voice, a voice that certainly did not belong to Monsieur Albert.

Pickett turned and saw Julia standing in the doorway, staring at him wide-eyed. Her obvious admiration acted as a balm to his wounded pride, until he reminded himself that of course she would like it; she had orchestrated the whole thing, and had done so without his knowledge or permission. He turned away from her, hardening his heart.

"Thank you, Monsieur Albert," Julia told the hair-dresser quickly, realizing at once that all was not well with her husband. "How much do I owe you?"

"I will send *madame* my bill," he promised, being wise enough in the ways of the aristocracy to know that his noble clients would consider it shockingly vulgar for him to demand payment at the time his services were rendered.

176

As soon as the Frenchman had taken his leave, Julia turned to Pickett. "Darling, what is the matter?"

"What's the matter?" he echoed incredulously. "*What's the matter? Julia, I didn't want* my hair cut! I never *said* I wanted my hair cut!"

"You did," she reminded him, taken aback by his vehemence. "I offered to send for Monsieur Albert, since he'd always cut Frederick's hair, and asked if you would prefer me to ask Emily Dunnington who cuts her husband's, and you said it wouldn't be necessary. So I sent for Monsieur."

"I said it wouldn't be necessary to send for anyone at all!"

"You didn't!" she insisted. "I'm sure you didn't!"

"Well, it's what I meant!"

"And am I supposed to be able to read your thoughts?"

"No, but you might at least have *asked!*"

A hollow feeling in the pit of her stomach suggested to Julia that he might have a point. Still, she had spent long six years deferring to a husband who always managed to put her in the wrong, and she had no intention of falling back into the same pattern with her second husband. "For heaven's sake, John, it's *hair!* If you don't like it, you can always grow it out again." Seeing he was not convinced, she wrapped her arms around him and ran her fingers through the short curls at the back of his neck. "I think it looks splendid. Can you not at least *try* to like it?"

"I like *you*," he said, heaving a sigh of resignation as he returned her embrace. "If you're happy, I'm happy."

And it must be said to his credit that he tried hard to believe it.

* * *

Pickett arose the next morning with his good humor apparently restored, but it seemed to Julia that there was an invisible wall between them that had not been there before, and she knew (the warmth of his farewell kiss notwithstanding) that she was not entirely forgiven. After he had set out for Bow Street, Julia decided to try and restore herself to his good graces with a little investigating of her own. With this end in view, she dressed for the day in a Pomona green walking dress with a matching spencer, and set out on foot for Grosvenor Square. Upon arriving at the Washbourn residence, she sent up her card, and within a very few minutes was ushered into the drawing room where Lady Washbourn sat waiting to receive her.

"My dear Mrs. Pickett," the countess said, rising to drop a curtsy. "How kind of you to call! Won't you sit down?"

The walk had not been long, but the sun was warm, and Julia was only too thankful to sink onto the brocade sofa, conscious once again of the sense of fatigue that had plagued her all too frequently of late.

"Would you care for tea?" asked her hostess, reaching

for the bell pull. "Or something a bit stronger—sherry, perhaps, or a glass of peach ratafia?"

"*No!*" Recalling her husband's suspicions regarding the peach ratafia, Julia was certain she would never be able to drink it again, and certainly not under Lady Washbourn's roof. Seeing her hostess regarding her with raised brows, she added in a more moderate tone, "That is, tea would be lovely, thank you."

Lady Washbourn gave the necessary orders to the butler, along with her instructions that he was to deny her to any other callers. After he had left the room, she turned back to Julia. "Dare I hope—that is, have you some news for me?"

"I'm afraid you are laboring under a misapprehension," Julia said. "I have not come as an emissary for my husband. I only wanted to thank you for your hospitality in inviting Mr. Pickett and me to your entertainment, and to express my regret that it ended in such a tragedy." Which was not entirely accurate, Julia reflected, but it was true insofar as it went.

"Oh. I see. Yes, I thought it was going rather well, until—until what happened to poor Annie." Lady Washbourn gave her a strained smile. "I fear I am not quite comfortable in company. It was my husband's mother who suggested that we host a party to allow me to practice entertaining."

Privately Julia thought an intimate dinner or two, followed by perhaps a card party or a musical evening, would be less demanding for an inexperienced hostess, and therefore more suitable, than a large masked affair at which guests would be prone to take advantage of their anonymity in order to conduct themselves in ways they never would have risked, had their identities been immediately apparent. Aloud, however, she merely said, "You are fortunate, then, in your mother-in-law. I wish mine had been as understanding."

"Mother Washbourn has been everything that is kind," the countess agreed, "which is all the more remarkable when one considers that she was once Lady Beatrice Frampton, the daughter of the Duke of Moring, whose holdings apparently include most of Hampshire."

"But—forgive me, your ladyship—"

"Oh, pray call me Eliza."

Julia thought their acquaintance was rather slight to have progressed already to the use of Christian names, but credited it to the poor little countess's hunger for friendship, rather than any intentional impropriety on her part.

"Eliza, then," she said, acceding to this request, "I was under the impression that you and Lord Washbourn had been married for two years already. How is it that you have only now begun entertaining?"

Lady Washbourn nodded. "Yes, we married in the

summer of '07. But Washbourn's father died very shortly after the wedding—he had been ill for some time, and was particularly wishful to see his son wed before he died—and then my own father died not long after, so we have spent most of our marriage in mourning."

Julia searched these words for any implied criticism of her own failure to mourn her first husband for the full twelve months Society judged proper, but found nothing beyond a simple statement of fact. "A sad beginning to your life together," she said sympathetically. "Let us hope the end of your mourning marks the beginning of happier days ahead."

"I hope so." The countess's bleak expression held very little hope for this desirable outcome. "Mrs. Pickett, may I—may I ask you a personal question?"

"I suppose so," Julia said warily.

"How long after your marriage—your first marriage, that is—was it before you realized you'd made a mistake?"

Julia blinked, taken aback by the question in spite of her hostess's warning as to the personal nature of her query. Julia would most likely have given a sharp set-down to anyone else presumptuous enough to press for such con-fidentialities on so short an acquaintance, but decided to indulge Lady Washbourn for the sake of her husband's investigation. After all, if Lady Washbourn were to receive such confidences, then she could hardly balk at answering Julia's own inquiries.

"It was not so bad at first," Julia recalled, casting her mind back to that time almost seven years earlier when she and her first husband had been newly married. "Indeed, our wedding trip was quite—quite pleasant." Pleasant, yes, but six weeks with Lord Fieldhurst in Paris during the brief Peace of Amiens had been nothing to compare to six days with John Pickett in a shabby two-room flat in Drury Lane. Still, she had been a bedazzled nineteen-year-old girl, with no knowledge yet of how glorious—or how painful—marriage could be.

Lady Washbourn eagerly leaned forward in her seat. "Oh, yes! Our honeymoon was lovely, too." A shadow crossed her face. "I knew Washbourn did not love me, of course. He had hoped to marry Lady Barbara Stafford, but in spite of her father's exalted rank, Lady Barbara's dowry was no more than respectable, and Washbourn had to wed a fortune if he hoped to salvage his family's heritage. I knew I was not his first choice, and yet I thought—I hoped, anyway—that I could make him happy, that in time he might learn to love me."

"But honeymoons have to end sometime, don't they?" Julia remarked sympathetically. "In my case, it was a summer in Brighton that sounded the death knell, for it was there that I discovered Fieldhurst had a predilection for opera dancers. We had been married for almost a year by that time, and while there had been signs that he was unfaithful—

unexplained absences, women of the *demi-monde* who smiled at him a bit too familiarly when we encountered them at the theatre or in the park—he assured me I was worried about nothing, and I was only too ready to believe him. Then, too, I was unable to conceive a child, and that eventually drove a wedge between us."

"In my case, there was nothing so definite as that," Lady Washbourn recalled sadly. "By the time we returned from our honeymoon, we were—friends—or at least I thought we could be, in time. I had every reason to believe we might learn to be happy together. But after we returned to Washbourn Abbey, something changed. Little things began to annoy him, and although I'd had charge of my father's household after Mama died, I didn't do things at the Abbey the way Washbourn's mother, and his grandmother, and his great-grandmother had done."

"And I suppose your predecessor's remaining beneath the same roof hardly helped matters," Julia remarked, belatedly thankful that her own mother-in-law had removed to the Dower House in anticipation of their return from Paris.

"No, no, you do Mother Washbourn an injustice," the countess protested. "She has been nothing but supportive. Whenever I committed some *faux pas* through ignorance, she always defended me. I remember one incident shortly after we returned from our wedding trip, when I ordered that the medieval tapestries in the hall should be taken down so they could be cleaned and repaired. Washbourn was beside himself when he saw they were gone, and it was Mother Washbourn who reminded him that I was brought up with a different set of values, and did not understand the significance of an ancient tradition and 'elegant decay,' as she put it. And I must say she was right," she added with unexpected candor. "I cannot see the sense of letting one's family treasures fall apart through respectful neglect when they could be saved by a discreet stitch or two on the back, where no one could possibly notice."

Julia was inclined to agree, provided the restoration could be done in such a way as to render the repairs invisible, but she suspected the Fieldhursts would not have agreed with this philosophy any more than the Washbourns had done.

"And then," continued Lady Washbourn, "Lady Barbara's husband died in a hunting accident. Now she is free, and Washbourn—isn't."

"Your ladyship—er, Eliza," Julia began, choosing her words with care. "My husband told me that he suggested you might leave London for a time, and that you refused even to consider it. Under the circumstances, would it not be better—?"

"No!" Lady Washbourn shook her head emphatically. "I won't run away and leave Lady Barbara a clear field. Perhaps I might do so if I thought she truly cared for him, if I thought he might find with her the happiness he has not been able to find with me. But she is an odious creature who cares for nothing but herself! He might be unhappy with me, but he would be utterly miserable with her."

"Perhaps if you were to go away for a time and leave him to her, he might discover that for himself," Julia suggested, trying another tack. "It is quite possible that without the lure of the forbidden, the lady would lose much of her appeal."

"I understand what you are saying, but I cannot," the countess insisted. "Besides Washbourn, there is our daughter to consider, you know."

"And for your daughter's sake, you must do what you can to stay alive," Julia pointed out with some asperity.

She might have saved her breath. While Lady Washbourn was perfectly willing to concede Julia's point, she remained adamant. In the end, Julia was forced to admit defeat, and took her leave without persuading her hostess to take what steps she might to save herself. Still, she could not feel the visit was a complete waste, for she had made one interesting discovery: Lady Washbourn, in spite of her suspicions, was deeply in love with her husband.

13

In Which Comedy Turns to Tragedy

P ickett, meanwhile, entered the Bow Street Public
Office to considerable fanfare.

"Will you look at Lord John!" one member of the Foot
Patrol exclaimed loudly enough to be heard over a chorus of
appreciative whistles. "His lady wife is going to make a
gentleman of him yet."

"Turn around," commanded Mr. Dixon, making a
spinning motion with his hand. "Let us see the back."

Suppressing a huff of annoyance, Pickett turned.

"Very smart," said Mr. Colquhoun, observing this
exchange from the bench. "Still, you might have warned us.
Mr. Carson here might have arrested you as an imposter."

"You had as much warning as I did," Pickett said with
some asperity. "When I got home last night, Julia had a curst
Frenchman waiting for me with scissors in hand."

"Ah well, you may find you like it, once you get used to

it. And if not, well, it will always grow back. It's only hair, you know."

"So she said," Pickett grumbled.

"All jesting aside, what do you intend to do today regarding the Washbourn investigation?"

Pickett resisted the urge to protest that it was no jesting matter, and instead described for the magistrate his meeting with the doctor. "Which sounds rather suspicious, given that there's a large portrait in the Washbourn drawing room which shows her ladyship wearing a blue dress," he concluded. "I intend to call in Grosvenor Square and find out who painted it, and when."

Mr. Colquhoun nodded in approval, and Pickett set out for Grosvenor Square. Upon reaching the Washbourn residence, however, he suffered a check.

"Her ladyship is otherwise engaged," the butler informed him, "but if you would care to leave a message—?"

Pickett was tempted, but reminded himself that any such message might reach the ears of Lord Washbourn or the dowager countess. He shook his head. "No, no message, thank you."

Deprived of his primary object, Pickett satisfied himself instead with calling at a nearby art supply house, and inquiring of the proprietor whether he included Prussian blue among his inventory.

"Oh, aye," the shopkeeper informed him. "It's one of

my most requested paints, and no wonder. A hundred years ago, you know, the only blues available to artists tended toward gray or green, like cerulean, or else were so costly, like ultramarine, that only well-established artists could afford them."

In fact, Pickett had *not* known, but the information gave him an angle from which to introduce his next question.

"I'd never thought of painting as being so expensive a pastime," he remarked, and wondered aloud whether the shopkeeper numbered any of the aristocracy among his clientele.

"Aye, several," the man said proudly. "Especially those with daughters who paint in watercolors."

As Lord Washbourn's daughter was still an infant, Pickett doubted she was painting much of anything except the seat of her clouts. "I wonder if you've ever done business with an acquaintance of mine," he said. "Lady Washbourn, whose husband is the earl of that name."

"Washbourn," the shopkeeper echoed thoughtfully, his brow creased in concentration. At last he shook his head. "No, I can't say I recall her ladyship, nor her lord, neither."

"Ah well, their daughter is a bit young for art lessons as yet," Pickett said, displaying a talent for understatement.

"When her little ladyship is ready, I hope you'll put in a word for me with her parents."

Pickett agreed to this, privately hoping that the girl's

mother would still be alive at that point to take his advice, and took his leave. He repeated this exercise at some half-dozen art supply houses in all, each one chosen for their proximity to the Washbourn residence, and received the very same answers. He gained a new understanding of the difficulties of reproducing Nature's hues on canvas, which had apparently become somewhat easier with the accidental discovery of Prussian blue a century earlier, but came away with no firm knowledge of how Lord Washbourn might have come by this substance.

At last, finding himself in the vicinity of Curzon Street (and painfully aware that he had parted from Julia on less than idyllic terms), he set out for Number 22 with the intention of having a bite to eat in the company of his wife before returning to Bow Street. He entered the house, and found her in the hall, just putting off her bonnet and pelisse.

"Why, John, what a pleasant surprise," she said, lifting her face for his kiss. "Are you hungry? Shall I ring for tea and sandwiches?"

He agreed to this plan, and within a very few minutes they were seated side by side on the drawing room sofa.

"Only think, if I had been five minutes later, or you five minutes earlier, we should have missed one another," she remarked as she dispensed tea into two delicate Sèvres cups. "I have spent most of the morning closeted with Lady Washbourn."

Pickett set his plate down with a clatter. "You *what?*"

"I called on Lady Washbourn," she said again, bewildered by his reaction. "I knew her refusal to leave her husband had you baffled, and I thought—quite correctly, as it turned out—that she might be more inclined to confide in the widow of a viscount than in a Bow Street Runner."

"Thank you for reminding me of my place, my lady," he said, tight-lipped. "For a while there I was in danger of forgetting it."

She set down the teapot and gave him a reproachful look. "Oh, John, don't be that way! Your 'place' has nothing to do with it. Poor Lady Washbourn has so few friends, thanks in large part to the machinations of 'Aunt Mildred,' that I thought she might welcome a confidante." Seeing he was not satisfied with this explanation, she added coaxingly, "You used to like my help."

"It was my only excuse for spending any time with you," he pointed out.

"Oh, was *that* it? How stupid of me! I actually thought I was being useful!"

"Of course you were," he amended hastily. "But on those occasions we worked *together*. You didn't go haring off on your own like this without so much as a by-your-leave!"

"Oh, so now I must ask your permission before I pay a simple morning call?" she demanded, her bosom swelling with indignation.

"Not a *simple* morning call, no. But this was something more than just a simple morning call, wasn't it?"

"It is only common courtesy to call on one's hostess the day after an event to thank her for her hospitality!"

"This isn't the day after the event," he pointed out.

"No, for an inquest was held the morning after. And I don't see why you are making such a great to-do over nothing! I should have thought you would be grateful to me for discovering the real reason for Lady Washbourn's refusal to leave Town, while you were wasting your time calling on that horrid Lady Gerald Broadbridge!"

"I wasn't calling on Sophy; I was calling on her father, and she just happened to stop in."

"She actually paid a morning call?" Julia exclaimed in scandalized tones. "I hope she had her husband's permission!"

"Will you please leave Sophy out of this? As it happens, I tried to call on Lady Washbourn myself—I wanted to ask her who painted that enormous portrait over the mantel—but I was turned away with the information that her ladyship was otherwise engaged."

"But that's easy," Julia insisted. "The artist was Mr. Henry Tomkins, of the Royal Academy."

He blinked at her in confusion. "Lady Washbourn told you this?"

"She didn't have to. Mr. Tomkins is the most fashionable portraitist in London at the moment, and his depiction of light and texture is quite distinctive. So you see, you didn't have to ask Lady Washbourn, after all. You had only to ask your wife."

Perhaps it was the note of triumph in her voice, or maybe her rather smug smile, that goaded him beyond endurance. "Very well," he retorted. "Perhaps my wife can also tell me when it was painted, and whether Lord Washbourn watched the proceedings, or showed any undue interest, or whether Mr. Tomkins happened to misplace any of his paints during the process." Finding her lost for speech, he prompted, "Well, Mrs. Pickett? Am I not to have the benefit of your expertise?"

Whereupon Julia, to her own dismay and her husband's horror, promptly burst into tears.

"*Julia?*" Pickett slid from the sofa and dropped to his knees before her, taking her hands in his and alternately chafing and kissing them in a futile effort to stem the flood. "Julia, sweetheart, don't—please don't cry," he pleaded helplessly, utterly floored by the sight of the same woman who had only a year ago faced the prospect of the gallows with an almost stoic calm now dissolving into tears at a few cross words (at least, he *thought* there had only been a few— hadn't there?) from her husband. "Never mind, my love, you had no way of knowing I meant to call on her ladyship. I'm a beast to speak to you so."

Her tears showed no signs of abating, and he transferred both her hands to one of his own, so that he might have a hand free to reach into his coat pocket for a handkerchief. Unfortunately, this proved to be a relic of the days before his marriage, when he had been obliged to purchase such things at secondhand; consequently, it bore someone else's monogram in one corner. Apparently the sight of it disturbed her, for it seemed to Pickett that her tears fell all the harder.

"Look," he said in increasing desperation, recalling something else he'd felt in his pocket while fumbling for his handkerchief. He reached in once more, and drew out a small coin purse. "Today I got my wages for the week—twenty-five shillings. Let's blue it all, shall we?"

This suggestion, it seemed, was unusual enough to make her emerge, puffy of eyes and red of nose, from the folds of his secondhand handkerchief. "What, all of it?"

"As you said yourself, it's not as if we need it to live on." He was rather proud of the careful neutrality in his voice. "What do you say? Dinner at Grillon's? The theatre? Not Drury Lane, obviously, since it burned to the ground, but they must be staging something at Covent Garden."

"Oh, John, do you mean it?" she asked, smiling tremulously through her tears.

Her eagerness made him feel ashamed. Since returning from their wedding trip, they had made only one social appearance—the Washbourn masquerade—and even that had been a matter of professional necessity. For his part, he could think of nothing more pleasurable than coming home to his wife at the end of the day; he tended to forget that she was accustomed to evenings filled with social engagements, to which his solitary companionship must pale in comparison.

"I do," he announced recklessly. "I'll take you anywhere you like, and you may dress me up however you wish." He glanced at the clock on the mantelpiece. "I have to be getting back to Bow Street now, but shall I stop by Covent Garden Theatre and purchase tickets?"

She readily agreed to this plan, and kissed him fondly (several times) in between profuse apologies for wrecking his plans for the investigation. He was obliged to insist, with perhaps more diplomacy than truth, that she had done no such thing, and they parted on such exceedingly good terms that he was halfway to Bow Street before it occurred to him that he just might have been played for a fool.

No, his heart argued with his mind, *it isn't possible. She's not that sort of woman.*

But his misgivings were not allayed when he stopped by the box office at Covent Garden Theatre, and discovered that the evening's offering was a comedy with the inauspicious title of *The Bridegroom Deceived*.

* * *

Julia, for her part, reflected upon the incident with mingled shame and bewilderment. Why, she had never done such a thing before in her life! In fact, she despised the sort of female who resorted to tears and hysterics in order to get her own way. She had no idea what had brought on the sudden bout of crying, much less the reason for its equally sudden cessation, but in retrospect she could see how her uncharacteristic outburst might be interpreted in just such a light. It was too galling to think he might believe her capable of such manipulative scheming.

There was only one thing to do, then, to make sure she was restored to her husband's good graces: she would spend the afternoon lying down with cold compresses over her eyes to reduce the swelling, and then, when he returned to Curzon Street that evening, she would devote herself to the task of captivating him anew.

* * *

Thus it was that, when Pickett returned to Curzon Street that evening with a large bouquet of flowers in his arm (having purchased this from the same market at Covent Garden where, in his younger days, he had once picked pockets or pinched the occasional apple), Rogers relieved him of his hat and gloves and informed him that he might find madam upstairs preparing to go out for the evening.

Pickett thanked the butler for the information, then took the stairs two at a time. He tapped lightly on the bedroom door, then opened it, stepped inside—

And froze, the flowers in his hand forgotten. His lady stood by the window (was it possible that she had been watching for him?), dressed for the evening's entertainment in a high-waisted, low-necked gown of some diaphanous white fabric that appeared golden in the light from the setting sun. He had seen her like this once before, only on that other occasion it had been the fire in the grate that had gilded her like the touch of Midas.

"You remember," she observed with some satisfaction, seeing the recognition in his eyes.

He opened his mouth to answer, but no words came. He shut his mouth, swallowed, and tried again. "You were wearing that dress on the night we met." It was a curiously romantic interpretation of the evening of a man's murder, but perhaps understandable under the circumstances. Pickett shook his head in wonder. "If anyone had told me then that in less than a year you and I would be married, I would have thought he belonged in Bedlam."

"The best thing Frederick ever did for me was lead me to you." Her gaze dropped to the burden in his arms. "But what's all this?"

He looked down at the flowers he held as if surprised to see them there, and then stuck them out awkwardly in her direction. "They're for you. It's just that, well, I've never made you cry before. I never want to do it again."

She found herself blinking back tears as she took the flowers from him. "Too late," she said, laughing a little at her own foolishness. "It was sweet of you, John. I'll have Rogers put them in water, shall I?"

"Rogers can wait," Pickett said, and pulled her into his arms and kissed her in a way that posed a considerable threat to the flowers trapped between them.

At length she felt his fingers dislodging her hairpins, and was moved to protest. "John, you're wrecking my coiffure."

"Hang your coiffure," he retorted, making no very noticeable attempt to mend his ways.

"What a domineering man I've married," she complained with a marked lack of regret. "But you had best change your clothes, if we are to reach Covent Garden Theatre before the curtain call."

Reluctantly agreeing to this plan, Pickett shrugged off his workaday brown serge coat and washed up, then rang for Thomas to assist him into the evening clothes he'd worn for his wedding. When this operation was complete (and Pickett was forced to concede that it took less time with Thomas's assistance than it would have taken him alone), the Picketts, man and wife, set out for Covent Garden.

And if it occurred to either of them that they were both trying perhaps a bit too hard to avoid resuming the subject of their earlier disagreement, it is doubtful that they would have recognized this as anything but a good thing.

* * *

Upon being set down before the theatre at Covent Garden, Pickett and Julia were the objects of cheers and not a few jesting remarks by members of the Night Patrol just coming on duty at the Bow Street Public Office adjacent to the theatre.

"Ignore them," Pickett said, glaring at his colleagues before escorting his wife inside.

She left her new evening wrap in the cloakroom (hoping that it might be spared the fate of its predecessor, which had perished in the Drury Lane Theatre fire), and then took Pickett's arm as they climbed the stairs to the boxes above. She was rather taken aback to discover that her husband, usually so careful in matters of money, had spared no expense where this outing was concerned; the box he had hired for the evening was one of the best and, consequently, the most expensive. The tickets, together with the flowers he'd bought, must have made quite a dent in his twenty-five shillings.

After they had taken their seats, however, she noticed his gaze darting about the theatre, and realized he was less concerned with making a lavish gesture than he was with scouting out the exits and determining the best route of escape in case of emergency; clearly, she was not the only one who retained vivid memories of their flight from the

198

burning Drury Lane Theatre two months earlier. She could not help thinking this a good thing, as it served to distract his attention from the curious stares, raised quizzing glasses, and occasional pointing fingers leveled at them. Lifting her chin defiantly, she moved her chair closer to his and proceeded to flirt outrageously with him.

Or at least she tried. It was difficult to flirt with a man who wouldn't flirt back.

"What is it, John?" she asked at last, finding his gaze fixed on some point on the opposite side of the theatre.

"Look at that box—the fourth one from the proscenium. Is that Lord and Lady Washbourn?"

"I think so," she said, reaching instinctively for her reticule before remembering that the object she would have sought was not there. "I do wish I hadn't lost my opera glasses in the fire!"

He laced his fingers through hers. "I'm just glad that was *all* you lost."

"I lost my evening cloak, too," she reminded him, and then gave his hand a squeeze. "But only look what I found."

There was no opportunity to say more, for at that moment the curtain rose and the play began. The Washbourns and their troubles were forgotten until the interval between acts, at which time the boxes emptied as aristocrats decamped to the lobby for refreshments.

"Would you like something?" Pickett asked, gesturing

vaguely in the direction of the lobby. "Champagne, perhaps? I'm not on duty tonight, you know."

He did not seem precisely eager at the prospect of going downstairs to fetch it, and she realized that he had been more aware of the gawking looks than he had let on. She should not have been surprised; after all, his livelihood (at least until he had married her) depended upon his being observant. Although a glass of champagne sounded tempting, she would not subject him to the sort of scrutiny he would face were he to go in search of it.

"Thank you, darling, but I'm not thirsty," she said with less than perfect truth. "Let's just stay here, shall we? Oh, look! Now, what do you think of *that?*"

Without being so vulgar as to point, she contrived to position her fan so that it directed his attention to a box across the theatre, one level lower than the Washbourn box and some distance to its right. Lord Washbourn had just entered this enclosure, and stood talking to a lady whose ample bosom threatened to spill out of her low-cut gown.

"At a guess, I should say that was Lady Barbara Brennan," he said.

Julia nodded. "The very same. And in the meantime, there sits poor little Lady Washbourn all alone."

"There's something we can do about that, anyway," Pickett said, pushing back his chair and rising to his feet.

"What are you doing?"

200

"Everyone else appears to be visiting. Why shouldn't we?"

"An excellent notion." She gave him her hand and allowed him to pull her to her feet. "I can't help wondering, though, if it is simple human kindness that inspires you, or if you are hoping to learn something useful."

"A bit of both, perhaps."

She nodded wisely. "I suspected as much. Very well, Mr. Pickett, lead on!"

He did, and as they traversed the long, curving corridor to the other side of the theatre, she noticed once more that the awkwardness with which he faced purely social situations disappeared once he became a man on a mission. Pickett, for his part, counted doors as they passed, wondering how they would know the right box when they came to it. Thankfully, this dilemma was resolved when he recognized a footman in the Washbourn livery stationed outside one such door.

"Lord and Lady Washbourn?" Pickett inquired, just to be certain.

"His lordship has stepped out, but her ladyship is within."

"Excellent!"

The footman flung open the door and stepped back to allow them entrance.

"Back so soon, my dear?" Lady Washbourn began,

turning at the sound of the door opening. "Oh, Mr. Pickett! And Mrs. Pickett, I'm so pleased to see you." She rose from her chair and dipped a curtsy.

Greetings were exchanged, and then the countess gestured toward the chair vacated by her husband. "Washbourn is not here at the moment, but he should be back directly. In the meantime, will you not sit down?"

They seated themselves, and Pickett broached the subject he had been unable to raise with the countess that morning. "Your ladyship, my wife and I have been discussing the portrait hanging over your drawing room mantel," he said, which was certainly a novel way of describing the conversation that had taken place a few hours earlier. "Mrs. Pickett says it was done by a Mr. Tomkins."

"You have a good eye, Mrs. Pickett," she told Julia, then turned to Pickett. "Yes, Mr. Henry Tomkins of the Royal Academy."

"Was it painted shortly after your marriage, or more recently?"

Lady Washbourn regarded him keenly, realizing there was more behind his innocent questioning than an interest in art. "It was done six months ago, when we were in Town for the autumn session of Parliament. Mr. Tomkins is much in demand, you know, and his services are practically impossible to procure during the Season."

"Did your husband watch Mr. Tomkins at work?"

Realizing they might be overheard by curious ears in the adjacent boxes, Pickett added in an offhand manner, "I suspect his lordship paid a pretty penny, so I shouldn't be surprised at his wanting to make sure he was getting his money's worth."

"No, for Mr. Tomkins will not allow anyone to watch him paint. I confess I was more than a bit nervous about the finished product, for I don't need an artist to tell me I am no beauty. Still, I can't but be pleased with the results. It is an excessively flattering likeness, is it not?"

"On the contrary, I thought the artist captured you very well," Pickett said. Lowering his voice, he asked, "When Mr. Tomkins completed the commission and presented his bill, did he mention any of his paints being lost, or misplaced?"

"Why, no, Mr. Pickett," she responded in kind, but her expression was puzzled. "Should he have done?"

"That is what I would like to know, your ladyship. If you should happen to recall any such incident, will you send word to me, at either Bow or Curzon Street?"

"Of course." Correctly assuming the subject to be closed, at least for the nonce, she addressed Julia in a very different tone. "Tell me, Mrs. Pickett, what do you think of *The Bridegroom Deceived?*"

Julia shook her head. "It's a very amusing play, but I fear I cannot think much of the intelligence of any man who fails to recognize his wife through a disguise." She smiled up at Pickett. "I suspect my own husband would very quickly penetrate any such ruse."

"Yes, but then, you are wed to an unusually clever man," her ladyship pointed out. "Then, too, Mr. Goodman had no reason to suspect that his bride was a princess, and so he would have no reason to expect to see her in such a rôle."

"It will be interesting to see how he reacts when he finds out," Pickett remarked with perhaps undue solemnity, given that the play under discussion was a farce.

"You will not have long to wait, for the second act should begin soon. I do hope Washbourn will not be late— ah, there you are," she said a bit too brightly, looking at some point beyond Pickett's shoulder.

"Forgive me, my dear—Mrs. Pickett, Mr. Pickett," he added, nodding to each of the visitors in turn. "Some non- sense about a missing fan. Lady Barbara is convinced she must have lost it on the night of our masquerade."

"She summoned you to her box for the purpose of discussing a lost fan?" Lady Washbourn asked, apparently unable to prevent a trace of skepticism from creeping into her tone.

His lordship nodded. "This particular fan had been a gift from—a former suitor." His slight stumble left Pickett in no doubt as to the identity of the suitor in question. "I told her you had not mentioned finding such a thing—although poor Annie's death might well have driven it from your mind—and that she would do better to address her inquiries to you."

"Yes, of course," the countess agreed with an eagerness Pickett found both touching and pathetic. "I don't recall any such item turning up, but I shall ask the staff."

The conversation became more labored with the earl's arrival, and it seemed to Pickett that they were all trying a bit too hard to avoid the subject of Annie's death. All in all, it was a relief when the gong sounded to signal the theatre patrons to return to their seats for the second act.

Alas, Pickett only traded one set of problems for another. He escaped from the real-life drama of the Washbourn marriage only to be immersed in the fictional one being enacted onstage, in which the obtuse Mr. Goodman's dilemma reflected rather too closely Pickett's own situation.

Apparently Julia was equally conscious of the parallel, for they had scarcely settled themselves in their seats when she looked at him keenly and remarked, "I expect Mr. Goodman will be very pleased by his unexpected rise in the world."

"They could be quite happy living on his income," he pointed out. "It isn't as if they would be begging in the street."

"Yes, but why should they? Why should she have to give up her kingdom merely for the sake of his pride?"

" 'Mere' pride, Julia? There is also the little matter of deception, you know. They don't call it *The Bridegroom Deceived* for nothing. She should have told him."

"Perhaps she felt she could not," Julia retorted. "Perhaps she knew that if she had told him from the beginning, he would have been too—too confoundedly *noble* to marry her at all!"

"Blast it, Julia, he found out on his *honeymoon!* From his *father-in-law*, of all people!"

"What?" Utterly bewildered, she looked down at the printed program in her hand, whose description of the plot bore absolutely no resemblance to the scenario he had just described.

At that moment, perhaps thankfully, the curtain opened on the second act.

"Never mind," muttered Pickett as he fixed his eyes on the stage, uncomfortably aware of having said too much.

The play wound to its inevitable conclusion: the lovely Gwendolyn was revealed as the true princess of Sylvania, the handsome but dim Mr. Goodman took his place at her side with nary a qualm, and everyone lived happily ever after. Still, something of the evening's early promise had been lost. When they returned to Curzon Street and prepared for bed, Pickett gave Julia a perfunctory peck on the cheek, then snuffed the candle and rolled over. But it was a long time before he fell asleep.

14

*In Which John Pickett's Investigation
Takes an Unexpected Turn*

B efore reporting to Bow Street the next morning, Pickett called at the Bond Street studio of Mr. Henry Tomkins, R. A. As he opened the door, a bell mounted over the doorframe announced his entrance, and a masculine voice from the floor above called down to inquire as to the nature of his business.

"John Pickett, of Bow Street," he said, feeling more than a bit foolish at having to shout up the stairs in the direction of the unseen speaker. "I should like to ask a few questions, if I may."

"Bow Street, you say? Oh, very well," the disembodied voice conceded grudgingly. "I suppose you'd better come up."

Pickett mounted the stairs to the floor above where, he assumed, the artist would be working in the room at the front of the house in order to take advantage of the light from the large windows overlooking the street. This theory proved to be quite correct; alas, Pickett discovered to his chagrin that the artist had company. In fact, Mr. Tomkins was hard at work on a new portrait whose model was draped sinuously over a *chaise longue*, clad in nothing but a strategically placed scarf.

"Er, um, I'm sorry," Pickett stammered, blushing crimson and quickly turning his back on the overexposed and quite unembarrassed model. "I didn't know—I thought you were alone."

Mr. Tomkins laid down his brush, then picked up a cloth and began to wipe the paint from his hands. "It's quite all right, Mr. Pickett," he said with a sigh that indicated otherwise.

Too late, Pickett realized that he should have given his direction as Curzon Street, and offered some tale about wishing to engage the portraitist's services. The artist's next words, however, drove such petty considerations from his mind.

"If you will excuse me, Persephone, you may rest for a bit before we resume."

"*Persephone?*" At the mention of the name, Pickett whirled about to confront the artist's model, her lack of clothing forgotten.

But not for long. The woman had let her scarf fall to the seat of the *chaise longue* and picked up a satin dressing gown, which she appeared to be in no great hurry to put on. Upon hearing her name called in a voice of incredulous dismay, she looked up at Pickett and winked.

Mr. Tomkins looked from one to the other. "You two know each other?"

"We've, er, we've never been introduced, exactly," Pickett temporized.

"Of course we have," the artist's model put in, shrugging her arms into the sleeves of her dressing gown. "Dr. Humphrey introduced us. Don't you remember?"

In fact, Pickett tried his best not to think of that experience at all, but it was unlikely he would ever forget his encounter with Persephone or Electra, another member of the same sorority, who had been tasked with proving his virility (or, more specifically, any lack thereof) for the purpose of obtaining an annulment, while Dr. Edmund Humphrey observed the proceedings and took notes. Pickett had hoped never to clap eyes on any part of that unholy trinity again, and here he had crossed paths with two of the three in less than a fortnight.

"I, um, er—"

"Never mind, poppet, I won't tell," she assured him, her gaze drifting down his person in fond remembrance. "I trust that little business was settled satisfactorily?"

"Most—most satisfactorily," Pickett said with a hint of defiance. "In fact, the lady and I decided to stay married."

"Oh, well done," she purred approvingly. "I must say, I thought at the time that it was a right shame."

"If you'll wait for me in the other room," the artist interrupted impatiently, "I'd like to take care of this business with Mr. Pickett, so I can get back to work before I lose the morning sunlight."

"Of course, Hank," she cooed, then chasséd from the room.

"Now, Mr. Pickett, what can I do for you?"

"I believe you recently painted a portrait of the Countess of Washbourn."

Mr. Tomkins nodded. "Yes, about six months ago. What of it?"

Pickett regarded Persephone's abandoned *chaise longue* with some consternation as a new and unwelcome thought occurred to him. "Did Lady Washbourn come here to your studio for her sittings?"

"No, no, certainly not. The studio is all very well for persons of Persephone's stamp, but for a commission such as Lord Washbourn's, I am of course at his service—or her ladyship's, as the case may be."

"And having commissioned you to take his wife's likeness, did his lordship take any particular interest in the proceedings themselves—wanting to watch as you painted, for instance?"

"No, he didn't, and for that I'm grateful," confessed the

artist. "As a general rule, I don't allow others to watch me at work, but when one is paying as much as Lord Washbourn— well, it would have been an awkward prohibition to have to enforce."

Pickett glanced at the open paint box on a table positioned next to the artist's easel. "It must be a challenge, working somewhere other than your studio. You must have to be careful not to leave anything behind."

"Not so very much," Mr. Tomkins said, to Pickett's disappointment. "Long before I could afford to set up a studio, I made a practice of soliciting commissions from door to door, so I already had an established routine for working at various locations. The greater risk is that of leaving something at the studio, and then wishing I'd thought to put it in my paint box. Of course, that's not to say I never forget anything. In fact, a day or two after I'd completed the Washbourn commission, I realized I had left something at their house in Grosvenor Square."

"Did you indeed?" asked Pickett, his ears pricking up at this revelation. "A tube of paint, perhaps?"

The artist's eyebrows rose in surprise. "Why yes, as a matter of fact, it was. How did you know?"

"Lucky guess," Pickett said cryptically. "I trust you were able to get it back?"

Mr. Tomkins shook his head. "There was no need to trouble her ladyship over such a thing. The tube was almost empty, and ocher is cheap in any case, so"—he broke off with a shrug.

"Then the missing paint was not Prussian blue?" Pickett asked, conscious of a pang of disappointment.

"No, it was ocher, a yellowish-brown that I used—in combination with several other pigments, of course—to render her ladyship's hair, as well as certain parts of the background and the carpet at her feet."

"I see," Pickett said, abandoning with some regret what had appeared to be a very promising theory. "Well then, I'll take no more of your valuable time."

The artist nodded in dismissal, clearly impatient to get back to work, and Pickett quitted the premises. When he returned to Bow Street, he found Dr. Gilroy lying in wait for him with a thick book under one arm, its leather binding cracked and its pages dog-eared from much use.

"The good doctor here wants a word with you, Mr. Pickett," Mr. Colquhoun informed him without preamble. You can use my chambers for privacy, if you wish."

Pickett nodded. "Thank you, sir." He showed the doctor into the magistrate's private office, and then closed the door behind them. "I'm sorry to have kept you waiting, Dr. Gilroy. You have information for me?"

"I believe I may, although you will be the best judge of whether it is any use or not." The physician set the heavy book on the desk and began flipping pages. "I took the liberty of looking up prussic acid in my medical texts to make sure I hadn't missed anything that might have been of use to you."

"And?"

"And it appears the pigment Prussian blue is not the only source of the poison. It also occurs naturally in certain plants, including the seeds of common fruits."

"What fruits?" asked Pickett, as a new and entirely unexpected possibility began to take form in his brain.

The doctor ran a finger down the page. "Apples, for one, as well as stone fruits such as apricots, cherries, peaches, plums—" Dr. Gilroy interrupted his reading to inquire, "Are you all right, Mr. Pickett?"

"Yes, I'm—I'm quite all right," Pickett stammered, squeezing his eyes shut against the blinding light of revelation.

He could not recall afterwards exactly what he'd said to the doctor. He hoped he had thanked the man for the information before sending him on his way, but he could not have sworn to it. He did, however, remember waiting with his head spinning until Mr. Colquhoun concluded his business at the bench.

"I've been looking at it backwards," he told the magistrate, as soon as he could have a word alone with his mentor.

"Have you, now?" asked Mr. Colquhoun, his bushy

white brows lowering thoughtfully. "In what way?"

"Lord Washbourn is not trying to kill his wife. Lady Washbourn is trying to kill her husband."

"Bless my soul! Are you sure?"

"No, not entirely, but it certainly looks that way." He ticked the sequence of events off on his fingers. "Lady Washbourn—whose father was a brewer, let's not forget that—makes her own ratafia flavored with peaches and almonds; shortly before the masquerade, her ladyship goes downstairs and instructs the staff to serve this in addition to the champagne and negus she'd ordered for the party; Lord Washbourn brings her a glass of that same beverage, which she sets down untouched; and, finally, an unsuspecting maid picks up a glass of ratafia, drinks it down, and dies within minutes."

"We don't know that it was the same glass," the magistrate pointed out.

"That's true, sir, but if I were a betting man, I wouldn't lay you very long odds."

"Even if that were the case, wouldn't it be Lady Washbourn giving the glass to her husband, rather than the other way 'round?"

"I haven't worked out all the details yet," Pickett confessed. "I hadn't even considered the possibility until just now."

"I see," Mr. Colquhoun said, nodding. "In the

meantime, perhaps you can tell me why her ladyship would wish to do so, and why she would set a Bow Street Runner on the trail."

Pickett thought of Lady Washbourn, sitting in miserable solitude while her husband indulged in a *tête-à-tête* with the lady he had once hoped to marry. "The oldest story in the world," he told the magistrate. "She's in love with her husband, but he loves another woman, one whom he had thought at one time to marry, and who may even now be his mistress. Lady Washbourn decides that if she can't have him—*all* of him—then no one will."

"And her reasons for bringing you into the matter?"

"To establish her own innocence. She sets herself up as the intended victim, and then, if a tragic 'accident' were to befall his lordship, what would I think but that he'd been hoist with his own petard, so to speak? The maid's death even helps her in that regard. After all, there's already been one unintended victim; why not another?"

The magistrate shook his head. "It makes a certain sort of sense, but she would be taking a terrible risk. She couldn't know for sure that you wouldn't tumble to the truth."

Pickett's lips twisted in a wry smile. "Yes, well, it wouldn't be the first time I've been underestimated."

"So, assuming this theory of yours is correct, how do you intend to prove it?"

"There's the rub, sir," Pickett said with a sigh. "To start

with, I should like to have a look about Lady Washbourn's still-room, where she makes the stuff. So I suppose it's back to Grosvenor Square."

"No, that won't do."

"Begging your pardon, sir, but why not?"

"Because a house in Town wouldn't be equipped with such a thing. Think, man! Lady Washbourn's still-room would be attached to the country house, where his lordship's orchards are."

"Oh," said Pickett, rather nonplussed. "Yes, I see."

"So I expect you'll be wanting to go to Surrey, to Washbourn Abbey." Mr. Colquhoun turned in his chair and looked up at the large clock mounted on the wall over his bench. "If you hurry, you can catch the noon stage from Cheapside, and reach Croydon by nightfall."

"You don't mind?" Pickett asked, taken aback by his magistrate's ready capitulation to a scheme which he'd thought would take considerable persuasion.

"I'm not entirely convinced, mind you, but your theory holds enough validity that it must be eliminated, anyway. I only hope you can find sufficient evidence to either condemn her ladyship or confirm her innocence."

"So do I," said Pickett with feeling.

"And now, you'd best be going home." The magistrate regarded his most junior Runner with a twinkle in his blue eyes. "Besides packing your bags for the journey, I expect your farewells are likely to take some time."

* * *

"I wish you were not going back to Sussex so soon, Emily," Julia complained to Lady Dunnington when she called in Audley Street that morning. "Whatever shall I do without you?"

"The same things you were doing before I arrived," Emily pointed out. "Shopping, visiting Hookham's Library, walking in St. James's—" She broke off this catalog of entertainments to make a practical observation. "Even if I were to stay in London, I would not be able to accompany you for much longer. Little Lady Genie is making her presence increasingly difficult to hide—and I do mean *increasingly*," she added, and although she made a moue of distaste, she patted the bulge of her abdomen with affection.

"But I wasn't doing anything before," Julia confessed. "Not really. There are only so many times one may arrange flowers for the hall, or plan meals for the week, or give instructions to the housekeeper, or darn one's husband's stockings—oh, but I must mark that one off my list, for I bought him new ones, and got rid of the old. Monogramming handkerchiefs, perhaps," she murmured, recalling the one with which he had dried her tears.

Lady Dunnington wrinkled her nose. "Monogramming handkerchiefs does not sound like my idea of being giddy to the point of dissipation, but so long as it gets you out of the house"—she shrugged her shoulders.

"Actually, I would probably have the haberdasher send over half a dozen—or perhaps a full dozen," Julia amended, thinking of the additional hours the extra embroidery would fill.

"Julia Runyon Fieldhurst Pickett, are you *in hiding?*" Emily demanded.

"Of course I'm not! Well—yes—I suppose I am—that is, sort of," Julia confessed sheepishly.

"Then you *are* regretting your *mésalliance!*"

"No, not at all! If anything, my feelings for John have grown stronger over the last two months. It is only that if I go out, I am sure to be stared at, and whispered about, and pointed out—if I am not given the cut direct, which is equally likely."

"You knew it would be that way," Emily pointed out, albeit not unkindly. "Still, you went to the theatre last night, did you not?"

"Yes, but that was different, for John was with me. I can face anything so long as we are together. I have only to look at him to know he is worth ten of whomever is doing the snubbing." She sighed. "But he has to work during the day, and so I am left rather at loose ends."

"He might give it up," the countess pointed out. "Your jointure was set up in such a way that it continued even after your remarriage, did it not?"

"Yes, and I suggested that." She shuddered at the memory. "It did not go well."

"No, I daresay he is not the sort of man who would be content to live as Mr. Julia Fieldhurst."

Julia came swiftly to her husband's defense. "Nor would I want him to be!"

"I must say, I think the better of him for it. But my dear, you cannot hide from the *ton* forever. You must face them down. The sooner you do so, the sooner they will find something—or someone!—else to gossip about."

"I know you're right," Julia conceded. "Still, it is a great deal easier said than done."

Emily leaped to her feet as quickly as her increasing bulk would allow, and held out her hand to Julia. "Then let's confront them together, shall we?"

With some misgiving, Julia took her friend's hand. "And what of little Lady Genie?" she asked, gesturing with her free hand toward Emily's middle.

"I shall wear my fullest pelisse, and unless we are walking into a stiff wind, I daresay no one will notice. And if they do, they will have *two* shocking women to talk about, instead of one!"

Emily in full flow was a force to be reckoned with, and she shot down one by one every objection Julia put forward. By the time they reached St. James's Park, Julia was more than reconciled to the outing; in fact, she actually looked forward to it. The trees in the park were unfurling their new greenery, and the flowers were beginning to bloom, and it seemed to Julia that the abundance of Nature served to reflect the promise of her new marriage.

Alas, they had not gone far along the path before her earlier fears were confirmed. Several ladies of long acquaintance took great pains not to meet her eye, and others gave her only the curtest of nods in passing, while two young bloods ogled her quite boldly through their quizzing glasses, as if her descent in the world excused them from showing her even the most basic forms of courtesy.

Her detractors, however, had reckoned without the Countess of Dunnington. "Why, Mrs. Langford-Hicks!" Emily exclaimed, hurrying forward to seize the hands of a starchy-looking female who had shown every indication of drawing her skirts aside lest she be contaminated by some accidental contact with the former viscountess. "How delightful to see you looking so well!"

"Lady Dunnington," acknowledged the woman, detaching herself gingerly from Emily's grasp. "How do you do?"

"All the better for having my dear Julia's company," she declared, dragging Julia into the conversation, will she or nill she. "You are acquainted, are you not?"

Having no choice, Mrs. Langford-Hicks nodded stiffly. "Your ladyship—er—that is—"

"Mrs. Pickett," Julia said, supplying the proper term of

address with more than a hint of defiance.

"Yes, for she has recently remarried, you know," Emily put in.

"So I had heard," their companion said, wrinkling her nose as if she smelled something that offended her. "To a Bow Street Runner, or some such person, if rumor doesn't lie."

"Oh, but not just any Bow Street Runner, for her Mr. Pickett is quite the cleverest of the lot, and very likely the handsomest as well." Lady Dunnington went on to describe Pickett's person and prospects in such glowing terms that that young man would scarcely have recognized himself. "I should not be at all surprised if he is made a magistrate by the time he is thirty, and knighted by forty," she concluded. "Then all those who snubbed him in his Bow Street days will look a pretty set of fools, won't they?"

"Really, Emily," Julia chided, choking back her laughter until Mrs. Langford-Hicks had withdrawn stunned and reeling from the assault. "I had no idea your opinion of John was so high!"

"No, and if you ever tell him I said such a thing, I shall deny it with my last breath! But Mrs. Langford-Hicks's pretensions needed depressing, for what was she before her marriage but Mr. Langford-Hicks's housekeeper?" Seeing Julia's expression of shocked delight, she added, "Oh, didn't you know? Quite the scandal of '92, it was—or do I mean

221

'93? Either way, she has no room to look down her nose at anyone. And the fact that you made your come-out ten years later and had never heard the tale only proves what I have been trying to tell you: people will forget—or at least lose interest—when some new scandal comes along."

Whatever Julia might have said to this assertion was to remain unspoken, for at that moment she was hailed by a feminine voice.

"Mrs. Pickett! You are Mrs. John Pickett, are you not?"

Gratified that *someone*, at least, seemed eager to acknowledge her, Julia turned and beheld a young woman with crimped dark ringlets and a walking dress so lavishly decorated with frogs and braid that the crimson sarcenet beneath the ornamentation was scarcely visible. "Yes, I am Mrs. Pickett. How may I be of service to you?"

"Lud, I'm sure there's nothing *you* can do for *me!* I'm Lady Gerald Broadbridge, you know."

In fact, Julia had recognized her husband's first love from the moment she saw her approaching, but she refused to stroke the young woman's vanity by letting on. "I'm pleased to meet you, Lady Gerald," she said, curtsying. "Tell me, are you acquainted with Lady Dunnington?"

Sophy appeared less than gratified by the introduction, no doubt because a countess must take precedence over the wife of a mere fourth son, even if his father was a duke. "Lady Dunnington," she said without enthusiasm, dipping the briefest of curtsies.

"Lady Gerald." Emily, who knew to a nicety how to dampen pretensions, gave Lady Gerald Broadbridge a curtsy that somehow combined the dictates of courtesy with just the right amount of condescension.

"I'm pleased to make your acquaintance, both of you," Sophy said, turning to Julia with a mixture of eagerness and malice. "But especially you, Mrs. Pickett. I knew your husband, you see."

"Yes, I know," Julia said, maintaining her smile with an effort. "He once worked for your father, I believe."

Sophy was not best pleased with this reminder of her own humble origins, but, having claimed acquaintance with John Pickett, she could hardly deny the charge. "Yes, he was Papa's apprentice. How you would have laughed, if you could have seen him as I did, all black with coal dust! He was quite mad for me, you know—in fact, he begged me to marry him."

"Yes, so he told me," Julia said, determined to rid Sophy of any illusion that John Pickett still nursed his youthful passion as a deep, dark secret. "What a good thing it is that we are not allowed to marry our first loves! When I was sixteen, I conceived a grand passion for one of the stable hands."

"For me it was my dancing master," Emily agreed.

"Yes, but John was nineteen," Sophy pointed out.

"Worse and worse!" exclaimed Julia. "When I was nineteen, I married Fieldhurst!"

Emily nodded. "It is curious, is it not, that young ladies are considered marriageable at nineteen, or even younger, but how many young men of that age do you see embarking upon matrimony? One might assume it takes them longer to mature."

"Perhaps it is Nature's way of preventing them from making disastrous marriages," Julia suggested blandly.

"Like yours with Lord Fieldhurst?" Sophy suggested with a brittle smile. "I only hope poor John lasts longer than your first husband did."

"So do I," agreed Julia, resolutely ignoring Sophy's too-intimate use of her husband's first name, as well as the implication that she had been responsible for Lord Field-hurst's death. "But if—God forbid!—he does not, at least he will have the satisfaction of dying happy. I only hope Lord Gerald may be as fortunate."

Sophy looked a bit puzzled by this remark, as if sensing some insult she could not quite pin down. "Speaking of my dear Gerry, I mustn't keep him waiting," Sophy said a bit too brightly, glancing over her shoulder at the portly, red-faced gentleman tottering along the path in their direction. "So pleased to make your acquaintance, Lady Dunnington, Mrs. Pickett."

She spun on her heel and hurried away in Lord Gerald's

direction, the dyed ostrich plumes on her bonnet bobbing indignantly with every step.

"Cat!" said Emily, choking back her laughter.

Julia glared at Sophy's retreating back. "Yes, isn't she?"

"I was talking about you, my dear. 'I only hope Lord Gerald may be as fortunate!' Really, Julia, I didn't know you had it in you."

"I suppose I should be ashamed of myself, but I could *not* let her flatter herself that John has been wearing the willow for her all these years!" She sighed. "It's very lowering to think that one's husband, who is in all other respects an exceptionally clever man, could have succumbed to the wiles of such a creature!"

"Did *you* flatter yourself that because you were the first woman in his bed, you must also have been the first to touch his heart?" Emily shook her head. "Your Mr. Pickett may be young, but he is a healthy, red-blooded Englishman, you know, and if it's true that he was once a collier's apprentice, I daresay few respectable females came his way. I should have thought it more remarkable if he had *not* succumbed. In any case, it seems to me that you, with your stable hand, have little room to talk."

Julia looked rather shamefaced. "There was no stable hand. Well, there were, of course, but I never had the slightest romantic interest in any of them. I only wanted to put that dreadful female in her place." She shot a resentful glance at Lord Gerald Broadbridge, his belly straining the buttons of his flowered waistcoat as he ambled along with labored steps that suggested his lordship suffered from gout. "Look at him! He must be more than twice her age, for Lord Gerald is fifty if he is a day—and looks every bit of it, thanks to years of running with Prinny's Carlton House set. And yet he is held to be a prize catch, while my poor John is an anathema, so far as Society is concerned—at least until they have need of him," she added bitterly.

"It's the way of the world, Julia," Emily said, not without sympathy. "You may flout the rules at your peril, but you will never change them."

15

In Which the Honeymoon Comes to an Abrupt End

After leaving Bow Street, Pickett did not head for Curzon Street at once, but instead set out for Grosvenor Square. There was one bit of business that had to be addressed before his journey. He knew it was a necessary preface to his inquiries at Washbourn Abbey, but this knowledge did nothing to lessen the feeling that he was betraying Lady Washbourn in suspecting her of the very crime against which she had engaged him to protect her.

He shook his head as if to clear it. Mr. Colquhoun had cautioned him long ago against becoming personally involved in the cases that would come his way—and those warnings had been repeated with a vengeance when the newly widowed Lady Fieldhurst had first crossed his path. In all other cases (well, most of them, anyway, at least those that had not involved the lady who was now his wife), he believed he had succeeded in maintaining a professional distance. But something about Lady Washbourn's situation echoed a bit too closely his own. Like the countess, he too had wed above his station, and although the parallels were not exact—he had no fortune, for one thing, nor did he believe Julia harbored the slightest desire to put a period to his existence—the failure of the Washbourns' marriage seemed somehow to bode ill for that of the Picketts.

Having reached the Washbourn residence in Grosvenor Square, he sent up his card to her ladyship, and was soon shown into the now-familiar drawing room.

"Good morning, Mr. Pickett," the countess said, rising to greet him. "Have you any news for me today?"

"I'm afraid not," he said, waiting until the butler had closed the door behind him to continue. "I must go to Washbourn Abbey to follow a—a possible lead, however."

"A lead? At Washbourn Abbey? What—?"

"I can say no more at present, your ladyship," Pickett said hastily. "Pray don't ask me questions I can't answer. In the meantime, though, I wonder if you might give me a letter to take to your staff there. I should hate to travel all the way to Croydon only to be turned away at the door."

"Yes, of course."

The countess moved without hesitation to the writing desk before the window, apparently never suspecting that in granting his request, she might be sealing her own fate. Either his suspicions were wide of the mark, Pickett reflected, or the lady was confident he would find nothing that might implicate her. He rather hoped it was the former.

For the next several minutes, there was no sound save for the scratching of pen on paper. At last Lady Washbourn returned the pen to its standish and sprinkled sand over the wet ink, then folded the single sheet and sealed it with a wafer.

"That should suffice, Mr. Pickett," said her ladyship, handing him the letter. "I have given instructions that everyone on the staff is to cooperate fully with your investigations, including answering any questions you might ask or showing you anything you may wish to see. I trust that will be sufficient."

"Yes, thank you, your ladyship."

He tucked the letter into the inside breast pocket of his coat and took his leave, feeling rather like Judas must have done.

* * *

He returned to Curzon Street to find Julia absent, and was conscious of a pang of disappointment; given that they were soon to be separated, he didn't want to lose a minute of her company in the meantime.

"She should be back very soon," Rogers assured him. "She has gone to Audley Street to call on the Countess of Dunnington. If you would care to send a message, sir, I shall have young Andrew, the new footman, deliver it."

"No, that won't be necessary," Pickett said, suppressing a sigh. "I'll just go upstairs and pack my bag. With any luck, she will have returned by the time I've finished."

"You are going away, sir? Will you require Thomas to accompany you?"

"Good heavens, no!" Pickett said, alarmed at the very idea of trying to conduct a discreet investigation with a valet in tow. "I don't expect to be gone above a day, so I can manage very well on my own."

"Thomas will be disappointed, sir," observed Rogers.

"Very likely, but I'm afraid it can't be helped."

Having dealt firmly with the matter of Thomas's delicate sensibilities, Pickett betook himself up the stairs and finally ran his battered valise to ground in one of the unfurnished rooms. He carried this back to his bedchamber, where he laid it out on the bed, then opened the clothespress and dragged out fresh linens sufficient for an overnight stay. And it was here, a quarter of an hour later, that Julia found him.

"John?" Her gaze fell on the half-filled bag on the bed. "Are you going away?"

"I have to make a short trip to Croydon."

Her face lit up. "Excellent! I'll send for Betsy to pack my things. When do we leave?"

" 'We' don't, my lady," he said apologetically, abandoning his packing long enough to take her in his arms. "I'm sorry to have to go without you, but if all goes well, I should be back by tomorrow evening."

Twenty-four hours earlier, Julia would have accepted this dismissal with a good grace. But twenty-four hours earlier, she had not been snubbed by the very same people who had once courted her favor, nor been condescended to by Lady Gerald Broadbridge. Suddenly the prospect of being left alone in London, abandoned to the mercies of such people as these, was more than she could bear.

"Won't you take me with you?" she pleaded, clinging to him when he would have returned to his packing.

"I'm going on Bow Street's shilling," he reminded her. "I have only enough to cover one fare on the stage, and God only knows what sort of lodgings I'll be obliged to put up in once I reach Croydon."

"I won't be a burden," she said coaxingly. "After all, I can pay my own way."

It was the worst thing she could have said. "This is not about your money, Julia," he said in a voice that brooked no argument. "Even if you were to pay your own fare, I could hardly drag you along on the common stage. We'd have to arrange for the hire a post-chaise, and then locate an inn suitable for a lady. I could be there and back by the time all the arrangements were in place."

"Your flat in Drury Lane wasn't suitable for a lady, and yet I lived there quite happily for almost a fortnight," she reminded him. "We would be together, and that, surely, would more than make up for any discomfort."

"But we *wouldn't* be together," he pointed out. "I would be at Washbourn Abbey, and until I finished my business there, you would be obliged to wait at the inn, where you would no doubt be bored to tears. I'm sorry, Julia. Perhaps another time, but not today." Considering the matter closed, he turned back to the clothing on the bed, picked up a shirt, and began to fold it.

"But I could help you," she insisted, clutching at his sleeve.

"Like you 'helped' me by calling on Lady Washbourn?" Recalling his suspicions about the countess, he added in quite another voice, "Speaking of her ladyship, I must ask you not to call on her again until I return."

"Oh, must you?" she challenged, her bosom swelling in indignation. "In that case, I wonder you don't *want* to take me with you, so you can be sure I don't do anything of which you might disapprove!"

"Julia—"

"I see what it is!" she said accusingly, bright spots of color burning in her cheeks. "You're jealous! You're jealous because *I'm* the one who knew who painted Lady Washbourn's portrait, and *I'm* the one who found out she was in love with her husband, and now you're afraid I may discover something else of importance before you do!"

"Julia, that's utter nonsense, and you know it!" he snapped, flinging the shirt into the bag with a force that completely undid his careful folding job.

"Oh, do I? What other reason can you have for—for shutting me out like this?"

At this grossly unfair accusation, the dam of his patience ruptured, and a dozen small resentments, each one suppressed for the sake of marital harmony, all burst forth. "*Shutting you out?* I should like to see me try! For God's sake, look at me! I don't even look like myself anymore!" His angry gesture took in everything from the new garments hanging in the clothespress to his newly shorn head. "You've got me living in your house, you've got me dressing like your first husband, you've got your first husband's barber cutting my hair, you won't let me eat dinner until I tog myself out like the Prince of Wales, and now you won't let me conduct a simple investigation— which I was doing very well long before I ever met you!— without getting your fingers on that, too. Good God, am I to have no part of my life that's strictly *mine?*"

His voice had risen in volume with each new allegation, and Julia responded in kind. "If you feel that way, I wonder you wished to marry me at all!"

"I don't recall that I was given much choice in the matter!"

"No, but you consummated it readily enough when you

had the opportunity!"

"*What?* I was barely conscious at the time!"

"Well, *that* explains a lot!"

He opened his mouth to make some retort, but froze as her implication became clear. Julia saw the stricken look in his eyes, and would have given up every last farthing of the fortune he so deplored, if by doing so she could have called the words back. But they could not be unsaid; once uttered, they hung in the air like an invisible barrier, substantial as any wall and just as impenetrable.

"I see," Pickett said at last in a cool, detached voice quite unlike his own. "In that case, my lady, I suppose there is nothing more to be said. I'm sorry I couldn't oblige you by being impotent, but maybe your solicitor can think of something. Apparently it's near enough as makes no odds."

He snapped the valise shut and hefted it off the bed, then turned and left the room without another word. Everything in her urged Julia to go after him, to call him back, but she stood rooted to the spot. She had played variations of this particular scene before, with her first husband, and although the matters at issue had varied, the ending had always been the same: she had always been the one to beg his pardon, even if it had been Lord Fieldhurst who was responsible for forcing the quarrel in the first place. She refused to set such a precedent in her second marriage, even though a small voice inside her head whispered accusingly that she had wounded her beloved second husband as much as, if not more than, her first husband had ever wounded her. She heard Pickett's footsteps echoing down the stairs, heard him exchange some word with Rogers (who had no doubt got an earful), and, finally, heard the faint thud of the door closing behind him.

I will not cry, she told herself as she moved to the window, watching his retreating form until her own breath fogged the glass. She wiped away the condensation with her sleeve and pressed her face to the windowpane, following his departure until he turned the corner and disappeared from view. *I will not cry*, she told herself as she turned away from the window and approached the bed, which still bore the imprint of his valise on the counterpane. *I will not cry.*

She collapsed onto the bed and sobbed until no more tears would come.

* * *

Pickett was obliged to take a seat on the roof of the crowded stagecoach for the first part of the journey, and found himself in the unusual position of being grateful for the discomfort this entailed. So long as he was forced to hug his coat closed for warmth, or keep a hand on his hat to prevent its blowing off, he could forget, even if only for a moment, the rift with Julia and the open wound left by her parting words. He had feared from the first that she would eventually come to regret their hasty marriage, but in his imagination it had always been her loss of status in the eyes of Society at the root of her remorse. The reality, now that it had come, was infinitely worse. It was not his social standing that she found lacking; it was himself.

He had not known she felt that way. He had never even suspected. The early days of their marriage, spent in his Drury Lane flat, had been the happiest of his life, and he had assumed she'd felt the same. If she had found his inexperienced lovemaking clumsy—and he acknowledged that she must have done—she had never let on. She had given him a bit of gentle guidance when it was needed, and because she had been tactful (or—lowering thought!—had suffered in silence), he had flattered himself that he'd been a quick study. But then, he had no previous experience against which to measure it; she had, and it was clear that he did not appear to advantage in the comparison.

It occurred to him that, if only he had allowed her to accompany him, he might still be living in happy ignorance, and bitterly regretted his own stubbornness in not acceding to her wishes in the matter. He'd yielded to her in so many other areas—in fact, therein lay the whole problem—surely one more would not have hurt, not if by doing so he might have saved his marriage. Why hadn't he given in, when he saw how much it meant to her? As if in answer, her accusation came back to him. *You're jealous . . . you're afraid I may discover something else of importance before you do . . .*

Could she have been right? Was he really that petty? No, he could not believe it. Long before they were married (before they had *known* they were married, in any case), they had formed an unusual partnership, with her finding out things that, due to the difference in their stations, he would have no way of discovering. It had not troubled him in the least. On the contrary, he recalled, smiling a little at the memory, it had been rather gratifying to see her begin to realize she had capabilities far beyond the merely orna-mental, and to think he'd had something to do with that. His smile faded abruptly. At least he had done that much for her, even if he could not satisfy her in other ways. No, painful as it was, he had done the right thing by insisting he make the journey without her, and thereby forcing the ensuing quarrel. It was better, surely, to face the bitter truth than to go on living even the sweetest of lies.

The stagecoach drew into the yard of the Blue Boar just as the sun was setting. The inside passengers disembarked first, and Pickett and his fellow sufferers on the roof fol-lowed somewhat stiffly from the heights. He waited while the bags were removed from the boot, then claimed his valise and followed the crowd shuffling inside to bespeak rooms for the night. He was directed at last to a tiny attic chamber with a ceiling so low that he could not stand up straight without banging his head on the rafters. Far from deploring these primitive lodgings, he felt vindicated; this was certainly no place for a lady, and Julia would no doubt have been appalled at the prospect of sleeping in such humble surroundings. Ruthlessly rejecting the memory of his first week of marriage, when he and his lady wife had blissfully shared a bed certainly no wider than the one this room offered, he deposited his valise at the foot of the narrow cot and went back downstairs to the public room in search of dinner, feeling a small—a *very* small—sense of satisfaction in sitting down to eat in rumpled and travel-stained clothes.

The Bull's Head prided itself on two things: the Yorkshire pudding which was prepared daily by the proprietor's wife, and the strength of its home-brewed ale. While it cannot be said that Pickett actually tasted any of the former (although as he blinked at the empty plate on the table before him, he realized he must have done so), he was considerably more receptive to the latter. In fact, when he realized with some surprise that his tankard was empty, he asked the barmaid to fetch him another. And then another. And still another. Alas, whatever its fine qualities, the beverage proved insufficient to erase from his mind the memory of Julia, or the last words he would ever hear her speak. For it was obvious he could never go back, not now, not knowing how she felt about him, about their marriage. He must return to Bow Street, of course—he still had a position there, even if he had lost the only other thing that had given his life meaning—but he could not go back to Julia. Never again. Never . . .

"Sir? Beg pardon, sir, but we're closing up for the night."

Gradually Pickett became aware of someone shaking him by the shoulder, and realized he had gone to sleep with his head on the table. He opened one bleary eye, and saw a young woman who looked vaguely familiar. In one hand—the one that wasn't shaking his shoulder—she held a pewter tankard. His razor-sharp brain instantly deduced that she must be the barmaid who had been keeping him lubricated all evening.

"I know who you are," he informed her, realizing with mild curiosity that his words were oddly slurred.

"I don't wonder at it, sir, for you've kept me busy most the night," she said. "But we're closing now, so you'd best go home."

"Can't go home," he said. "Can't ever . . . go home . . ."

He would have put his head back down on the table, but the girl still had him by the shoulder, and hauled him upright again.

"You have a room for the night here? Do you need some help getting up the stairs to it?"

"Upstairs," Pickett echoed stupidly, and heaved himself to his feet.

"Do you need some help?" the barmaid asked again.

"No, thank you," Pickett said. He took a step forward, and realized he'd spoken too soon, for the wooden floor beneath his feet would not behave as a floor should. It refused to stay still, for one thing, and the boards persisted in crisscrossing one another in a way that made every step a potential hazard.

"Let me help you, sir," the barmaid said, slipping beneath his shoulder to support him with his arm draped across the back of her neck.

His first step had been sufficient to inform Pickett that accepting the girl's assistance was probably a wise move. He made no further protest, but allowed the young woman to turn them both in the direction of the door. Climbing the stairs presented a challenge, but with the railing on his right hand and the girl on his left, he managed to reach his small room without mishap.

"There you go," she pronounced at last, easing out from under him. Deprived of her support, he collapsed onto the narrow bed, where he expressed a fervent desire to die.

"Nonsense!" she said briskly, tugging off his boots. "You'll have an aching head in the morning, but otherwise you'll be fine. It's the ale, you know. It takes some folks that way, 'specially if they aren't used to it." She regarded his recumbent form with a speculative gleam in her eye. "It's right cold in here with no fire. If you like, I could stay for awhile. Keep you warm, you might say."

Drunk he might be, but Pickett was not so far gone that he did not understand exactly what she was offering. He opened his eyes and regarded her sadly.

"You wouldn't enjoy it anyway," he said with surprising clarity, then closed his eyes once more and surrendered to oblivion.

16

*In Which Julia Receives Surprising News,
but Has No One with Whom to Share It*

J ulia awoke the following morning heavy-eyed from
lack of sleep. Granted, she had not slept particularly
well in several weeks, but the previous night had been by far
the worst. She had tossed and turned all night, and when she
had finally drifted off, her slumber had been troubled by
unpleasant dreams that were surely no worse than the
waking nightmare she now faced. She rolled over in bed
(unsurprised to discover that at some point she had reached
for her husband's pillow and apparently passed the rest of
the night with it clutched to her breast) and looked at the
ormolu clock over the mantel. It was not yet eight; he had
said he would return before nightfall. How long, she
wondered, might she have to wait? Eight hours, perhaps?
Ten? Twelve?

She wished she might remain abed longer, to sleep
away as many of the empty hours as possible, but she knew

too well what would happen: sleep, so elusive even during the dark watches of the night, would evade her entirely in the light of day, and she would lie awake reliving in her memory every word of their quarrel. With the clarity that inevitably came with morning, she recalled every one of his accusations, and realized to her chagrin that he had every right to resent her. She had known, of course—although the discovery had come too late to change anything—that she had overstepped in arranging for a barber to cut his hair, but she had not recognized how this relatively minor infraction must appear when taken in sum with the others. She had only wanted to help him adapt to the new world into which their marriage had thrust him. He, on the other hand, had received a very different message: *You are not good enough for me the way you are . . . you must change if you are to appear worthy of me . . .* It was the last thing she had meant, of course, but she should have known he might interpret it that way, especially in the light of his past experience with Sophia Broadbridge.

But she could not blame Sophia for their quarrel, for the blame fell squarely onto her own shoulders. Mr. Colquhoun had tried to warn her, and she had ignored him, certain that she knew her own marriage best.

With a sigh of resignation, she threw back the covers and reached for her pink satin wrapper. She shrugged her arms through the sleeves, tied the belt around her waist, and made her way downstairs to the breakfast room. The sunlight streaming through the windows hurt her eyes, and she instructed Rogers to draw the curtains.

"And Rogers," she added thoughtfully, when he had carried out this request, "what did Mr. Pickett say to you when he left the house yesterday?"

He gave her a look of wordless sympathy. They had a long history, she and Rogers, dating back to the time of her first marriage. "He merely thanked me, madam. I had just given him his hat and gloves, you know, so he thanked me."

"I see," she said, conscious of a pang of disappointment. She was not quite certain what she had hoped for—some word regarding his return, perhaps, or some message of apology or forgiveness—but it was clear that despite his humble origins, her husband knew instinctively not to air his dirty linen before the servants.

The butler gave a discreet cough. "Er, madam—"

"Yes, Rogers?"

"If you will forgive me, madam, it is not unusual for newly married couples to quarrel. It can be difficult, learning to live with another person, no matter how deep the affection one feels for them."

She should have delivered some crushing rebuke designed to put the butler in his place, but she found she could not do so. They were old allies, she and Rogers, dating back to the early days of her marriage to Lord Fieldhurst, and following the viscount's murder, Rogers had stood in Mr. Pickett's debt, just as she had; in fact, she suspected that the deference the butler had shown his new master from the day of Pickett's arrival in Curzon Street went beyond mere professional courtesy.

"Thank you, Rogers," she said, giving him a grateful little smile.

She turned her attention to the breakfast laid out on the sideboard, and lifted the lid of a silver chafing dish. The aroma of freshly cooked bacon, usually so pleasant in the morning, now assailed her, an offense against her nostrils. She dropped the lid back in place with a clatter, and turned away just in time to be violently ill all over the floor. As if things could not possibly get any worse, a knock sounded on the door at the front of the house.

The butler glanced helplessly at his mistress and then in the direction of the front door, clearly torn as to where his duty lay.

"See who that is, Rogers," Julia gasped between retches. "Tell them I am indisposed."

"Yes, madam," he said, and hurried from the room.

He returned a very short time later, hovering awkwardly in the doorway. "Begging your pardon, madam, but it is the doctor—Mr. Gilroy. Under the circumstances, I thought perhaps you might wish to see him."

As if on cue, the physician's head appeared over

Rogers's shoulder. Julia removed the napkin she had pressed to her mouth. "Forgive me, Doctor. I don't know what happened, but it appears to be over now—all except for cleaning up the mess," she added, grimacing at the disgusting puddle at her feet.

Rogers assured her of his willingness to see to this task, and suggested that she might perhaps be more comfortable in the drawing room. Dr. Gilroy took her arm to assist her to this chamber, adding over his shoulder that the butler might bring his mistress a little—a *very* little—dry toast.

"In fact, I came in the hopes of finding your husband at home," the doctor said as he guided her into the drawing room. "It occurred to me that he might wish to borrow my medical text for its information on prussic acid, at least until he has completed his investigation of that particular case. But while I seem to have missed Mr. Pickett, it appears I've come at a good time nonetheless."

"I'm quite all right now, truly I am," Julia said shakily, allowing the physician to settle her on a chair. "It is only that I have not been sleeping well recently, and have not had much appetite of late. As for the other, well, I fear it does not take much to make me 'cast up my accounts,' as the saying goes." It was true. On one occasion not so very long ago, the mere sight of John Pickett in a passionate embrace with another female had provoked just such a reaction. Small wonder, then, that so bitter a quarrel as they'd had the

246

previous day should eventually yield the same result.

The doctor, however, seemed uninterested in this disclaimer. "Never mind, Mrs. Pickett. You'll find that such symptoms are not uncommon for a woman in your condition, but they usually pass after the first few months."

"My 'condition'?" echoed Julia, bewildered. She hadn't been aware that quarreling with one's husband constituted a "condition," much less that it manifested certain telltale symptoms. "What condition is that?"

"I beg your pardon," the doctor said in some consternation. "It appears I may have spoken too soon. Naturally, I assumed—but—forgive me for asking so personal a question, Mrs. Pickett, but when did you last have your menses?"

"It was—" She broke off abruptly. When had it been? Not while she had been nursing the injured John Pickett in Drury Lane—she certainly would have remembered that!— nor had it occurred while they were visiting her parents in Somersetshire following the wedding. "February," she said at last. "I don't recall the exact date, but I was certainly finished by the twenty-fourth, for that was the night of the fire at Drury Lane Theatre."

"Some women occasionally miss a month," he remarked.

She shook her head. "Not I. Mine are usually like clockwork." Her eyes widened in dismay as the doctor's implication became clear. "Dr. Gilroy, if you mean to suggest—"

"Just so, Mrs. Pickett," he replied, bestowing an avuncular smile upon her. "It is perhaps a bit too early to be entirely certain, but I am reasonably sure that you are going to have a child, very likely by Christmas."

She gave a bitter little laugh. "I can assure you, Doctor, it is no such thing."

"What makes you say so?"

"To put it bluntly, Dr. Gilroy, I am barren. In six years with my first husband, I never showed the slightest sign of being *enceinte*."

"I see. And did it never occur to you that the fault might lie with your first husband, rather than yourself?"

"Oh, no," she said decisively. "The physician was quite clear on that point."

"Was he? How did he know?"

She looked at him blankly. "I beg your pardon?"

"Unless there is some obvious indicator—an absence of menses on the woman's part, for instance, or a lack of vital fluids on the man's—it is practically impossible to assign a definite cause to a couple's childlessness. So again I ask: how did the physician know?"

"He never said," she confessed. "He informed Lord Fieldhurst—my first husband—that the deficiency was mine, and that it was doubtful anything could be done to correct it, but he never stated the basis for his conclusion. I assumed it must be some complicated medical reason that we would not have understood, even had he attempted an explanation."

The doctor nodded sagely. "I suspected as much."

"But why? Why would Dr. Humphrey lie about such a thing?"

"Humphrey? Do you mean Dr. *Edmund* Humphrey, by any chance?"

"Why, yes. Do you know him?"

"Only by reputation, but that is enough. Dr. Humphrey has made a long and lucrative career out of telling aristocrats what they most want to hear. He would not want to jeopardize a valuable source of income by informing Lord Fieldhurst that he was sterile."

Julia was glad to be sitting, for she suddenly felt faint. Now that she thought of it, in spite of her first husband's serial infidelities, she had never heard the slightest whisper of his having fathered a child on any of his mistresses. And no wonder: Frederick had been sterile. All those years, it had been he, not she, who was responsible for his lack of an heir and his cousin's eventual assumption of the title.

"Fieldhurst knew, nonetheless," she said at last. "He must have known. And yet he let me bear the blame all those years!"

"It was very wrong of him, of course," the doctor said, "shamefully so. And yet, if I may offer a word of advice, Mrs. Pickett, Lord Fieldhurst is dead. Let his sins against you die with him, and concentrate instead on celebrating the birth of your child with your new husband."

She nodded. "Yes, that is good advice, Doctor. Thank you. But you spoke of 'symptoms,' in the plural. What other symptoms may I expect?"

"It appears you are experiencing some of them already." He ticked them off on his fingers. "Alterations in sleep patterns, loss of appetite, and nausea, particularly in the morning. Some women also notice changes in temperament —emotional outbursts, for instance, such as sudden bouts of tears or uncharacteristic querulousness . . ."

"I see," she said slowly, recalling several incidents over the past weeks that appeared very different in the light of this revelation. Perhaps her husband might forgive her more readily, once he knew the reason for her inexplicable moodiness. She glanced up at the clock, and saw that it was not yet nine. *Hurry home,* she silently begged across the miles. *Please, please hurry.*

* * *

Pickett, for his part, awoke that same morning in some confusion as to where he was and why he had apparently slept in his clothes, as well as why he should be possessed of a pounding head and a mouth that felt as if it had been stuffed with cotton wool. Gradually, however, the memories returned: the quarrel with Julia which had ended in the realization that he was unable to satisfy her; the stagecoach journey to Croydon; the previous evening's overindulgence.

Bracing himself against the pain he knew would follow, he sat up in bed, clutching his hands to his head. He had been drunk exactly twice in his life, and those experiences had been sufficient to demonstrate why he had no desire to cultivate the habit. The first had occurred a year earlier, while he was investigating Lord Fieldhurst's murder, and had been purely unintentional: he had been questioning a person of interest in a public house, and had not realized until much too late that the man was attempting to drink him under the table. Last night's excesses, however, had been quite deliberate, a desperate attempt to forget, if only for a few hours, all that he had lost. The only trouble with drinking to forget, he reflected bitterly, was that one returned to sobriety only to discover that nothing had changed: the thing one had hoped to forget was still there, and in the meantime, one felt considerably less able to face it. Then, too, there was still the investigation that had necessitated the journey in the first place; he could hardly show up at the door of Washbourn Abbey in his present condition. Responding reluctantly to the call of duty, he swung his legs to the floor, stood up—and cracked his pounding head against the rafters.

He let out a ragged sigh. It was going to be one of those days.

Half an hour later, feeling somewhat the better for

having washed, shaved, and consumed several cups of strong coffee, he inquired of the innkeeper the direction of Washbourn Abbey and set out on foot. A Londoner born and bred, Pickett was no great lover of country living, and did not look forward to a seven-mile trek along rutted country lanes, especially when his head pounded anew with every step. Consequently, when a farm wagon drew alongside him and the driver offered to take him up, he accepted the offer with gratitude; besides accomplishing the journey in much less time, the obligatory small talk which courtesy demanded he make with the farmer served to distract him from endlessly rehashing the angry words he'd exchanged with his wife, and her final accusation.

At length the wagon rounded a curve, and the vista that came into view inspired Pickett to interrupt the driver's engrossing account of how Farmer Dawson's cow had given birth to a calf with two heads.

"Is *that* Washbourn Abbey?"

"Aye." The driver leaned over the side of the box so that he might spit onto the road below. "That's it."

Away to their right, the ground rose in a long, gentle swell of green meadow. A massive house of weathered grey stone commanded the rise as if looking down on the lesser beings in the valley below, its powerful lines reflected in the ornamental lake spread out beneath it like a robe at a monarch's feet. Behind it, the dark green of a line of trees stood in stark contrast to the pale stone of the house as well as the blue of the sky beyond. Staring at it, Pickett could not help feeling a pang of sympathy for Lady Washbourn; it must have been quite a shock to go from being Miss Eliza Mucklow, daughter of a wealthy brewer, to the mistress of such a pile. His own rise from Drury Lane to Curzon Street, while disconcerting in its own way, was nothing to this. Perhaps if he had admitted his ignorance, had asked . . . But no, the same pride that balked at living as his wife's pensioner forbade his asking her for instruction on a matter at which, to his mind, any man worthy of the name would have excelled instinctively. Well, he hoped he and his pride would be very happy together.

He shook off the unproductive train of thought and dragged his attention back to the matter at hand. Julia had claimed that Lady Washbourn was in love with her husband, having coaxed such a confession from the lady's own lips; what, then, had the poor little countess endured to drive her to so desperate an action as plotting the murder of her husband? He found himself in the curious position of hoping he did not find the evidence against her that he had come from London to seek.

"Mind you, five years ago it didn't look so fine as this," the driver remarked. "The old place was well nigh falling to rack and ruin before his lordship was wed. But a regular Midas, her ladyship's father was, and a whole army of workmen descended on the house and its outbuildings before the ink on the marriage lines was dry. Kept half the countryside in work for more than a year, it did."

"I see," Pickett said. "If you'll set me down here, I can walk the rest of the way."

The driver drew up his horses, and Pickett thanked him and offered him a shilling for his pains, which the man rejected with the easy generosity of country people. Pickett thanked him once again and climbed down. He stood watching as the wagon lurched out of sight, then turned and set out for the grey house on the hill.

He did not approach the massive double doors at the front of the house, but followed the raked gravel drive around the eastern façade to an unassuming door at the rear. Recognizing this as the service entrance, he stepped up to it and rapped sharply. A moment later it was opened by a young maidservant in a mobcap and a voluminous apron.

"Yes, sir?" she asked, gaping at him.

"My name is John Pickett. I've come from Bow Street, in London." He gave the girl his card, wondering as he did so if she could read it. "I should like to have a word with the housekeeper, if I may."

"Yes, sir," the girl said again. "If you'll come this way, I'll fetch Mrs. Hawkins."

She bobbed a curtsy and left him just inside the door. When she returned a short time later, she was accompanied by a gaunt female of indeterminate years. "This is Mr. Pickett, mum," she said, then bobbed another curtsy and took herself off.

"Well, Mr. Pickett? Betty says you've come from Bow Street." Mrs. Hawkins eyed him with disfavor, as if she suspected this tale was nothing more than an excuse to conceal his nefarious intention of seducing the female staff. *If only she knew,* Pickett thought with a sigh.

In fact, the prospect of explaining the reason for his visit to the Abbey had caused him considerable unease. As there was no possible way he could justify this as part of an inquiry into Lady Washbourn's missing rubies, he had no choice but to reveal his continuing investigation into a death which a coroner's jury had determined was no murder. He only hoped Lord Washbourn would forgive him, given the possibility that his findings might save his lordship's life.

"I'm looking into the death of one of Lady Washbourn's housemaids, Ann Barton by name." The identity of the dead girl inspired no spark of recognition in the housekeeper's eyes, and Pickett realized that, with the probable exceptions of his lordship's valet and her ladyship's abigail, Lord Washbourn maintained two completely separate household staffs, one for his Town residence and the other for his country estate.

"Yes, what of it?" challenged Mrs. Hawkins, still on her guard.

Fortunately, Pickett had expected this response, and now withdrew Lady Washbourn's letter from the inside pocket of his coat. "I have here a letter from her ladyship stating that I am to be given the full cooperation of the staff during the course of my investigation." Recognizing that this news would hardly endear him to the very people upon whose cooperation the investigation depended, he added, "I will not require much, Mrs. Hawkins. In fact, I hope to be out of your way very shortly."

"Very well, Mr. Pickett," she conceded with a cautious nod. "What do you want of us?"

"Very little. I only want to have a look about her ladyship's still-room."

"Her still-room?" echoed the housekeeper, with a skeptical lift of one eyebrow. "Whatever for?"

"I'm sure you can understand that I am unable to discuss the case in detail," Pickett said. "Suffice it to say that the girl was known to have drunk a glass of her ladyship's own peach ratafia just before she died."

Mrs. Hawkins gave a disdainful sniff. "Her ladyship has made that particular beverage for years, from her own mother's receipt, and gives the vicar a bottle every Christmas! If there were anything wrong with it, he and his wife would have been dead these ten years and more."

As Lord and Lady Washbourn had married only two years earlier, Pickett knew this for an exaggeration.

"Nevertheless, I should like to see it," he reiterated, standing his ground.

"Very well."

With the air of one bestowing an undeserved favor, she led Pickett through the kitchens to a small room whose windows looked out onto the herb garden. A work table of plain deal was positioned beneath the window to catch the light, while overhead, bunches of herbs and flowers hung from the rafters, giving off a faint but pleasant odor as they dried. All in all, it seemed a rather cheerful place to plot a murder.

"Thank you, Mrs. Hawkins," Pickett said firmly, seeing the housekeeper showed no inclination to leave. "If I require anything else, I will be sure to ask."

Mrs. Hawkins gave him one final glare, but left the room without argument. Alone in the small chamber, Pickett closed the door and looked about him, unsure exactly what he was looking for, let alone how he should go about finding it. He selected a glass jar at random and unstoppered the cork, wrinkling his nose at the sharp aroma that rose from the fine reddish-brown powder inside. Conceding that Ann Barton was unlikely to have been poisoned by cinnamon, he replaced the cork stopper and returned the jar to the shelf. In truth, he was more than a bit daunted by the task that he had traveled all the way from London to complete; he had not expected to be confronted with floor-to-ceiling shelves filled with unlabeled jars, bottles, and boxes, each containing some unfamiliar and faintly sinister-looking powder or liquid. It would have been helpful to discover one marked "prussic acid," "poison," or even a more general "keep out," but Pickett put the chances of such a felicitous discovery somewhere between slim and none. He thought wistfully how much more quickly the search might have been accomplished—to say nothing of how much more pleasurable the task would have been—if Julia had been there to examine the shelves on the right-hand side of the room, while he took those on the left.

Banishing from his mind an image too painful to dwell on, he began with the nearest shelf and began inspecting the containers one by one, sniffing this one and shaking that, and wondering all the while if he would even recognize the substance if he were to happen upon it. Dr. Gilroy had said the substance was derived from a blue pigment; did that mean it would appear blue? But no, surely any obvious color would have turned the peach ratafia dark or cloudy, alerting any potential victim—intentional or accidental—that something was amiss with the beverage. Besides, the doctor had also said it occurred naturally in peach pits, apple seeds, and cherry stones, none of which possessed any such hue. Abandoning this promising idea, he resigned himself to the necessity of recognizing the substance by the same bitter almond odor he'd recognized on the maid's body.

Alas, his nostrils were soon so inundated with the pungent scents of cloves, anise, and peppermint—among others—that he was obliged to open a window and take several great gulps of fresh air before returning to his task. As he turned away from the window, his gaze fell on a small book bound in black leather, a book so old that its cover was spotted and stained, and its binding cracked. Pickett was suddenly seized with the fanciful notion that he beheld a witch's book of spells, and that if he were to open it, he would find its pages inscribed with directions for placing curses on one's enemies or concocting charms to open the heart of one's beloved. The latter reminded him, not unnaturally, of his estrangement from his wife, and he flipped open the pages with a rather wistful sigh.

He was disappointed (though hardly surprised) to discover that it yielded no such useful information. Here was a receipt for black butter made from apples, and here was one for quince preserves, both transcribed in a graceful, feminine hand. Unwilling to turn back to his odoriferous investigations just yet, he spent a few minutes flipping through the pages, noting that the book contained directions for concocting medicines and beauty aids as well as jams and jellies. He grinned as he read one such entry, wondering what Julia would have to say about a face powder whose main ingredient appeared to be dried horse manure. His smile faded as he remembered he would never have an opportunity to describe this concoction to her.

He found, too, that it was easy to see which entries were the most popular: while some of the pages resisted his attempts to part them, others all but fell open at a touch. At last he found the receipt he sought, the one describing the preparation of peach ratafia flavored with almonds. While it was interesting in its way, it was of little use to him as far as the investigation went; there was certainly no mention of the fact that one might use the leftover peach pits to create a poison whose effects would be hidden by the flavor imparted by the almonds. Heaving a sigh, Pickett closed the back cover (for he was almost at the end of the book by now) and turned it over, prepared to set it aside and return to his examination of the still-room shelves. But he failed to grasp the front cover securely, and so only succeeded in flipping the book open to the flyleaf, where the owner had written her name, along with the year in which she had begun compiling her herbal.

Instead of Eliza Mucklow, the title page bore the inscription *Mildred Frampton, 1747.*

17

In Which Victory Turns to Ashes

T he stagecoach rattled into the stable yard of the Swan with Two Necks in Gresham Street, Cheapside, just as darkness descended over Town. Pickett, perched once again on the roof, waited with ill-concealed impatience as the inside passengers disembarked, then scrambled down, claimed his valise as it was tossed from the boot, and entered the inn. Here he was obliged once again to wait his turn while those passengers meaning to break their journey for the night were assigned rooms. At length, when the last of these arrivals had been directed upstairs, the innkeeper turned to Pickett.

"I'm sorry, sir, but we haven't any more room."

"That's all right," Pickett said with a sigh, mentally revising his plans for the night. "But I wonder if you might be willing to hold my luggage until I send—until I call for it," he amended lamely, belatedly remembering that there would be no dispatching a footman on such an errand. Like his marriage, those days of prosperity were over, just as if they had been nothing but a vivid dream. Maybe it was better to think of his brief taste of marital bliss (when he had to think of it at all) as just that: a dream, and one from which he'd been rudely awakened.

Having arranged for the storage of his bag, he set out on foot for the Grosvenor Square residence of Lord and Lady Washbourn. He sent up his card and was soon shown to the drawing room, where he found not only the lady of the house, but her husband and her mother-in-law as well.

"Why, Mr. Pickett," exclaimed the countess, rising to greet him. "How fortunate that I should be home tonight to receive you! We—we have good news, you see. Only today my husband has been appointed to the British embassy at Constantinople, and we are to sail within a se'ennight. Washbourn wished to have this evening to celebrate quietly with his family before facing the congratulations of his friends." Her gaze fell to Pickett's brown coat, wrinkled from travel and almost white with the dust churned up from horses' hooves and carriage wheels. "Am I to understand that you have just returned from—from your errand, and have some new information?"

Pickett glanced down at his person. "You are, ma'am, else I would not have inflicted myself upon you in all my dirt."

"Never mind that." She turned to her husband. "My dear, if you and Mother Washbourn will please excuse us—"

"Forgive me, your ladyship," Pickett interrupted, "but what I have to say concerns them, too."

"Have you found the Washbourn rubies, then?" Lord Washbourn demanded eagerly. "Good man!"

Pickett made no reply, but addressed himself to the countess, who sat ramrod straight at one end of the sofa. "Throughout this investigation, your servants have made mention of the peach ratafia which 'her ladyship' makes with her own hands. I always assumed they meant you, given your father's occupation. I have since asked the housekeeper at Washbourn Abbey for confirmation, but I should like to have the truth from your own lips, if you please: who made the peach ratafia that was served on the night of the masquerade?"

"Why, Mother Washbourn," said the countess, gesturing toward her mother-in-law. "Everything having to do with the still-room falls under her authority. She is far better at that sort of thing than I will ever be, so everyone benefits from the arrangement."

Not quite everyone, Pickett thought. *It hadn't worked out so well for Annie.* Aloud, he merely said, "Thank you. And whose idea was it that the ratafia should be served at the masquerade?"

"Mother Washbourn suggested it. She is justifiably

proud of it, you know, for it is very good, and the receipt was handed down from her mama."

"So I've been told." Pickett turned to the dowager. "What was your mother's name, ma'am?"

The older lady looked down her aristocratic nose at him. "My mother was a Frampton of the Hampshire Framptons, Mr. Pickett, but what it can possibly have to do with my daughter-in-law's loss of the Washbourn rubies quite escapes me!"

"And her Christian name?"

The dowager's haughty gaze never wavered. "Mildred."

The young countess, apparently seeing the direction of his questioning, made a faint whimpering sound.

"Look here," Lord Washbourn protested. "Surely you can't mean to imply that my mother had something to do with the disappearance of the rubies!"

Pickett glanced toward Lady Washbourn for consent, and found her staring at her mother-in-law with a stricken expression. He turned back to the earl. "No, your lordship, your mother had nothing to do with the missing rubies. In fact, they aren't missing at all. They are in my wife's jewel case."

"*What?*" Lord Washbourn whirled about in his chair to confront his wife. "I trust you have some good reason for this, Eliza."

"Yes," she said unsteadily, her eyes never leaving the

dowager's face. "At least, it appears that I did."

"With your permission, your ladyship?" Pickett asked. Receiving a distracted nod from the countess, he addressed himself to her husband. "The rubies were never missing, my lord. Their absence was nothing more than an excuse for me to confer with your wife on another matter entirely."

The earl's face darkened. "If this has to do with that maid, Annie, then let me remind you that the coroner's inquest found her death to be due to natural causes! Now either you will let the poor girl rest in peace and cease persecuting my wife, or I will go to your magistrate and lodge a complaint against you!"

"Annie's death enters into it only indirectly," Pickett told him. "In fact, her ladyship sent for me because she feared her own life was in danger."

"Can this be true, Eliza?" demanded the earl in some consternation. "As I told you before, they were nothing more than unfortunate accidents. I had no idea they had upset you so much. My dear, why didn't you tell me?"

Lady Washbourn found her tongue at last. "Because I thought—I thought it was you," she confessed, her voice low and breathless.

"*Me?* You thought *I* was trying to kill you?" Lord Washbourn sounded more injured than angry.

"Lady Barbara's husband had just died," the countess said in her own defense. "If you could only be rid of me, there would be nothing to prevent you from marrying her."

She gave him a brave and, Pickett thought, rather pathetic smile. "I know it was she you had wanted all along."

"My dear Eliza!" The earl took her hand in both of his. "My father was ill. He insisted that I marry before he died, and I had long ago come to realize that marriage for me must mean an alliance with a woman of property, no matter my feelings for the lady herself—or hers for me, for that matter. My fascination with Lady Barbara was nothing more than a stubborn man's last act of rebellion against the fate that had been forced on him by his ancestors' extravagance."

"You answered the summons to her theatre box readily enough," she reminded him.

"Only because I wanted to make it clear to her that whatever had once existed between us was over, and to beseech her to put an end to advances that could serve no purpose but to embarrass us both." He grimaced at the memory. "If you desire proof, you have only to ask the people in the boxes on either side, for she did not accept the rebuff quietly. No, Eliza, within forty-eight hours of the wedding ceremony, I knew that any marriage between Lady Barbara and me would have been an unmitigated disaster. By the time you and I returned from our wedding trip, I was in the unexpected position of blessing my forebears for the profligacy that made it necessary for me to make a match which otherwise I would never have had the wisdom to

Sseek." He lifted her hand to his lips. "So you see, my dear, your fears have been groundless."

Pickett, feeling very much *de trop* by this time, cleared his throat. "Not quite groundless, your lordship."

Lord Washbourn turned toward Pickett as if surprised to see him still there. "Eh, what's that?"

"In fact, there *was* someone who wanted your wife dead—someone who pretended to be her friend while losing no opportunity to poison first her reputation, then her marriage, and, finally, her peach ratafia."

"You brought me the glass, my love," Lady Washbourn reminded her husband. "I was obliged to set it down untouched, but Annie drank it—and Annie died. You can see how it looked—why I thought—"

Lord Washbourn's gaze slewed from Pickett to the countess, and back again. "Is this true, Mr. Pickett?"

"Quite true, your lordship, no matter what any coroner's jury might have said to the contrary. I'd heard of a poison that left behind an odor of bitter almonds, and when I learned that a beverage flavored with almonds had been added to the menu at the last minute, I couldn't help thinking it would have been a very convenient medium in which to hide a poison. Although I failed to convince the coroner of its significance, I did a little investigating on my own, with her ladyship's permission. I recently learned from a physician that the poison I had in mind occurs naturally in the pits

S

of peaches, and so I traveled to Washbourn Abbey in search of some evidence that might confirm my suspicions."

He wisely neglected to mention the fact that his suspicions at that time had centered on Lady Washbourn herself. Instead, he reached into the inside pocket of his coat and withdrew a small book bound in worn black leather.

"I found this in the still-room there. I'd been told that 'her ladyship' made the peach ratafia from her mother's old receipt, and I found the receipt here, so well-used that the page has almost detached from the binding. But when I saw the name and date inside, I realized that it hadn't belonged to Lady Washbourn—her maiden name had been Mucklow— but to the dowager countess. Then, too, it is dated 1747—too early to have belonged to Lady Washbourn's mother, even if Mrs. Mucklow had borne a child very late in life." He turned to the dowager, who sat as if turned to stone. "Well, ma'am? What made you do it?"

"Have the goodness to leave my mother alone!" put in Lord Washbourn, very much on his dignity. "Why, Mama has been nothing but kind to my wife since the day I brought my bride home to Washbourn Abbey!"

"Kind to her face, perhaps, I'll grant you that," conceded Pickett with a nod. "And all the while spreading the most vicious half-truths designed to cast her in as unfavorable a light as possible." He looked to the dowager for confirmation. "Isn't that right, your ladyship—or should

I say, 'Aunt Mildred'?"

The earl stiffened. "You are offensive, sir! How dare you suggest that my mother has anything to do with that scandal-rag?"

"That—that was you, too, Mother Washbourn?" the countess stammered, addressing her mother-in-law for the first time since Pickett had entered the room.

The older woman regarded the younger as if she might a particularly repulsive species of insect. "I am not your mother, you—you common little adventuress! I never have been, and I never shall be!"

"And—and you killed Annie—"

The dowager pressed an affronted hand to her bosom, and the red stone on her finger winked accusingly in the light. "Is it *my* fault you are so lax with your servants that they think they can help themselves to whatever they please?"

Lord Washbourn, who had listened in mounting horror to this exchange, now stared at her in revulsion, as if his parent had suddenly turned into a serpent before his eyes. "You gave me that glass and bade me take it to Eliza, saying she must not be allowed to tire herself out," he recalled in stunned disbelief. "You were so thoughtful, so solicitous of her, and yet—all the while—"

"Oh, do be quiet, Charles!" interrupted his mother. "I did it for your sake! What do you think it does to a mother's heart, to see her son forced to give up the woman he loves? And all for what? Why, to wed the daughter of a *tradesman!*" She all but spat the word. "Your father and his father before him needed money no less than you did, and yet they married daughters of the aristocracy. They knew what was worthy of their name!"

Lord Washbourn practically erupted from his chair, and began pacing restlessly back and forth. "In other words, they closed their eyes to the looming disaster, all the while congratulating themselves on their exalted lineage!"

"Yes, they married to please themselves, and they chose women deserving of their lofty rank," the dowager insisted. "My dowry may not have been large, but I was accounted a great beauty in my younger days, and descended from the Framptons of Hampshire, whose ancestors sailed to England with the Conqueror! Why should you alone of all the Washbourns be forced to sacrifice yourself? It was not fair, it was not right!"

He had reached the end of the room by now, and whirled about to confront her. "Not right, Mama? *Not right?* What, pray, is 'right' about marrying an innocent young woman, possessing myself of her inheritance, and then plotting her death so that I might be free to lay my ill-gotten gain at the feet of another lady? What is 'fair' about that? No, don't interrupt," he said quickly, when she opened her mouth to answer. "Since you feel my wife is so far beneath you, I will not force you to remain in her presence. If you recall, I have a small Scottish holding, a castle in the Outer Hebrides, which I believe will suit you very well. If I remember correctly, it came to our family through my great-grandfather's marriage with the laird's daughter; I'm sure you will appreciate the irony."

"Begging your pardon, your lordship," Pickett put in, "but the only place your mother will be going is Newgate."

The dowager wrung her hands, and the large red stone on her finger flashed erratically. "I won't! I won't go to prison, and I won't be exiled to some ruin while that vulgar little creature takes my place!"

Before anyone realized what she was about, she wrenched the gem to one side, tipped her head back, and poured down her throat the powdery substance that had been concealed inside her ring. Pickett leapt toward her, even as he recognized the futility of intervention. Within seconds, the dowager was choking and gasping for breath even as the earl pounded her frantically on the back; within minutes, she lay twitching convulsively on the floor in her son's arms, unresponsive to his attempts to revive her. At last she lay still and the room fell silent, the quiet sobs of the countess the only sound.

"Hush, my love, don't cry," Lord Washbourn chided gently. He carefully lowered his mother's head to the floor, then rose to his feet and took his trembling wife in his arms.

"Perhaps it's better this way. We will return to the Abbey long enough to see Mama laid to rest next to Papa in the family vault, and then we will prepare for the journey to Constantinople. By the time we return to England, I hope to have persuaded you to forgive me for my blindness."

"There is nothing to forgive," she insisted, "at least not from you. No one could suspect his mother of such a thing, or even believe her capable of it."

"Perhaps not, but I dismissed your very real concerns as nothing more than foolish megrims, and you might well have paid for my obstinacy with your life. I will not soon forgive myself for that."

"If you will pardon the interruption," Pickett put in, "may I suggest that the coroner be sent for?"

"What? Yes, I suppose there is no way around it," the earl said with a sigh, recalled to his responsibilities. "But how Mama would have hated it!"

Pickett glanced down at the woman's body. Her face had assumed an unnaturally rosy hue, and he had no doubt that, if he were to bend over the body, he would catch the scent of bitter almonds. But he remained determinedly upright. While he had been set on obtaining justice for Annie Barton, he felt no such compulsion where the dowager countess was concerned. Her troubles had been of her own making, and in his opinion, the sooner her son and daughter-in-law could begin to repair the damage she'd done to their marriage, the better off they would be. Lord Washbourn's appointment to the British embassy at Constantinople seemed a good place to start.

"It is not uncommon for persons of the dowager's age to go off in an apoplexy," Pickett observed blandly. "After all, she was facing the prospect of being left alone in England while her beloved son and his family spent the next few years abroad. If you point this out to the coroner, I'm sure you'll get no argument from Mr. Bagley."

"But you know it isn't true, Mr. Pickett," objected Lady Washbourn.

Pickett shrugged. "I won't be here to protest any such conclusion. Aside from the fact that Mr. Bagley would not be pleased to find me here, I believe I've trespassed on your hospitality quite enough already."

"I see," the earl said, and the creases in his forehead lessened somewhat. "Thank you, Mr. Pickett. My wife and I are much obliged to you."

"Oh, I almost forgot," exclaimed her ladyship, recalling the pretense by which she had first engaged his services, "what about the rubies, Mr. Pickett?"

"I'll send them—" He broke off abruptly. With the resolution of the case, the death of the dowager, and the reconciliation of Lord and Lady Washbourn, he had been able to forget, if only for a little while, the shambles that was his own marriage. He could not send a footman to Grosvenor

Square with the rubies, or even return them himself; he would not be going back to Curzon Street, not ever again. He wondered if, in the midst of all the preparations for burying the dowager and then going abroad, either of the Washbourns would remember the reward he had been promised, and realized he really didn't care. Through his own incompetence, he had lost something worth far more than fifty pounds. Nothing else seemed to matter anymore. "If you'll call on—on my wife—in the morning, she will restore them to you."

The Washbourns thanked him again and bade him farewell. Pickett said all that was proper (at least he hoped he did; he could never afterwards remember) and stumbled out into the night, unsure where to go or what to do with himself. Reminding himself that he had, after all, just solved a troublesome case, he resolved to inform Mr. Colquhoun of his findings, and with this end in view, set out for the magistrate's residence.

Mr. Colquhoun was rather surprised to receive a visit from his most junior Runner at so late an hour, but he instructed the butler to admit the caller, and listened attentively to Pickett's account of his visit to Washbourn Abbey and its aftermath. At the end of this recital, he shook his head.

"I don't like it, Mr. Pickett," he growled. "You should have waited until morning, got an arrest warrant, and followed the proper procedure. The dowager should have had to stand trial. Instead she managed to cheat the hangman, and that with your assistance. It was badly done of you."

"Begging your pardon, sir, but I can't agree. Who is to say she might not have had another go at killing Lady Washbourn—and a more successful one—overnight, while I was waiting to go through the proper channels? As for the lack of a trial, well, she's dead either way, so does it really matter how? Besides, his lordship is to take up a diplomatic post in Constantinople; surely such a blemish on his family's reputation could do nothing to strengthen national relations with the Turks. I'm sorry to disappoint you, sir—I'm well aware of how much I stand in your debt—but if I had it to do over, I can't honestly say I wouldn't do the same thing."

The magistrate regarded him appraisingly for a long moment. "You've grown up, John," he said at last. "To tell you the truth, I'm not quite sure how I feel about that. Ah well, it's getting late, and we both have to be back at Bow Street in the morning."

Mr. Colquhoun heaved himself out of his chair as he spoke, giving Pickett to understand that the interview was at an end. Unable to think of any reason for delaying his departure, he took his leave of the magistrate and stepped from the warmth of the house into the dark and un-welcoming night. He turned his steps eastward with no particular destination in mind, and soon found himself in the vicinity of Covent Garden, where he had once picked pockets as a boy. The theatre had apparently let out only a short time earlier, for a throng of well-dressed patrons milled about the streets, their presence a jarring contrast to those members of the lower classes who hawked flowers, hired themselves out as chair men, or eked out a living by less legal means. It was hard to believe that only a few days ago he might have been found amongst the former group, after having spent his formative years as one of the latter. Now, he reflected morosely, he belonged to neither. The aristocrats ignored him, and the flower women and chair men, several of whom were old acquaintances, no longer seemed to recognize him. The habit of years reasserted itself, and he found himself watching the people lingering about the street even at so late an hour, appraising which ones would make the easiest mark for a practitioner of his former trade. Suddenly a boy barreled into him, a skinny lad with curly brown hair stuffed beneath a shapeless cap.

"Sorry, gov'nor." The youth gave him a cheeky grin and tugged his forelock. "My mistake."

"Yes, it was," Pickett agreed, grabbing him by the wrist and twisting his arm behind his back. "I'll thank you to give back whatever it was that you just pinched from my pocket."

The boy raised limpid brown eyes to his. "I didn't take nuffink! I'm innocent, I tell you!"

"And I'm the tsar of all the Russias," Pickett scoffed. "Next time you decide to lighten someone's pockets, you might do well to choose someone besides a Bow Street Runner. Now, are you going to give me back what's mine, or do I haul you before the magistrate?"

Reluctantly, the boy opened his hand. Three ha'pence and a farthing lay within his grimy palm. "How did you know?" he asked in grudging admiration.

"Because I was on the budge myself long before you were ever born," replied Pickett, slipping easily back into the language of his youth. "And making a better job of it, too. I had three guineas on me, and yet you come up with nothing but a handful of copper."

"Well, how was I supposed to know?" retorted the boy. "It's not like you was gonna stand still while I turned out your pockets, is it?"

"You learn by feel," Pickett answered impatiently. "I can tell you never had my father for instructor! He made me practice blindfolded until I could tell one coin from another with just the tips of my fingers—and he rapped my knuckles for me if I guessed wrong. You're going to end up dancing at the end of a rope someday if you don't improve your technique."

It occurred to him that Mr. Colquhoun would hardly approve of him giving professional advice to a fledgling member of his erstwhile profession, but then, he knew better than most that the boy's illegal activities most likely owed less to moral deficiency than they did to the simple need to put food in his belly. He himself had been lucky; for most young criminals, there was no Mr. Colquhoun to take an interest in setting their feet on a better path.

"On second thought, here." He took the boy's arm and poured the coins back into his hand. "Go and get yourself something to eat. Not Blue Ruin, mind, but something good—something filling."

The boy regarded him suspiciously. "Why? So's you can haul me into Bow Street and tell the magistrate I stole it?"

"No, so you don't have to pick any more pockets, at least not tonight." His expression softened, and he added more gently, "I remember what it's like, you know—being hungry."

His words fell on empty air, for the boy had taken to his heels as if afraid his unexpected benefactor might change his mind. He need not have worried. Pickett had seen something of himself in the young pickpocket, something of the boy he had once been. Ten years ago, he reflected, it might have been him, right down to the curly brown hair and the big brown eyes trying their best to look innocent.

Ten years ago . . . It had been almost eleven years since his father had been transported to Botany Bay, but if Moll—Da's woman and his own *de facto* stepmother—had conceived shortly before he'd been shipped off . . .

Pickett shook his head as if to dismiss the unproductive train of thought, and set his mind to the more urgent task of finding a place to stay. It was perhaps inevitable that his steps should lead him eventually to Drury Lane, where he had once resided in a two-room flat over a chandler's shop. In fact, it had been in these unprepossessing surroundings that he and Julia had consummated their irregular Scottish marriage, putting an end to the plans that had already been made for an annulment. At the bittersweet memory, a dull ache settled somewhere in his chest, and his gaze drifted down the lane, past the Cock and Magpie to the chandler's shop beyond, and then upward to the flat above, where a light burned in the window like a beacon.

He froze. A light! She had come for him! He ran down the lane to the shop, groped for the key hidden over the doorframe, then unlocked the door and took the stairs two at a time until he reached the door at the top. He would have flung it open, but this, too, was locked. He was glad of it; these were hardly the most salubrious of surroundings for a lady alone. He pounded on the door until he heard the click of the key turning in the lock, and a moment later it opened. There in the doorway stood a worn-looking woman with a baby on her hip and a toddler clinging to her skirts. Pickett had never seen her before in his life.

"Well?" she asked impatiently. "What do you want?"

"I—I'm sorry," Pickett stammered. "I thought you were—I hoped—I beg your—my—my mistake."

The baby began to wail, and she turned her attention to it, closing the door on Pickett. He turned and staggered back down the stairs, the pain of blighted hopes lancing his belly like a knife. He had thought it would be Julia, had believed for one brief, shining moment that she'd been as miserable as he was, and was waiting for him in the flat where they'd once been so happy. He plodded his way down to the Strand and stood on the corner, lost as to where to go or what to do in this city he knew so well. The air was heavy and damp with the promise of rain and the fishy smell of the Thames, just out of sight beyond Somerset House.

He had not been aware of following the familiar odor, but eventually he found himself standing on the quay looking out over the water. The darkness was broken at intervals by the lanterns of boats riding at anchor, their faint lights tipping each tiny wave with gold. Soon, he knew, the lighters of coal would be arriving from Newcastle, and at dawn the heavers would swarm aboard with their shovels and sacks, ready to fill the wagons that would deliver the fuel to warm London's homes. He should know; he had spent five years of his life at the grueling work, and might have been there still, had not Mr. Colquhoun seen some potential in him and taken an interest.

Perhaps, he thought bitterly, he would have been better

off if Mr. Colquhoun had left him there. He had been only too willing to leave the Granger household at the time, but the pain of Sophy's rejection had been mere child's play next to what he felt now. Surely it would have been better never to have known Julia at all than to—

He realized with a start that if he had never come to Bow Street, Julia—Lady Fieldhurst, as she was then—might well have been hanged for the murder of her husband. She would be dead now, would have been dead for almost a year, and he would never have been the wiser. No, he could not regret knowing her, not regret loving her, even knowing how it must end.

He looked down at the black water at his feet. The tide was just beginning to ebb, and by dawn the muddy riverbank would be visible. Some of his earliest memories were of mudlarking along the banks of the Thames at low tide, scavenging for any scrap of bone or metal that might be exchanged for coin. It would be fitting in a way, for his life to end here, where so much of it had been spent. And Julia would be free of him, but on his own terms, with no need for pettifogging by the Fieldhursts' solicitor.

He frowned at the thought of Julia. However un-satisfactory she found him as a husband, he had to believe that she had loved him once. He would have to make the thing look like an accident, for her sake. His magistrate, however, would be more difficult to deceive. Julia might wonder, but Mr. Colquhoun would *know*, or quickly deduce, what had happened, and would blame Julia for it, however unfairly. Pickett had no desire for his death to become a bone of contention between the two people he loved most in the world. He let out a ragged sigh. It appeared that even this final door was closed to him.

And then, just when he thought things could not possibly get any worse, the heavens opened and the floods descended. He pulled his hat forward to keep the rain out of his eyes, and shuddered as the cold water trickled down the back of his neck where his queue used to be. Head down, he concentrated on putting one foot in front of the other, scarcely knowing or caring where he was going until he found himself standing on a familiar front stoop. He rang the bell, and a moment later was shown into the drawing room.

The master of the house sat before the fire in his slippers, reading a journal, but upon the entrance of a creature more closely resembling a drowned rat than a human being, he flung down his magazine and shot to his feet. "John? Good God, man, what's happened?"

The look Pickett gave him was one of utter desolation. "I think—I think I've left my wife."

18

*In Which Julia Fieldhurst Pickett
Takes Matters into Her Own Hands*

S colding like a mother hen, Mr. Colquhoun soon had
Pickett out of his sodden coat and steered him to a
chair drawn up before the fire, where he might warm himself
and dry off.

"Now," he said at last, having dispatched the butler for
brandy, "what's all this nonsense about you and Mrs.
Pickett?"

Pickett shook his head. "I'm sure you did your best, sir,
but it looks like I'm still my father's son, after all." Except,
of course, that the elder Pickett's faithlessness stemmed from
his being too appealing to women; the younger, it seemed,
could not even please the one woman he loved, and who had
professed to love him in return. Even love, it seemed, had its
limits.

"Nonsense!" his mentor repeated briskly. "Even the
most devoted couples have lovers' quarrels now and again.

283

It's not the end of the world."

"No," Pickett said bleakly. "Just the end of a marriage."

The magistrate forbore to comment. He had seen this rift approaching ever since the couple's wedding day, when he'd discovered, quite by accident, that John Pickett labored under the mistaken belief that his wife's jointure would end with her remarriage, and that he fully intended to support her as best he could on his own meager wages. Mr. Colquhoun's misgivings had increased exponentially when he had spoken to the lady herself and realized she hadn't the slightest notion as to the blow the reality had dealt to her young husband's pride, much less the need for softening it as much as possible. When the inevitable confrontation had come, it had apparently come with a vengeance.

"But where is your bag?" he asked bracingly. "Surely you didn't travel to Croydon with nothing but the clothes on your back!"

"No, sir," Pickett said, staring morosely into the flames. "I had a valise, but I left it at the Swan and promised to call for it later. They had no more rooms, and I—I didn't know where else to go."

"I'll send a footman to fetch it, and have the house-keeper make up a room for you."

"Thank you, sir. I'm sorry—"

His apologies fell on deaf ears. Mr. Colquhoun betook himself from the room, but made no visible effort to summon his housekeeper. Instead, he went across the hall to his study, where he composed a short note that made no mention of Pickett's bag at all. Having shaken sand over this missive, folded it, and sealed it with a wafer, he rang for a footman and surrendered this correspondence into his keeping, with very specific instructions as to its delivery.

"You want me to take the carriage, sir?" the footman asked stupidly, experience—as well as the name of his position—having long since taught him that such errands usually entailed trudging across Town, even in the midst of such a rainstorm as this one.

His employer lifted one bushy white eyebrow. "Didn't I just say so?"

"Yes, sir. But—am I to wait for a reply?"

"Unless I miss my guess," the magistrate predicted, "you will need to wait for a passenger."

* * *

He was not coming back. As she stared out the window onto the darkness that was Curzon Street at midnight, Julia finally admitted to herself what she had feared ever since he had departed the previous morning. She had not dared to leave the house all day for fear of being absent when he returned, and she had listened for his footsteps in the hall long before she had any realistic expectation of hearing them. But afternoon had turned to evening and evening to night with still no sign of him, and she had finally pushed her dinner plate away untouched and sent Thomas to Cheapside to inquire whether the stagecoach from Croydon and points south had arrived yet. Thomas had returned some time later with the information that the stagecoach had indeed reached London three hours earlier ("safe and on time," the booking agent had reported proudly), and that a passenger fitting Mr. Pickett's description had disembarked just before nightfall, leaving his bag at the inn until such a time as he should call for it.

"Should I have fetched it home while I was there?" Thomas asked uncertainly. "I would have done, but I thought maybe he wouldn't like coming for it and finding it gone."

"No, you did right." Julia turned away from the window and summoned up a feeble smile. "If he has made other plans, I am sure he would not thank us for interfering with them."

Julia dismissed the footman and turned back to the window, watching the rain that beat against the glass panes, unceasing as a widow's tears. She rehearsed in her mind every word, every gesture in the quarrel that had culminated in his leaving without even saying goodbye. She had spoken in anger, she thought desperately, she hadn't meant any of it. Surely he must have known that! *Oh, must he?* a small voice whispered back accusingly. *How? How would he have known?* Unlike herself, he had never been married before, never even had a longtime sweetheart unless one counted the faithless Sophia. She had been well aware, of course, that he feared she might someday come to regret their marriage; perhaps, believing his worst fears had come to pass, he had thought to salvage what remained of his pride by leaving her before she could order him to go.

Now he was out there alone in the darkness somewhere, and she had no idea where he was or even if he had sufficient funds remaining from his journey to procure a roof over his head for the night. Every instinct cried out to her to go after him, to search every thoroughfare and backstreet of London until she found him, but it was not safe for a woman to go gadding about Town alone at such an hour, even if she'd had any idea where to begin looking for him. She pressed a hand to her abdomen. Had it been only her own safety at risk, no danger would have been too great, no peril too hazardous. Now, however, she had someone else's welfare to think of, someone whose existence would be the only thing that might comfort her for his loss.

A hollow feeling formed in the pit of her stomach at the thought of the new life she carried. Someday, when the child was old enough, she would have to tell it about its father: who he was, and how very much she had loved him—and, finally, how she had driven him away. She pressed her forehead to the cool glass, and closed her eyes against the tears that threatened.

Her bleak reflections were interrupted by a light

scratching at the door.

"Begging your pardon, madam," Rogers said apologetically, "but had you not best turn in? It is quite late, you know, and the young master will not want you wearing yourself out waiting for his return. I will be happy to stay up to admit him myself, or to receive any message concerning him—in which case I should naturally apprise you at once."

She cast one last, longing glance up the rain-soaked street before turning reluctantly away from the window. "Yes, I suppose I should. But you need not wait up, Rogers." She gave the butler a forlorn little smile. "I do not think we will see Mr. Pickett again."

"Mrs. Pickett—madam—" He was spared the futile attempt at consolation by the sound of a vehicle drawing to a stop before the front door. "Forgive me, madam," he said, bowing himself from the room as someone in the street below wielded the door knocker with vigor.

Propriety, of course, required that she wait patiently in the drawing room until Rogers returned to announce the visitor, or until (as she infinitely preferred) her husband should join her, expressing his profound apologies for the long delay. But propriety made no allowances for the agonies endured by a woman estranged from her husband for more than thirty-six hours, the last four of which had been spent in envisioning increasingly grim scenarios ranging from a permanent, irreparable breach to the discovery of his lifeless body in a back alley off Drury Lane.

"Oh, *hang* propriety!" she muttered under her breath.

Picking up her skirts, she ran from the room and raced down the stairs, reaching the hall below just as Rogers opened the door to admit the caller. It was not, as she had hoped, her husband who entered the house, but a stranger in servants' livery who stood there holding a letter in his hand. Rogers spoke to him in hushed tones, then took the epistle and conveyed it to his mistress.

"From Mr. Colquhoun, madam," the butler murmured.

She broke the seal with hands that shook, and unfolded the single sheet. *There is a very unhappy young man at my house,* it read. *If you want him, please come and get him. P. Colquhoun, Esq.*

"Will there be any reply, ma'am?" asked the footman, observing her sparkling eyes and flushed cheeks.

"Yes, there will," she said resolutely. "But I shall deliver it in person. I'm coming with you!"

She disembarked before the magistrate's house a short time later. Heedless of the cold rain that now fell in sheets, she hurried up the stairs onto the portico with such haste that the footman was hard pressed to reach the front door ahead of her. He flung it open, and she stumbled over the threshold into the hall, where Mr. Colquhoun waited.

"Where is he?" she asked without preamble.

He nodded in the direction of a closed door opening off

the hall. "Am I to understand, then, that you've come to fetch him back home?"

"Yes." Now that the moment of reunion was at hand, however, she hesitated. "I have much to thank you for, Mr. Colquhoun, and much for which to beg your pardon. You tried to warn me, but I wouldn't listen." She glanced toward the uncommunicative door. "If he refuses to come with me, I shall have only myself to blame."

The magistrate's bushy eyebrows arched toward his hairline. "Surely it isn't as bad as all that!"

"I was angry and hurt," she said, hanging her head in shame at the memory. "I said—I said something un-forgivable."

"In my experience, there are very few things unforgivable, provided the love is there," he said, more gently than was his wont.

"Yes, but I knew he was—I knew he had not—"

"It seems to me, Mrs. Pickett, that these self-recriminations would be better addressed to the young man beyond that door," suggested the magistrate.

"Yes." She took a deep, steadying breath. "Yes, I'm sure you are right."

She slowly crossed the hall and put her hand on the panel. She glanced over her shoulder at Mr. Colquhoun, then, receiving a reassuring nod, pushed the door open and stepped inside.

He had removed his coat, and now sat before the fire in his shirtsleeves, with his back to the door. She could not see his face, but the slump of his shoulders, outlined sharply against the damp linen of his shirt, told its own tale. She advanced tentatively into the room and gently closed the door behind her.

"I'm sorry to impose on you at this hour, sir," he said without looking around. "If you can put me up for the night, I'll see about finding a place of my own first thing in the morning. Someone else has my old flat now and, well, I didn't know where else to go."

"You could always go back to your wife," she said softly.

He whirled around to stare at her, his expressive countenance a curious mixture of hunger and fear, as if he dared not believe the evidence of his own eyes.

"Please, John—I'm so very sorry—"

She got no further. He crossed the room in three strides, caught her up in his arms and began raining frenetic kisses on her lips, cheeks, eyes, hair, and anything else with which his mouth came in contact.

"Oh John, I've been so worried—don't you ever—*ever* do such a thing again!" she said in between frenzied kisses, softening this scold by clinging to him all the more tightly.

"No—I won't—I'm sorry—I'm so sorry—"

"It wasn't your fault. It was mine, all mine," she

insisted, and once the passion of reconciliation had spent itself and coherent conversation was possible, she enlarged upon this theme. "You tried to tell me, even Mr. Colquhoun tried to warn me, but I wouldn't listen. I've been so happy, I didn't want to think that you—weren't."

"But not because of you, my lady—never because of you. From the moment we met, you've had my whole heart, Julia, but I can't be the man you deserve. You're going to have to tell me what to do—what you want—"

Her face had been buried in the front of his shirt, but at that she looked up. "Darling, what are you talking about?" she asked, very much afraid she already knew.

"I don't please you." The pain contained in those four simple words was plainly written on his face.

She drew a ragged breath. "I was right, then, in thinking that was what drove you away. John, to say I owe you an apology doesn't even begin to cover it. When I came home yesterday and found you packing, I was still smarting over a—an unpleasant encounter I'd had in the park. Then I realized you meant to go away and leave me to the mercy of such people—" But that episode seemed a lifetime ago, and it was absurd now to think that they had parted, even temporarily, over anything so unimportant. "At that moment I wanted to hurt you as I had been hurt—and I did. I said something cruel and stupid, something that wasn't even true. It is very precious to me, the knowledge that you have been with no other woman but me, and however inexperienced you may have been when we married, I can say in all honesty that I have never known such happiness as I have found in your arms. You may be my second husband in terms of chronology, but you are first in my heart, and you always will be. And *that*, my darling, is the truth."

Pickett could find no words with which to answer this declaration. There was a gesture, however, one that he had promised more than half in jest, but that seemed to be the only response that would even begin to express what was in his heart. And so he dropped to one knee and lifted the lower edge of her gown, then bent his head and pressed it to his lips.

"No, John, don't," she protested, tugging at him. "We're equals in every way that counts. Besides, there is something we must discuss. It—it concerns the matter of finances. I knew you were troubled by it, but I didn't realize how much."

At her urging, he rose to his feet. "Julia, I will never be completely reconciled to the fact that I can't support my wife in the manner to which she's accustomed, but neither do I want you to give up any more than you already have in marrying me. If that's the price I have to pay, then I'll pay it willingly."

"Nevertheless, I have a proposition to put to you. For the next six months, we will live wherever you wish: in

Drury Lane, or Covent Garden, or under a bridge, if that is what you want—"

"I think we can eliminate the bridge," he put in.

"Don't interrupt," she said, pressing a finger to his lips. "As I said, for the next six months we will live in whatever lodgings may be had for twenty-five shillings a week. But after that, I must insist we find somewhere else to live—if not Curzon Street, then some other house we will choose together. I will not compromise on this."

"Your proposition sounds remarkably like an ultimatum, my lady," he said, although the tenderness in his voice robbed the words of any belligerence.

"Does it? Oh dear, I suppose it does," she confessed, conscience-stricken. "Still, you must admit your Drury Lane flat is rather small for three people."

"On the contrary, I could show you whole families living in—wait—what—three? Who—?"

The radiance of her smile rivaled the sun. "You're going to be a father, John Pickett."

He took a step backwards, staring at her. "But—but that's impossible!"

"Yes—except that it isn't."

"You told me you were unable to have children," he insisted, "that in six years with Lord Fieldhurst—"

"With Fieldhurst, yes. It turns out that the failing was not mine, but his—a failing, furthermore, that my second husband does not share."

"A baby," Pickett said stupidly, still trying to take it in. A baby, which meant that a nursery must be furnished and a nurse engaged, and perhaps another laundry maid as well, to wash all the clouts the baby would tear through every day, and then, when the child was older, there would be the matter of schooling—none of which could be accomplished on twenty-five shillings a week, not in a manner befitting the child of his lady wife. And yet somehow it didn't seem to matter so much anymore, not when he looked into her glowing face. He had given her the one thing her first husband, for all his wealth and position, never could. And maybe, just maybe, that was enough. "When—? How soon—?"

Surprisingly, Julia had no trouble deciphering this disjointed query. "December—very likely before Christmas." She smiled up at him. "Not too shabby, for a woman who was supposed to be barren and a man who was supposed to be impotent."

Stunned as he was, Pickett was still capable of performing a simple mathematical calculation. "*December?* That— that didn't take long!"

"No, it didn't." She stood on tiptoe to press her lips to his slackened jaw. "So let us hear no more about your inadequacies as a husband."

Whatever he might have said to this was interrupted by

a light tap on the door. It inched open, and Mr. Colquhoun stuck his head in. Assessing the situation with a clinical eye, he noted that his protégé looked rather dazed, but the condition of the boy's cravat—to say nothing of his lady's hair, most of which had been pulled loose from its pins—was sufficient to inform the magistrate that the reconciliation was everything the lad might have wished.

"Forgive the interruption," he said, "but I have a coachman and a housekeeper awaiting instructions."

"Sir, we're having a baby!" Pickett blurted out.

"Well, don't have it here," recommended Mr. Colquhoun. "The offer of a room for the night still stands, but I rather think it will not be needed, is that correct?"

"Quite—quite correct," Pickett said, taking Julia's hand and looking down at her with a rather fatuous smile. "I think we'd best go home now, my wife and I."

"As you wish." Mr. Colquhoun turned to give the order to his coachman, and Julia picked up Pickett's still-damp coat and held it open as he shrugged his arms into the sleeves. There would be other misunderstandings, she knew —other quarrels, even—but next time they would be better prepared. As Mr. Colquhoun had said, the love was there, and it would see them through any storm.

Outside, the rain had stopped and the carriage waited in the newly washed street. The coachman opened the door and let down the step, but it was Pickett who handed Julia inside.

Once in the vehicle, however, she paused and turned back.

"But where *is* home, John?" she asked. "Have you decided?"

He looked up at her, and saw his whole world reflected in her eyes. "Home is where you are," he said simply, and turned to address the coachman. "Curzon Street. Number twenty-two," he said, then climbed into the carriage after her and shut the door.

Author's Note

Frequent readers of mysteries will no doubt have recognized cyanide as the almond-scented poison that featured so prominently in this book. People in Regency England would not have known it by that name, as the substance—derived from and named for the pigment Prussian blue, just as I've described it here—did not acquire its scientific name until 1826, almost two decades after the events in *Mystery Loves Company*. If you love words and their origins, as I do, you might be interested to know that the root word in *cyanide* is the same as the name given to the cartridge of blue ink in the color printer on your desk: *cyan*.

As for John Pickett, if you'd like to know more about his journey from juvenile delinquent to collier's apprentice to Bow Street Runner (including his ill-advised romance with his master's daughter), you can find it in *Pickpocket's Apprentice: A John Pickett Novella*, a companion piece to the mystery series, available in paperback, electronic, and audiobook formats.

About the Author

At age sixteen, Sheri Cobb South discovered Georgette Heyer, and came to the startling realization that she had been born into the wrong century. Although she doubtless would have been a chambermaid had she actually lived in Regency England, that didn't stop her from fantasizing about waltzing the night away in the arms of a handsome, wealthy, and titled gentleman.

Since Georgette Heyer was dead and could not write any more Regencies, Ms. South came to the conclusion she would have to do it herself. In addition to the John Pickett mysteries, she has also written several Regency romances.

A native of Alabama, she now lives in Loveland, Colorado. She loves to hear from readers via email at Cobbsouth@aol.com or her Facebook author page.

71103839R00179

Made in the USA
Middletown, DE
20 April 2018